Paws, Claws,
and
Magic Tales

A FELLOWSHIP OF FANTASY ANTHOLOGY

ISBN: 9781720055150
Cover Design by Julia Busko
Interior Design by Dragonpen Press

Dear Readers,

Welcome to *Paws, Claws, and Magic Tales*, the fifth anthology from the Fellowship of Fantasy. Because our admins are apparently crazy cat people, our theme for this excursion is the magical, fantastical beast known as the feline. Oh yes, the majestic house tigers we know as cats are on full display with their elegance, grace, and ability to chase tiny red dots.

Of course, this being the Fellowship of Fantasy, these aren't ordinary felines. They're crime fighters, guardian angels, and maybe even dragons. These furry friends open portals, play matchmaker, and save kingdoms.

Enjoy the furry, the funny, and the fantastic with sixteen original tales (or should it be tails?). There are many perilous journeys ahead of you, but no graphic content. All the stories here fall below a PG-13 rating.

The Fellowship of Fantasy is an online group of writers dedicated to presenting the best in clean fantasy stories of any stripe. Some tackle epic quests to save the world, while others prefer more urban settings. Whether you enjoy contemporary tales, romantic retellings, or something else entirely, you're sure to find stories that speak to you.

Happy Reading, and may your reading be meowvelous!

Sincerely,
The Fellowship of Fantasy Authors
www.fellowshipoffantasy.com

Contents

The Witching Hour

SAVANNAH JEZOWSKI

I sat on the window seat of my human's personal chambers, trying to soak in the last rays of the evening sun which I believed rose for my benefit over all others. Did that make me conceited? Most definitely, but the superiority of cats could not be argued with. As far as tomcats went, I happened to be an unusually fine specimen.

The heat glancing off the glass rooftops and spires of Lite's capital city used to warm me right to the core, but lately—as the Alignment approached yet *again*—the heat couldn't find its way through the ceilings. The glass had been growing dingy, corroded, and covered in frost due to an unusual cold spell. I'd overheard the humans complaining the last of the crops had failed.

They blamed my human, because a crown princess couldn't take over the throne until she found a partner, and because Isabel couldn't seem to find one, everything must be her fault. It wasn't that the people thought women incapable or anything, but the strain of what was required of the royal couple simply proved more than one person could handle alone. I didn't understand the science or magic of how it worked, but the city drew its power from the king and queen. The strain on a single person proved indescribable. As we knew all too well.

Poor Queen Sylvia had been laboring for ten years on her own, after King Rupert suffered an untimely accident with a horse. Isabel was chosen to replace Sylvia the year after his death, but no replacement king had yet been found. Sylvia wouldn't dream of placing the burden on Isabel until she was fully grown and had found her helper.

I suspected the future king simply didn't *want* to be found, but the silly humans blamed my Isabel.

I scratched or peed on anyone who whispered it in my presence. Isabel wasn't perfect—she was a human being, after all—but she was *my* human, and I tolerated no disrespect from hairless two-leggers. I was doing everything I could to help her find a suitor, but there was only one I thought might suit us, and nobody in Lite would ever agree with me.

Even I had to concur the glass rooftops didn't glitter in the sun the way they used to. And this dog-eaten cold... Lite was one of the few havens left in the world. The darkness encroached on everything, draining life from the earth and bringing terrible things out of the shadows.

I imagined I could hear the howls of the hounds scouring the darkened lands beyond our border.

A gentle but firm hand brushed against my back. I stiffened involuntarily then relaxed into Isabel's touch. I couldn't help it. Even when I was in the foulest of tempers, the way her clever fingers began at my ears and stroked the length of my spine right to the tip of my tail was pure heaven. I felt a rumble growing in my middle and embraced it.

Isabel sighed and dropped her hand. I turned my head to stare at her, halting mid-purr. She gazed at the wall, head propped against the window frame. She was a homely thing, without a speck of fur, but she had nice, thick hair that tickled my nose when she leaned over me.

"At least I have you, Romeo," she said in a sad, quiet way that made even my lofty heart ache for her.

Romeo wasn't really my name of course, but humans simply didn't have the vocal capacity for cat speech. They couldn't growl and hiss properly at all. Which, consequently, meant I had been saddled with an awful name like Romeo.

Yack.

"The chimney seems to be working better," Isabel continued with a long, unhappy sigh. "Perhaps I won't need the chimney sweep after all."

I shot a glare toward the stone chimney in question. Great plumes of black soot coughed across the stone hearth, into the chamber, and across the marble floor.

Isabel perked up. "Oh, good," she said as she gave me a quick scratch under the chin. "It's still broken."

I hunkered again, keeping a wary eye on the chimney. I wasn't about to let my careful planning and hard work go to waste.

Isabel smiled for a moment, but the expression fleeted like a dog's ability to focus. She bent over to pick her wooden lyre off the floor and settled it into her lap. I cringed and moved to take its place, but she adjusted the instrument and kept plucking at the strings. The deep, discordant notes rattled my canines. I flexed my claws and dug them into the thick fabric of her gown.

The plucking jolted with a grating twang.

"Romeo, be nice," she commanded.

I ignored her, and she went back to plucking at the lyre with a resigned sigh. The notes, badly strewn together, sounded familiar. I pondered them as I flexed my claws, the purr returning. The humans had a name for that particular arrangement of notes.

8

The Witching Song. Now I remembered it. Of course, my human would play this song today. It was the day of the Alignment. An icy draft swept from somewhere and chilled me right to the bone.

No wonder Isabel was so unhappy.

I turned to peer through the frosted glass, out into the gray twilight. The courtyard resembled a cauldron of Cook's harvest stew—filled to the brim with every vegetable imaginable—fat and skinny, rare and common. Every eligible bachelor in Lite lined up in the cold waiting to be presented to the future queen.

It was Choosing Day.

"What am I going to do, Romeo?" I hadn't even noticed when she stopped playing. Her fingers fiddled with my left ear. "The queen is getting so tired. What if I can't find my partner?"

I felt sorry for her. If she couldn't find him, the lights would probably go out. Queen Sylvia knew what needed to be done, but the lights were still dimming. And Isabel? Young, inexperienced, chosen at the age of six? She didn't stand a chance on her own. Every year, she went to the Choosing, hoping to find her partner, but the Alignment came and went with the same results. The humans went home muttering their frustration, and Isabel wept great, horrible tears into my fur.

If she couldn't find a husband before old Queen Sylvia passed away, the burden would fall onto her narrow shoulders. I feared the strain would break her.

This, surprisingly, caused me a great deal of distress. I'd never been one for unnecessary sentiment, but I made an exception for Isabel.

A knock interrupted my musings. I glared as the old butler tottered into the room, his long hair brushing his shoulders as he peeked inside.

"Poor duck," the old butler mumbled with a sorrowful look toward us. "You didn't ask for this, and yet here we are."

Isabel sighed. "Go away, Gran. I don't want company." She plucked at the lyre again, eyes downcast. Her lower lip began to wobble.

I stared at the grungy windowpane, wondering what would happen if my plans fell through. I didn't just want her to be successful, I wanted her to be happy. I'd scoured the kingdom for the right boy, and there was only one that seemed to spark interest in her.

And that was complicated.

Gran clucked his tongue and inched the door open a smidge more. "You shouldn't be playing that song," he said. "You'll cry and scare away the boys."

Isabel scooped up a pillow and hurled it toward him. It fell sorely

9

short and lay in the middle of the stone floor. I sauntered over to investigate, sniffing the tassels before winding in a circle and perching on the pillow to take a bath. They both looked at me, Gran with consternation, and Isabel with something that might have been embarrassment. Or pride. I wasn't sure which and didn't care.

"A goose gave his feathers for that pillow," Gran scolded, looking miffed. He bent, groaning, to shoo me away and retrieve it. His rough fingers caught on the tassels. I swatted half-heartedly at his white knee socks and buckled shoes.

"Send him my thanks." Isabel sounded annoyed.

"He's dead." Gran frowned. "You probably ate him for dinner yesterday."

I licked my lips as I imagined one of Cook's fat, roasted gooses. Or was it geese? The human language was so hard to keep straight.

Isabel twisted to scowl at the busy courtyard below and the fellows in their fur coats and fancy boots, stamping around in circles to keep warm. "You would think with all those men down there I would be able to find *one* who would suit."

I almost padded over to comfort her. I didn't like this side of her, the girl who cowered in her chambers with her nose pressed against the glass, watching the world spin by without her.

She rarely took me out to sniff the flowers anymore. Especially now that the frost had killed them all off. The gardens were a wilted, slimy mess. They smelled quite interesting, actually.

"Honestly, Gran, why do I bother? We should just cancel the Choosing; we all know I won't find a match." The princess flopped against the pillows with the air of a martyr. I gave Gran's shiny shoe one last swat before sauntering back to the window seat and hopping up beside her. This comforting business was a trying chore, but someone had to do it. I lifted my nose for a chin scratch, which she obliged giving.

"It's chilly in here," she complained as her finger rubbed that hollow place beneath my jaw. "Hasn't the sweep arrived yet?"

"Oh, yes," Gran said as if he'd only just remembered the fact.

I opened my eyes just a slit, satisfied when I saw the interested gleam in my human's pale eyes.

"Then why isn't he *here*?" She jabbed an imperious finger toward the floor. A bit of pride stirred inside me. I liked this side of her; it was almost feline.

Gran looked baffled. I pictured the memory escaping him, frolicking just out of reach like dandelion seeds on a summer breeze. I flicked my tail, and the memory burrowed deeper out of reach.

10

But then a knock sounded on the door. The memory flared to life the way a spark catches fire in dry kindling.

"Ah!" The old butler lifted a gnarly finger. He remembered now.

I huffed and returned to my bath. There was a patch of fur just under my front leg that refused to lay right. "He sent me ahead to announce him."

"Thank you, Gran," Isabel said with a sigh. "That's most helpful."

"I live to serve."

"I'm sure you try. Now, please show the sweep in before I freeze to death." She fluffed her hair and ran a hand down the front of her day gown—the one with the scratchy lace around the collar I despised.

I left the window seat and darted behind the door as the old man swung it open, my paws itching with anticipation. Something pleasant churned in my belly as I hunkered down to wait for the chimney sweep to enter.

"You've been announced," Gran whispered noisily to the person waiting outside the door.

The sweep known as Ives inched into the room, head appearing first and tipping side to side as he scanned the room. He was even more homely than Isabel, a tall, skinny fellow with unruly dark hair and large ears. He paused, staring at Isabel, hair partially covering his eyes. The silence became tangible and tasted of repressed longing. I rolled my eyes as Ives eased into the room, shoulders hitched as if he were expecting an imminent blow. Loath to disappoint him, I launched out of my hiding place and pounced on his boot as he passed, raking his ankle with my claws. He bellowed and shook me off, but I sank my claws through his trousers and into his leg.

Other than Isabel, Ives was my favorite human in all of Lite.

"Oh, Romeo!" Isabel cried.

Hands grabbed me roughly around the middle. Confused, I tightened my grip on the human's leg. I gave in after several good yanks, mostly because the hands squeezing my bulging stomach made me feel like I needed to hurl. My attacker lifted me by the scruff of the neck until I was eye level with a human male I'd never seen before, but his resemblance to Ives suggested he must be related.

"What a nice cat," the newcomer exclaimed. He stared at me, hard, something glinting in his pale eyes. "Oh, you are a beauty, aren't you?"

I hissed and tried to swipe a paw at his nose, but the way he had me scruffed afforded little mobility. "Feisty old girl, too." He glanced at me and then amended with an apologetic smile, "Old boy. So sorry. Does this one give you much trouble?"

"Oh, loads, but he's a dear," Isabel said as she approached and held out her arms to take me. She hugged me against her chest, my face mashed against that dratted lace, and I twisted to glare at the two sweeps.

"Bad cat! That was very naughty. Very, very naughty." She shook me gently before lifting her eyes to the chimney sweep, suddenly shy. "Good morning, Ives."

The chimney sweep inched toward the fireplace, eyes downcast but flickering toward us. "Good morning, your highness." Another painful silence dangled between them.

I yowled pointedly. Ives's face turned an unsightly shade of red. I pierced him with an unrelenting stare until his shoulders wilted in submission.

"Good morning, Romeo," he finally muttered. "This is my brother, Cyril."

I glared at the newcomer and fretted he would ruin my plans. *Why was he here?*

Cyril winked at us and offered a mock bow. "I'm here to help Ives with this chimney and am delighted to assist a fair maiden and her charming kitty." I couldn't believe his cheek. A growling sound churned deep inside my chest.

"That cat's a menace," Ives warned as he made his way to the fireplace. "Don't try to pet it. You'll get rabies."

"Oh, really," Isabel said, sounding exasperated, but the beginnings of a smile tweaked the corners of her mouth, her pale cheeks flushed with color. They usually were whenever Ives showed up to fix the chimney. She liked him. This, more than anything, made him the perfect choice. He was astonishingly aloof for a human, a trait only cats can truly appreciate. He knew his place and fought desperately to stay in it. I wouldn't mind if he dandied himself up a bit or flirted with Isabel occasionally, but it was too much to expect him to become a cat.

Ah, but *that* would have made him perfect.

Cyril shot me another inscrutable smile before following Ives. "How long has this chimney been giving you trouble?"

"Forever," Ives muttered.

At the same time, Isabel chimed, "Oh, not long."

The two humans exchanged an awkward look. Then, they blushed and glanced away from one another. I rolled my eyes.

"Well," Isabel began with a nervous laugh. "Perhaps it has been a rather long while." Her hand began petting me with more force than was necessary.

"This is the fourth time this month I've been summoned to fix a

12

chimney that logically doesn't have a thing wrong with it." Ives seemed to be clenching his teeth as he knelt on the hearth and opened his sack to distribute his tools in a tidy row. I coughed, and one of them slid sideways. He started, adjusted it, and pulled out another.

"Oh, cheer up, Ives." Cyril let his own pack of tools shift from his shoulder and clunk against the marble floor. "It won't be as bad as last time. I'm here."

Ives shot him a frustrated look. I relaxed into Isabel with a satisfied purr. Last week, after Ives labored over the chimney for most of the day, the clog in the chimney shaft disintegrated, exploding out both ends of the chimney. It was said the soot cloud puffing from the tower could be seen for miles, and Ives had left the palace as black as a chunk of coal, convinced the thing was out to get him.

I'd been rather proud of that one.

"Obliged for the reminder," Ives said, quite bitterly.

"My pleasure." Cyril rocked back on his heels with a knowing smile. This human warranted watching.

"I do apologize about the chimney," Isabel said, sounding as if she were trying to justify its existence, "but it's always so nice when you come to fix it."

The way Ives looked at her then made me wonder if he knew what she was really trying to say. He looked like a hopeless, lost kitten staring at a bit of catnip dangling before his nose, knowing he could never have it.

Cyril snickered suddenly. I speared him with a glare, startled to find him staring right at me.

Ives turned abruptly and knelt in front of the fireplace. I licked my lips and suppressed an excited wiggle as a black cloud of smoke billowed into the room. Ives tumbled backward onto his bottom, coughing and waving his hands. He fished a dirty cloth from his pocket and smeared the soot around his face trying to get it off.

Cyril waited for the soot to settle before hunkering down beside him, narrow shoulders hunched around his ears as he leaned in to peer up the chimney shaft. "So tell me, old girl, what's troubling you?" He laid his hands on the stone hearth and leaned forward to listen.

I sat up with sudden interest. There was something odd about this brother, as if he knew things he shouldn't. Ives pretended to ignore him, but he seemed as interested as me in hearing Cyril's prognosis. Even Isabel was quiet, her hand still against my spine.

After several minutes of listening, Cyril settled back on his heels, dusting his hands against his work shirt. "Well, that explains a lot."

"What? Can you talk to chimneys?" Isabel asked with a shaky laugh.

Gran snorted from the doorway where he'd taken up his silent vigil, and Ives coughed.

Cyril only smiled at her, that annoyingly *knowing* smile. "On the contrary, I just know a bewitchment when I see it, and you've got a bad one, your highness."

I stiffened and then began yacking as if I needed to hack up a hairball. Isabel plopped me onto the floor. For the first time, she looked alarmed, but not at my imminent vomiting.

"Heavens, no. There's no enchantment," she said, but it was obvious by her pained look that there was an enchantment. And she had known about it.

We'd both known about it.

"Why didn't you tell me?" Ives exclaimed. "Here I've been wracking my brains over something I can't even fix. I've no gift for enchantments. You need a wizard, not a chimney sweep."

Isabel crossed her arms defensively. "There isn't anything wrong with my chimney." But her pitch was a tad too high, her coloring too pink. I resisted the urge to roll my eyes. Humans were such terrible actors. They possessed no nonchalance or style.

When Ives raised a sooty eyebrow, she had the good sense to blush and look away. "I mean, nothing that can't be fixed," she hedged. She looked at him from under her lashes, and I knew what she was thinking: she'd enjoyed his visits and hadn't *wanted* the chimney to be fixed.

"I understand your reasons for secrecy." Cyril fished a cloth from his pocket and wiped his hands. His gaze lingered on me and not Isabel. "But this chimney *is* enchanted."

I realized I'd forgotten about the hairball and resumed yacking. It wasn't anywhere near ready to be dislodged, but the humans wouldn't know that.

Cyril leaned over with a "Poor kitty" and tapped me hard between the ears. I narrowed my eyes at him but discovered my hairball had abruptly shifted and grown in size.

I began yacking in earnest. It took me a whole minute of agonized wheezing and dry heaves before the nasty thing came out. The narrow log of dark hair and unpleasant tummy things landed on the marble floor.

"Gross," Ives groaned.

Isabel sighed and pressed a hand over her eyes.

But Cyril gave me another firm tap on the head. "Good kitty," he said with a wink. I glared at him, a new sense of unease mingling with respect.

This human wasn't a common chimney sweep like Ives.

14

The door opened behind us, hinges creaking. Panic flooded through me as an elderly human entered the room, dressed in a fine gown, her pearl-white hair a pile of waves and poofs around her head.

Why was she so dog-eaten early?

Ives lurched to his feet, kicking over a bucket of ashes. His ears burned hotly as he tried to manage a bow that was as awkward as Cyril's was graceful. Under other circumstances, I would have found this hilarious, but today wasn't a day for frolicking. I had work to do, and the old queen was going to interfere.

"Oh," Queen Sylvia said, sounding surprised. Deep lines of exhaustion creased her weathered face. "You have guests. What a good thought, Isabel. It is good luck to see a sweep on your wedding day." The chimney puffed another cloud of soot into the room, but I made sure Ives received the brunt of it.

"They're here to fix my chimney," Isabel declared, sounding alarmed.

The queen laughed—even her laughter sounded weary. If Isabel didn't find a suitor this year and take over for the old girl... I shuddered to think what would happen if the darkness flooded over Lite. There'd be no more sunshine through windowpanes, that was for sure. And there'd be an alarming number of hounds—horrible, doggy things. "Don't be embarrassed, dear. A little extra luck can never hurt."

Considering it had been ten years since the princess's choosing and she was yet to find a potential husband, I couldn't argue with the queen's logic. My human needed all the luck she could get, which was why she had me.

And the chimney sweep.

"Will you be attending the ceremony?" the queen asked. She leaned on a pearl-handled cane, somewhat heavily. Her bearing was erect. She had been keeping the throne for nearly twelve years on her own, waiting for her successors to be chosen to replace her.

Ives kept his eyes trained on the floor. "No, my lady, I am but a common sweep."

"Everyone is invited to attend," she reminded him. "No man is beneath a kingship." I glanced between them, unable to believe my good fortune. Finally. A human who saw reason.

"Thank you for the invitation," Ives stammered, his gaze flickering upward briefly before returning to his sooty boots. "But we all know it wouldn't be a good idea."

Commoners had never been well received, as far as kings go. I could only recall two common kings, and it had been several centuries since the last one.

"Perhaps we are due for some changes around here," Queen Sylvia continued with dogged persistence.

"Please, your majesty," Ives said, his voice barely more than a whisper. "I've as much chance of being chosen as king as I have fixing this awful chimney."

Isabel coughed softly.

"I will attend," Cyril said, out of the blue, "to represent our family."

Ives stared at him, horrified.

"You will be most welcome," the queen said with another weary smile. "I am sure our gathering will be the better for it. You are welcome, as well, Master Ives," she said, turning back to him. "I've heard good things of your work. Our chimneys thank you."

I sniffed, and the fireplace poofed again. Ives went red all over and mumbled something noncommittal. The Queen took a hasty step back to avoid the plumes of soot dancing across the floor. Ives snatched up a handheld broom and tried to sweep them back toward the chimney, but they danced out of his reach and continued their revelry. Now that the cat was out of the bag, I didn't see the need to be subtle any longer.

"Well." The Queen lifted a dainty foot as a soot cloud danced past her out into the hall. She watched it go, unalarmed. This sort of thing happened rather frequently, and she'd probably gotten used to it. I couldn't help myself. "Ahem. Come now, Isabel, the Hour is approaching."

I looked out the window. Sure enough, the sun had sunk behind the city, a red orb of angry light reflecting off the smudged glass rooftops that dotted Lite's skyline. The Choosing would begin shortly and last until the clock struck midnight, when the Two Sisters aligned.

Then all activity would cease.

For the Witching Hour.

A shiver worked up my spine and seemed to buzz between my ears. A painful, stilted silence pervaded the room. They were all thinking about what might happen if Isabel failed to find her match tonight. The darkness pressed relentlessly against the borders, the hounds prowling just outside the city walls.

Waiting. Biding their time as ours ran out with each passing year.

At last, the Queen cleared her throat. "Come now, Isabel. We must prepare. Leave the lads to their work." Her heeled shoes clacked against the marble floors as she retreated from the room.

This time, Isabel obeyed, but with a reluctance she did little to hide.

Ives watched her progress, something lost and troubled in his expression. For a moment, one glorious one, he looked as if he might say something to her. His lips even parted, but then something dark filled his eyes, his jaw tightened, and he looked at the floor. Casting him a disgusted look, I padded after Isabel, mewing in distress, wishing I could console her and tell her all would be well, that I had a plan...

The door banged shut in my face.

"Let's get out of here," Ives said, a little too loudly. "Hurry, Cyril. Wave your arms or something and fix this stupid fireplace."

I spun about, spine arching. I hadn't worked this hard to have him spoil everything now. I hissed, and a wrenching groan belched from the mouth of the fireplace. Cyril slipped his hands into his pockets and took a step back. "I don't think the fireplace wants to be disenchanted," he said with a knowing look at me.

Ives began to throw his tools into his sack. "Then we'll come back and work on it tomorrow." There was something almost desperate in his movements. I stalked toward him, determined to drive him to the Choosing gagging on soot if I had to. Soot clouds churned down the chimney and advanced on him, but he had his nose in his tool bag and didn't see them coming.

"I think we should stay for the ceremony," Cyril announced.

I froze. The soot froze too, curled just above Ives's form like a giant paw about to smack him against the hearth. I was tempted to let it do just that, but I needed to figure out what game Cyril was playing. It almost seemed like he was trying to help me, but that was ridiculous.

Humans weren't clever enough to know what I was up to. Even Isabel hadn't figured it out yet, although she knew well enough I was to blame for her chimney.

"Are you crazy? They'd laugh us from the room."

Cyril rocked back on his heels, that knowing smile plastered across his infuriating face. Now *here* was a human with a style. "You heard the queen; *we were invited.*"

Ives rose from a crouch and yanked his tool bag closed. Frustration mottled his disproportioned features. "We're not staying."

I let the soot paw fall. Great plumes of smoke billowed into the room, but they curved around me and left me alone. Cyril swept a lazy hand, and the soot curled away from him as it settled to the marble floor around the perimeter of the room. That proved it, then.

Cyril was a wizard.

This explained why he wasn't a sweep like Ives. Wizards were rare in Lite and spent most of their time trying to bolster the protection spells around the perimeter of the city to keep the darkness and the hounds at bay. It explained why I'd never met him before today, even though Ives had been coming to fix our chimney for months.

When the cloud settled, Ives stood shaking on the hearth, as black as a man carved from pure coal. He blinked his eyes and rubbed at them. "I—I can't see a thing," he complained. A note of desperation seeped into his voice. "This chimney is out to get me. *It hates me.*"

"Somebody hates you, but it's not the chimney," Cyril said, as if he were discussing tea and biscuits and not an infuriated enchantment. He smiled at me as he walked to his brother and clasped his shoulder. Cyril gave him a gentle shake. "You can't go home yet, Ives. The princess will freeze if you don't get a fire going."

The sweep's shoulders wilted in resignation. The bag of tools hit the floor with a noisy clang. As Ives knelt to reopen his kit, I planted myself in front of the door, just to be safe. Cyril made himself comfortable in the window seat, eyes fastened on me with an intensity anyone but a cat would find disconcerting. For once in my life, I found myself almost a little thankful for a human.

This wizard was proving rather useful.

I held out until the music began filtering down the empty corridors from the throne room. The sky had grown dark outside the window, the only light coming from streetlamps and from within the buildings across Lite. The glow was feeble against the oppressive shadows. Cyril snored from the direction of the window seat, having finally grown bored with staring at me, and Ives muttered under his breath as he worked to get the damper open I'd been holding shut. The strain of maintaining the enchantment for so long was beginning to wear on me. I could feel the headache growing between my ears. I needed Isabel to give me a good petting.

With a meow of annoyance, I let the enchantment dissolve. The damper creaked open, and the mass of soot I'd been hoarding inside the chimney exploded into the room. Cyril woke in a fit of violent coughing.

"What's going on?" he asked around coughs. He left the comfort of the window seat and stumbled toward the fireplace.

Ives appeared out of the cloud, waving a hand in front of his face. "I think I fixed it," he growled. "No thanks to you."

"I don't envy the maids having to clean this up," the wizard said with

18

a dismissive laugh.

The soot settled at last, leaving a neat arc of untouched marble floor around me. I smiled to myself and licked a paw. Ives seemed to notice me for the first time, a frown pulling down his lips. But he said nothing—merely repacked his tools and hefted the bag over his shoulder.

"Let's get out of here," he muttered.

"You aren't going to the Choosing looking like that," Cyril said.

Ives reached the door and eyed me warily. "I'm not going to the Choosing at all."

I hissed and arched my back. I'd bet my last whisker I could change his mind on that score. He was going to show up for Isabel's Choosing, or one of us would be dead. He tried to edge me aside with his foot, but a hiss from me sent him skittering backward.

"Out of the way, Romeo!" His cheeks reddened beneath the soot. "I've no patience left for the likes of you."

"Be nice to the poor kitty," Cyril said with a yawn as he stepped around his brother and leaned to scoop me up. I yowled in dismay and scrabbled to get free, but he scruffed and pinned me against his chest, subjecting me to a rough, manly scratch under the chin.

Ives bolted for the door and out into the hall. Cyril followed, laughter reverberating inside his chest. "Oh, don't go that way," he said, still laughing to himself. When Ives paused with a questioning look over his shoulder, Cyril tightened his grip on my scruff. I glared at Ives, wishing I could chew his brother's hand off. "Not if you want everyone to see you. There's a back entrance we should use."

"Good idea," Ives muttered and pivoted on his heel.

I squirmed and tried to kick my back paws as Cyril moved after Ives, his steps surprisingly graceful for a human male. Most men of his species lumbered around like three-footed dogs who couldn't find their own tails. The females were little better, always sniggering and talking and never paying attention to where they put their pointy shoes.

"There, there, be a good cat," Cyril said.

"You should get rid of that thing while you can."

"He looks hungry. I thought I'd drop him in the kitchens on our way out."

I hissed and blinked rapidly, but instead of dropping me, Cyril rapped the top of my head, and a strange, fuzzy sensation seeped into me. The magic slipped just out of my reach. I grappled for it with a growing sense of panic. What was he doing?

We turned down another corridor and were halfway to the staircase at the opposite end when I realized where we were. The corridor Cyril suggested we use flanked the backside of the throne room. There were several doors along the hallway that led to small balconies overlooking the auditorium. If I could free myself from Cyril, I might toss Ives over one of the balcony railings and get him onto the main floor. Sure, he might break a leg when he landed, but it would be a small price to pay.

He'd forgive me once he realized kings didn't have to concern themselves with bewitched chimneys.

The mournful notes of the Witching Hour song filtered from behind the closed doorways.

"Ah," Cyril said, sounding smug. "The ceremony has begun."

I squirmed with renewed determination. As the Alignment approached, my time was running out.

Ives plodded onward with renewed vigor. "Terrific," he muttered. "No one will see us leaving then."

"Quite true. Let's pop into one of the balconies and watch."

"No, thanks."

But Cyril released his grip on me and snaked a hand out to scruff his brother instead. I felt the fog around my magic evaporating like dew in the morning sun. I smiled and twitched my tail. The nearest balcony door swung open with a bang. I considered summoning a nice whirlwind to bluster us out onto the balcony, but it wasn't needed. Once the door opened, Cyril hustled us out of the corridor in prompt order, Ives squirming and growling the whole way.

The balcony was empty, but for a thin maid with a broom peeking around one of the drapes. She gave us a cool stare and went back to spying on the events unfolding below. Cyril stopped once we reached the railing. I sprang free and flounced a foot or two away, where I sat preening at my indignity. Cyril leaned one elbow against the railing but kept a firm hold on Ives, who yanked against the hand on his shoulder, more determined than ever to be free of us both.

The royal musicians continued to play *The Witching Song*, and a human with a pleasant tenor sang the words. The melancholy notes pulled even at me, as if filled with a magic of their own.

> *Black is the Glass at midnight,*
> *Strong the shadow's power,*
> *Blacker the soul that falters*
> *When strikes the Witching Hour.*

Down below, Isabel stepped daintily along the long line of would-be suitors. She walked with squared shoulders, head lifted, as if she were daring the world to accuse her of anything other than doing her best. She looked remarkably pretty for a human, in a gauzy dress of pale blue and silver, her hair a cascade of curls around her narrow shoulders.

Ives stopped struggling as she continued walking down the line, a glowing orb of light bobbing above her head. It swayed side to side, as if inspecting or searching. The light possessed a life of its own, flickering and swirling. As it inspected each young man, the light dimmed as if in disappointment before bobbing to the next one. Isabel hardly looked at the faces she was passing as if she already knew the orb wouldn't choose them.

My heart ached for her; she was giving up on herself.

The man with the nice voice entered the second stanza, the strings and wood flutes building in volume.

Black is the Lite at midnight,
Black the shade and crow.
The song of bats and belfries
Brings blood with winter's snow.

Shadows crept over the throne room as the Alignment progressed. As the sisters joined, the light of the far moon shrank to a sliver. Soon, the moons would be as black as the midnight sky, and if Isabel didn't find a husband, the old queen would have to persevere another year.

I worried she didn't have it in her. For the first time, I began to doubt my plan. Ives was, after all, just *Ives*. I could see his better qualities—a strong sense of duty, hard-working, logical, determined—but I feared the rest of the kingdom may not be able to see beyond the soot of his unfortunate profession.

The singer moved into the final stanza, the notes reaching their highest, the music swelling to the deepest point. Even the glass windows and roof panels began to vibrate the notes back down to us, a desperate cacophony of words, notes, and longing.

Black are the tides at midnight,
Black the moon, her Sister.
The hounds are hungry—seeking—
Beware the Witching Hour.

A blur of elbows, drapes, and flailing paws interrupted the ceremony. One minute, I was perched on the balcony planning how to get Ives to ground level before Isabel reached the end of the line and the Alignment passed. The next thing, Cyril's elbow launched me over the edge. I yowled and grabbed for the massive scarlet drape that ran from the top of the balcony to the floor before, my claws raking for purchase in a desperate attempt to slow my descent. I caught myself halfway to the floor, heart beating so fast I thought I might be in danger of hyperventilating.

"Oh, that poor cat! Ives! You better save him!" Cyril's voice, far too chipper to be truly concerned, wafted from the balcony above me.

Worthless, devious, hateful human!

If I thought hanging from the drape was bad, it became ten times worse when Ives flopped over the railing and tumbled after me. I yelped as he careened downward, sooty hands grappling with the unwieldy fabric, long legs kicking and wheeling. Thick-soled boots skidded toward my head. It was flight or death, I was sure, so I released my hold on the drape and attached myself to Ives instead. We both yowled all the way down the drape and across the floor. We skidded to a halt before a pair of delicate white sandals with silver butterflies about the ankles.

I clung just behind Ives's shoulder, fur puffed and spine arched in disbelief of what had just happened.

I was going to kill that wizard and eat his innards for breakfast.

The sandals took a step closer. I craned my head to peer up into Isabel's horrified face. "Oh, Romeo," she whispered. Above her head, the Alignment reached its peak, every speck of moonlight disappearing behind the sister planet. Darkness fell upon the throne room.

It was now or never.

I hoped that Ives could manage to seem noble and worthy of a kingship, but I feared Cyril had ruined that chance. Ives lay on his belly, black as coal and smelling of sweat and smoke. Isabel's eyes swept over him. Something akin to compassion flooded her features as she leaned forward to offer him a hand, but the orb of light drifted over her shoulder and paused, pivoting.

She froze, as if she'd forgotten about it.

"Oh, crumb," Ives rasped. The orb hesitated above him and dipped down until it hovered mere inches from his upturned nose. It bobbed side to side—like it was trying to peer past the soot and into his soul—once, twice, and then settled.

It did not move again.

The pale white light began to pulse brighter, and brighter, and brighter until I squeezed my eyes closed to block its brilliance. Hands plucked me off the chimney sweep as gasps reverberated around the throne room.

"She's found him!"

"A commoner!"

"It's the chimney sweep!"

Firm fingers roughed me under the chin. I squinted up at Cyril through one eye and released my claws to give him a well-deserved spiking, but Ives stumbled to his feet just then and reeled backward. The orb followed him, merry and determined.

"It's you," Isabel breathed, sounding surprised and yet pleased. "Of course it is! I should have known." Her eyes moved to me in shocked pleasure, so I smiled smugly back. Now she understood about the chimney. She was clever; I knew she'd figure it out eventually. She offered me the faintest of smiles, and her expression promised much love and pettings for later.

Ives shook his head, the mule-head, swatting at the orb as if it were a lightning bug he might scare away. "It's not me," he sputtered. "It can't be me; I don't want to be a king!"

"The best kings never do," a regal voice called out, filled with amusement and also a desperate relief. The old queen approached, face blooming with a smile. I could almost smell her relief on the cool air. "Well done, Master Sweep."

"Well done, indeed," Cyril breathed, his fingers against my chin slowing from rough and playful to gentle and almost affectionate. I considered spiking him again, but now seemed poor timing with the entire kingdom looking on.

"It can't be me," Ives repeated, refusing to relent. "I'm just a sweep. My place is with my brushes. And you—you're a princess." His voice dropped to a husky whisper as he looked at her. Long-repressed emotions surfaced. It was clear to anyone with eyes that he'd already fallen in love with her.

How could he not? I wasn't the only fine specimen in Lite.

"Yes, it can," Isabel said as she lifted her skirts and followed him. She stepped closer, reached out to take his hands in both of hers. Her fingers were so pale, ghostly against his soot-blackened ones. For a moment, she seemed to be thinking the same thoughts, her eyes on their touching fingers. Then her gaze darted up to his. "Thank you," she whispered. "I'm glad it's you."

It was difficult to tell with him covered in soot, but I was pretty sure he blushed just then. This time, he didn't try to run away but let her grip his hands. They continued to stare at one another, having forgotten about the rest of us. I purred contentedly to myself, proud of a job well done.

Then, as the bell tolled the hour, every light in the room blazed to life. The fiery hot glow spread from one chandelier to the next, from one room to the one beyond it, until every light in the palace blazed. Then, the light flooded across the city, from one home to another, until even the feeble fires in the watchtowers blazed with sudden, violent heat.

The hounds howled their frustration beyond our borders.

The throne room—and the entire kingdom—erupted into cheers.

Ives and Isabel made their way to the dais—Isabel beaming and Ives looking embarrassed and a little green. Cyril remained where he was, at the back of the room, as if he were nothing more than a wallflower. The kingdom had us to thank, yet people pressed around us as if we didn't exist, unaware of the great service we'd done them.

Gran wandered over to stand beside us, beaming. "I saw this coming. I noticed a change in her a few weeks ago." He rocked up on the toes of his buckled shoes, gloved hands locked behind his back. "Young love."

I rolled my eyes and floofed my fur. Gran's ability to notice—and remember—anything was a matter of much debate. But he was kind to Isabel, so I allowed him his momentary and undeserved exultation. It didn't last long, anyway. Soon he wobbled away to scold some human offspring tearing about the throne room.

"We make a good pair," Cyril said, his knobby fingers tweaking my ears as he smiled over the crowd. I slanted a look at him, detesting his persistent pets. "We should do this more often."

Aligning myself with him enthralled me about as much as a dunking in Isabel's copper bathtub. I doubted I'd ever forgive him for hurling me over the balcony.

He bellowed a laugh as if he understood and gave me a firm pat on the head. Perhaps he could. To be on the safe side, I allowed myself to revel in some black thoughts about his worthless, ill-timed, unwelcomed interference. I could have accomplished the same thing without his help...and without the dog-eaten drape.

"You're welcome," the wizard said amiably. "You really are a nice kitty, aren't you? It's buried deep, and one has to look *very* hard to find it, but you're a dear, sweet puss beneath all that temper."

I yowled disagreeably but could forgive his condescending tone because he was right about one thing: I was a *very* good kitty.

I couldn't help myself; it just came naturally.

Savannah Jezowski lives in Amish country with her Knight in Shining Armor and a wee warrior princess. She is the author of *When Ravens Fall* and The Neverway Chronicles. Her work is also featured in *Five Enchanted Roses* and three Fellowship of Fantasy anthologies. "The Witching Hour" is a standalone short story that introduces a longer tale. To learn more about Romeo, his friends, and the dark hounds dwelling beyond Lite, keep an eye out for "The Witching Hour: the Continuing Story" coming 2019.

www.dragonpenpress.com

The Tail of Two Kitlings

Sharon Hughson

Once upon a full moon, Furlined Catdom's ruler prowled the Royal Study, awaiting the birth of his heir. His plush, silver tail flicked in increasing agitation. Today was the second day since his queen's labor began, and kitbirth never took so long.

A long-haired page skidded to a stop inside the door. His Highness Tomcat Leopold curled his tail toward the interruption.

"Majesty." The page slouched to his belly and stared at his forepaws, the respectful posture due his ruler.

The tomcat's tail whipped as he whirled to face his subject. "What news, page?"

"Her Highness has delivered..." The pause elicited an electric hum from the wind fae circulating above the tomcat's head. "Siamese twins."

"Twins." A rush of delight fluttered in the tomcat's chest. He puffed it out. "Toms?" He forced his tone to neutrality.

"Yes, Majesty."

"And the queen?" He relaxed onto his haunches.

"Well, considering the extended labor."

The tomcat nodded his dismissal, pacing a few lengths of the room. Names swirled through his mind. They'd tentatively agreed on Simon, after his great-grandfather, the fourth tomcat ruler of the island in the era of peace following the birding. Should the second name rhyme? Or should there be alliteration? His queen would have ideas.

Tomcat Leopold padded into the wide hallway. From a nearby alcove, his Chief Advisor rose from behind a tower of parchments and fell into step beside him.

"Congratulations, sir. Two sons are better than one."

"What do you know of Siamese twins?" The tomcat's whiskers twitched. He should know the terminology.

"Siamese twins." His advisor cleared his throat with something less than a growl. "They are conjoined at some part of their anatomy."

"Conjoined? As in attached to each other?" His alarmed tone sent a mouse maid scurrying into the nearest servant passageway.

"Indeed."

"Can they be separated?"

"Depending on where the joining occurs—anatomically—it might be surgically possible."

The air around the tomcat hummed and spun in circles. His bonded fae set his whiskers tingling. Never a good sign. Generally a precursor to doom.

The pair of cats wound through the wide hallways and up the graded ramps to the Royal Quarters. Servants bowed and melted away. Activity buzzed in the circular hallway outside the four bedroom suites. The guard toms rapped their claws twice on the slate flooring before one of them opened the door and announced the tomcat's presence with a rumbling yowl.

Inside, two nursemollies circled an oversized cradle that stood where the special crib artisans had sculpted during the queen's month of confinement had been. The tomcat's fae compelled him to spy his sons' conjoining, but he resisted. The physician hovered at the queen's bedside. His tail feathers ruffled at the tomcat's entrance, but his wing stayed near the queen's face, fur still matted from the strain of kitbirth.

"Darling. You've done well."

Her whiskers trembled, and tears pooled in her wide amber eyes. The tomcat denied his urge to smooth his tongue over her face. He compromised with an audience-appropriate greeting, ducking to butt his forehead gently against hers.

"They're handsome, but..."

"We've only one name." He cut off her quavering admission. She wasn't ashamed of the kitlings, surely. "Simon for the firstborn. It is a tomcatly name."

Her whiskers stilled. A pensive look chased the moisture from her eyes.

The tomcat turned wide eyes toward the physician. "Physic Owl, I understand the conjoining can be surgically undone."

The physic's unblinking stare made the tomcat's spine tingle. He refused to let it ruffle his fur. He ruled this room, even if he needed the owl's expert advice.

"Come see the kits."

To keep the physic from reaching the cradle first, the tomcat sprang over his wife's bed, landing soundlessly beside the cradle. The nurses cowered, backing away with bellies scraping the ground.

Two black-masked faces writhed beneath a heavy blanket. The kits had silver fur, lighter than his own, puffing beneath their chins. The unusual face markings sent his wind fae into another spinning gyration around his head.

The owl swept the blanket aside, exposing pale bellies and curled black paws.

"The coloring." He had a pale stomach, and his wife had light striping, but neither of them had such dark paws.

"A sign of the Siamese, Highness."

The tomcat scanned the mewling figures but only saw two wholly separate bodies. Although their hindquarters abutted each other. He shivered with dread.

With a sweep of his wing, the owl turned the kits over.

A single black tail with two silver rings near the tip curled across the two backs. They shared a tail? A glorious tail was the signature of royalty. His own fluffed and bristled with hair longer than that of his body. The queen's was black-tipped but elegant, waving proudly as they paraded through their daily lives.

"Only one of them can have it." The owl's voice was a mere hiss of sound.

The tomcat gulped, his sandpapery tongue glued to the roof of his mouth. Must he pronounce eternal disgrace on one of his sons? His chest ached at the thought.

"Which is the heir?" His advisor stood a step behind, his green gaze fixed on the owl's. Not a whisker twitched in his ginger-striped face.

The owl's wing brushed one head. The ache deepened. Tomcat Leopold could barely draw oxygen in his lungs. The wind fae bound to him fluttered around his nose, forcing in some air.

Without a tail, the spare would be shamed or shunned his entire life. Would it be a mercy to ask the physic to end him when the surgery was performed? The tomcat had commanded soldiers to their deaths, but could he do the same for an innocent kit? One of his long-awaited sons?

"Leopold." The queen's voice startled him from the dark thoughts.

He sat beside his wife and curled his tail around his paws—a simple action one of his sons would never perform. He tried to form his lips into a gentle smile, knowing she needed reassurance. But who would comfort him?

"My love. You've done well." He blinked to clear the haze from his vision.

"But Siamese." Her voice faded away. Moisture sparkled in her eyes. "Leo, my fae believes—"

The tomcat twitched his tail in a silencing motion. "Clear the room." His voice boomed the order.

"Highness, the kits need the nursemollies." The owl's tone screamed with disapproval.

"It will be only a few minutes." He glared imperiously at the room's occupants, and the nursemollies shuffled toward the servant passageway inside the queen's wardrobe.

When the physic and the advisor shut the exterior door, the tomcat gave in to his instincts, tenderly caressing his wife's forehead with his tongue. Heat flushed through him, and his dry mouth flooded with moisture thanks to his wife's water fae bonds.

After several moments of nothing but the slurp of his kisses, Leopold said, "It will be all right." If only he believed it.

"My fae know of a Water Spirit who can undo the Siamese curse."

The tomcat jerked away from his queen, eyes widening and then narrowing. "Spirits aren't to be trusted. They always require a high price for their spells."

The queen flattened her ears. "Is any price too high for our sons?" Their gazes clashed. "She is favorable to me because of my bonds."

After a silence buzzing with antagonized wind fae and unblinking stares, the tomcat's whiskers sagged. "I'll send an ambassador."

She shook her head, amber eyes flicking toward the cradle where the piteous mews clamored. "I must take them."

Leopold hated the relief that flooded him as authority's burden of responsibility sloughed from his shoulders. Did a wise ruler relegate such a task as this? He stared at the squirming bundles of fur, and warmth speared his chest. His children. Magic might save one of them from a lifetime of hiding and scorn.

"I'll need a royal decree." The queen twisted, holding a paw toward the cradle. "We can offer perpetual abstinence of pollutants into Mystic Lake."

The tomcat nodded. It would be a meaningless parchment if the seabirds returned. After a decade, their instincts still told the flocks Fur Isle was their wintering place.

For love, Leopold would wage this war again.

Four Years Later

Black paws pinned the thin dark tail, and spiny claws ground against the playroom's wooden floor. Tomkit Simon yowled and tried to scrabble away. He twisted to face his twin brother who held him hostage.

"Ha! Pinned your tail." Tomkit Diamon twitched a pale nub on his backside.

Simon hissed. "Let go."

Last week, he'd been the one pouncing on the tail while his brother wore it. But yesterday on their birthday, the tail had been returned to Simon. It was his turn to wear it for six months.

"Magic word." Diamon's blue eyes sparkled.

His brother was always teasing and playing. They spent every moment of every day together, laughing and learning. But the first few days Simon wore the tail, something hardened in his chest.

"Boys!" Their nanny flattened her ears and bared her teeth, nipping at Diamon.

The door to the nursery creaked open. Tawny fur filled the doorway. Warmth flooded into Simon's stomach. He loved his mother's visits.

"Why don't you take a break?" The queen's commands sounded like requests.

"Mother." Diamon scampered around the nanny and butted his head against their mother's fluffy forelegs.

Simon twitched his tail. He smoothed the ruffled hair with his tongue before prancing across the room. The black tail flicked and curled above his back.

"How about a story?" His brother almost purred the question.

The queen licked the spot between Diamon's ears and prodded him toward the divan situated in the golden sunlight streaming through the large window. Simon trotted beside her, pausing to let her rough tongue caress his ear.

Once their mother settled onto her haunches in the middle of the plush seat, Simon nudged his head against her side and burrowed into a spot behind her front leg. Diamon did the same on her other side.

"When the two handsome kitlings were only three days old—"

Simon yawned. "You always tell this one."

"Because it's important."

"Can't you make up something?" Diamon looked hopeful.

"With swordfights and feather war capes." Simon slapped his tail, recalling Father's recounting of Grandfather's heroics as he drove the water birds from their nesting grounds and claimed the island catdom.

Mother's rough tongue massaged the top of Simon's head. He purred at her ministrations, so much gentler than the nanny's. When her warm breath stopped fanning him, he blinked. Her tongue slashed across Diamon's face.

He could endure Mother's story if it kept her close. Father had stopped letting them cuddle into his sides a few weeks before.

"On an important quest, a certain queen carried the precious bundles." Simon told the second line of the story before stretching out his paws and settling his chin on them.

"Surrounded by a host of tomcat guardsmen." Diamon sneezed, butting his paws against Simon's.

Simon stared at the identical black-masked face, remembering the first time they'd gazed into the fishpond together. The only difference was that one wore the tail and the other did not.

"Am I telling this?" Mother purred, licking Diamon's ear again.

Simon tucked his tail around him and licked the end of the royal appendage. Diamon's purr rumbled to life.

Once they'd been silent for several moments, Mother lowered her voice. "The queen left the royal entourage on the highway. Leaden fear weighed her stomach. Her fae flitted and screeched beside her ears."

Magical fae bonds. Simon closed his eyes. On their next birthday, the kitlings would travel to the sacred grove. During a sunset ceremony, the fae would be invited forth and encouraged to bond with the tomcat's children. Powerful wind fae like his father's would adopt him.

A breeze ruffled his fur. His ear twitched. Was that his mother's wind bond teasing him? Could they read his thoughts? Until they were bonded, the kitlings couldn't ask about the mysterious joining or what powers it granted.

"Mystic Spirit rose with a tidal wave of mist forming a rainbow around her. Voices of water fae thundered. The queen crouched on the ground, and the kitlings in their hammocks stirred from slumber."

His brother stared at Mother. Why? They'd heard this story dozens of times. Simon's thoughts drifted with his heavy eyelids.

A sharp hiss startled him. His heart jumped into his throat.

"Never bargain with an immortal spirit." Mother's voice was a harsh whisper. The tale was nearly told. "Their wily words trick mortals into life-altering, binding vows."

"And the kitling without a tail?" Diamon sat up, eyes wide with anticipation.

Mother sighed. "Neither kitling would bear the curse alone—or indefinitely."

Simon swished the tail, yawning and stretching. The end curled and then straightened behind him. He blinked at his brother's twitching stub. Did he imagine the tail moving behind him? Simon always did.

But his mother wasn't finished. "What do the queen's actions teach us?"

"Don't bargain with spirits." Diamon sprung up, flexing his claws.

Mother's whiskers twitched. Her amber gaze pinned Simon in place. He raised his chin.

"Even immortals are bound by treaties."

Mist clouded her gaze. She blinked.

"As long as someone willingly pays the price."

Fifteen Years Later

Tomkit Simon bristled and paced his room. Had his six months passed already? He growled at the thought of returning to Mystic Lake and handing his tail over to his brother for the next half-year. Simon would be exiled to the slopes of Mt. Outlook, forced to prowl through the forest in shame and dwell in a treehouse.

He was rightful heir to the catdom, and his mother's bargain hindered his ability to rule. Bound to this spirit's spell forever? It couldn't be possible. With his mother's passing, his father had withdrawn and left the burden of public appearances to his sons. The tomcat issued edicts from his private chambers, rarely emerging.

Simon flicked the fluffy black appendage trailing him. Why should Diamon enjoy the privilege of wearing the mantle of heirship? Why did the tomcat-to-be hide like a criminal in the wild lands? He couldn't even fish from the lake because of his father's treaty with the water witch.

Careful. His air fae buzzed the warning into his ears. He flicked them away with a twitch. He would be tomcat, and his word would be law. It was time for his brother to bear the brunt of the Siamese curse. Surely, Diamon knew this day would come.

Simon howled. His steward rushed in, scraping his chin on the floor, his ears perked toward his master's command.

"A scribe and parchment, Whisky." With a submissive grunt, the steward backed out of the room. "I'll procure the Tomcat's Signet."

Simon stalked toward his father's rooms. No one would stop his mission to break the curse.

Kitling Diamon crouched in the brush, ears perked toward the mouth of the cave. His fox spies had given him correct intel. A pair of eagles had nested inside the cavern on the Growling Sea side of Mt. Outlook, a clear violation of the Treaty of Nesting that ended the birding thirty years before. His father wouldn't even permit the gulls to declutter the beaches because he feared anything that might infringe on his peace accord with the spirit of Mystic Lake.

Diamon's hindquarters flinched, a habit he couldn't stop. He twitched the nub of cartilage, staring at the scar he bore from the surgeon's careful removal of the tail he shared with his brother at birth. His mother had sold her water fae bond to grant him equal time wearing the royal appendage.

He'd learned to despise the tail, black as his paws with two rings a measure from its tip. The tail signaled both his royalty and his shame.

He preferred the twitching silvery nub, the mark of a Manx. The greatest irony of his life: he escaped the curse of the Siamese to inherit the scorn of the Manx. Couldn't he be Diamon for once? Did he have to be the Tomkit of Furlined Catdom? That was his brother's role, but Simon couldn't live it because they shared the tail.

The accursed tail.

"Mon, what's the plan?" The fox's shrill whisper jerked Diamon back into the moment, where he crouched in the brush, at home in the woods where he spent the peaceful half of his life.

"Guess we'll come back tomorrow. When I have the authority to run them off."

Authority, but only when he wore the tail.

"Why wait?" The second fox's teeth flashed in a villainous smile. "We've got teeth. You've got claws. Seems like authority enough to me."

Diamon's whiskers vibrated, and he flicked an ear toward his comrade. Bald eagles were enormous, and their talons made his claws look like puny sewing needles beside a broadsword. In truth, he didn't see what harm the birds brought. They fished from the shallow tide pools, so the treaty with Mystic Spirit went unbroken. Even if they snatched smaller prey from the woods, it didn't compromise the hunters from nearby villages. Most villagers survived on an agrarian diet, including pork, chicken, and beef they raised. Those were unenlightened creatures, but the eagles were as sentient as the feline and canine families.

"We'll wait." Diamon backed carefully away from the cave.

After a few minutes, the foxes followed, and they scouted the forest paths around him. All the way to Mystic Lake where Diamon would exchange his freedom for a tail.

Late autumn mist shrouded the lake. Water fae chanted, keeping the earth and wind fae at bay. Diamon heard the melodic warning and coaxed his menagerie of fire and earth fae to settle into the smooth rocks beneath his feet. The rocks were middle ground, earth that had been fired and compressed and often smoothed by water. Stones warmed the pads of his front paws, but he couldn't relax enough to settle on his haunches.

A party of felines, the Siamese masked face of his brother leading them, appeared on the narrow pathway that wound through the thinner portion of woods to the lake-bound roadway. Calling the livestock-mowed grassy stretch a road was a stretch when compared to the heat-smoothed stone highways near the castle. His brother's ginger-striped steward was two steps behind, and a bastion of silver-coated black gibs, trained from kittenhood to serve as guardsmen for the tomcat, flanked him.

Diamon's sixth sense ruffled the fur on his spine. From the brush behind him, one of his companions yipped, "Betrayal. Beware."

Diamon steeled himself and walked stiff-legged toward his twin. Blue eyes exactly like his own narrowed, and Simon halted, making his brother come to him. Every gesture a reminder of who was the spare and who was the heir.

Diamon's hair bristled again, but he forced the ruff away.

"Ready to join civilization, brother?" Simon's growl made the rhetorical nature of the question clear.

A pang twanged in the hollow of Diamon's stomach. He hadn't eaten for a day because the transformation made him queasy, and hacking up his last meal degraded him in front of those who expected a tomkit worthy of the catdom. He missed the days when his brother called him Mon, and he could address him as Sie. Days that had disappeared four years ago when Diamon dared to show up to his mother's burial parade without a tail. He'd been disguised, but Simon could always sense him, and his brother had been furious that he'd tainted the family honor by showing his face while bearing the curse of the Manx.

Diamon wouldn't dishonor his mother by missing her farewell to the next life. Would it be her ninth? Or was she an occupant of Paradise even now?

Diamon glanced pointedly at the crowd of soldiers. "Has there been trouble?"

Simon bared his fangs, a hideous excuse for a smile. "There will be."

Attack or retreat. Retreat or attack.

The fae buzzed beneath his feet, but Diamon refused their advice. He would not retreat from his brother.

The steward held out a rolled parchment.

A bobcat sheltered in a branch overhanging the group of soldiers hissed, "Tomcat Leopold's Seal."

The guardsmen nearest the tree whirled toward the voice.

"Spies, brother? How trite." Saliva glittered on one of Simon's fangs before he sucked it back into his mouth.

Diamon swallowed the bitterness rising from his gut. The vibrations in his whiskers intensified. Today, his brother intended to leave this place with the tail still attached to his posterior.

A wave lapped against the shoreline. Water fae began singing Mystic's serenade. Time for the semiannual transaction that segmented his life into independence and duty drew near.

Diamon twisted to face the lake. It wouldn't do to rile the spirit, but he angled himself to keep watch on his brother from the corner of his eye.

The foxes slunk closer, still under cover but their musky scent surely obvious to the felines in the clearing.

Diamon stilled at the whisper from his bonded earth fae. His ear twitched, wanting to flick backward and check the progress of his forest pals, but he wouldn't give away their positions. If the guardsmen allowed themselves to be outflanked, they deserved whatever mischief the red ones heaped on them.

As the immortal elemental rose from the depths, water cascaded off her iridescent gown. Her blue hair mirrored the clearing sky, and her green eyes echoed the murky depths. In the rising sunlight, her skin seemed transparent, making her ethereal form appear to float toward them, stopping at the earth boundary of her element.

"Kitlings." She widened her arms, as if inviting them for an embrace. Only a fool would accept such an invitation. "You come in keeping with your mother's bargain."

Diamon's calloused pads scraped against the warm stones as his paws edged closer without his bidding. He instructed his fae to hold him in place. It was the way of immortal spirits to compel mortals into their element. The kitlings didn't need to be that close for her magic to work.

Diamon's forward momentum halted. A flicker from his brother's direction drew his gaze. The steward belly-crawled forward, pink nose nearly scratching a path through the gravelly shoreline. His paw held the scroll toward the glittering elemental towering above them.

"Immortal Spirit of Water." His voice rang although his lips were toward the ground. An earth bond then? "The Tomcat of Furlined Catdom requests a parley."

In the pause that followed, a sprinkling of water sprayed the assembly.

"Tomcat Leopold is not present." Her voice roared like a tidal wave.

Diamon wasn't the only one to flinch at the trumpeting sound.

"This missive bears his seal." The steward's voice shook. "His kitlings and humble servants make this ambassadorial journey in his stead."

More mist sprayed him. Diamon's ears drooped, trying to slough off the moisture. Warmth sizzled through his fur, and the crackling of his fire bonds burned away the droplets.

The scroll flew out of the steward's paws and into a hand that emerged from the depths of Mystic's fluttering skirt. The steward scuttled back without a glance.

After a moment of perusal, the spirit peeled back the wax seal. The parchment unrolled before her fingers could even move, and sea-green eyes surveyed the missive. After a brief pause, a clapping sound concussed their ears. The parchment arced on a wave to slosh at Simon's paws.

"Heir to the catdom, I see your hand in this."

"I would renegotiate the terms of this arrangement—this sharing of the tail." Simon dropped his chin in respect, but his eyes stayed pinned to the ethereal form.

Diamon's ruff fluffed out, but he forced it smooth. His brother's pride could cost him a grievous price this day. Diamon's gaze flicked between the spirit and his twin, but he refused to look directly at the Spirit of the Lake.

"You are not satisfied to wear the tail for half a year?"

"How can a catdom be ruled for only half a year? My responsibilities—"

"Your father lives. Your twin can share the meager kitling duties. The curse is allayed." Her swelling words pounded against Diamon's sensitive ears.

"My father's health fails."

Diamon's thudding heart pinched at the remark. His friends from the palace had mentioned nothing of this. He narrowed his eyes at Simon. What was his brother playing at?

"It is agreed that on my 20th birthday, he will step aside."

"There are six months yet." The spirit's response whistled like a whirlwind.

"I must plan and prepare. I can't spend those months exiled," Simon hissed, "as a worthless Manx."

Waves smashed around the spirit. A rainbow arched in the mist surrounding her. Mystic's expression remained unchanged, but a dangerous ice characterized her tone when next she spoke.

"My bargain with Queen Desdemona is perpetual." Thunder clapped. "Unless you are willing to pay the price for a new bargain."

A chill ruffled Diamon's fur. Bargains with elemental spirits were costly. His mother had paid with her own fae bonds, making them servants of the water spirit for twice his mother's lifetime.

"I keep the tail. My brother pays the price." Simon's growl was triumphant.

Hair rippled to attention along Diamon's back. A fox sprang from the forest toward the tomkit only to be intercepted by a guard. Diamon curled his claws into the rocks to keep from leaping on the traitorous kit himself.

Betrayal. Betrayal. His fae's whispers burned in his ears.

"You think to bargain with a life other than your own?" The spray accompanying the question fell as shards of ice over Simon and his party.

The steward cringed further into the ground, which shivered as his earth fae rippled in agitation.

"The tail is mine. I am the heir."

"Your mother sacrificed much so your brother could live. You cheapen her love."

"She's dead." Simon inched closer to the shoreline. His silver fur fluttered, likely created by his wind fae holding him from the pull of the chanting water fae. "I am the heir. The tail belongs to me."

Wind blustered against them. Stones of hail drummed, ricocheting off the stony bank. Diamon called on his fae to increase their holding and warming powers. It was the only way to remain standing and untouched by the elements.

The stony gaze of Mystic anchored him. His bones and muscles tugged within him, feeling like they might splinter him into quarters.

"And you Kitling Diamon. What say you?" Her powerful gaze shocked him.

His tongue stuck to the roof of his mouth. What could he say? He didn't want to rule, and if that was the only reward the tail bought, he didn't want it. The forest clans accepted him and included him. If the felines in the villages, towns, and cities shunned him, what did that prove? That they couldn't look past the scope of a tail?

"The tail is a curse, Wise Mystic." Diamon's growl wasn't menacing, but all his throat could muster. "My brother can keep it."

A howl rose from the depths. Mist swirled, and the image of his mother reflected in the white curtain the water created. Her amber eyes looked moist, and her whiskers shivered, like she walked into a gale.

Her voice echoed through the air. "I pledge my bonds, for this life and the next. They will serve you in my stead."

The wind whipped his fur, chilling him. Immediately, he understood the consequences of his mother's bargain. To save his life, because his father wished him dead rather than disgraced, his mother became a common cat in her next life. If she lived her ninth life without elemental fae bonds, she could forfeit her place in Paradise.

His ears flicked, and his whiskers vibrated. *I never asked for this. How could you presume to know what I would want?*

"You understand, kitling." The water spirit's voice whispered on the lessening gale. "Your vision isn't blinded by power lust."

"Not lust!" Simon's predatory roar silenced the noise of the forest. "It is my duty to administer the feline future of this catdom."

The tail had cursed them both, robbing them of brotherly affection and warping their idea of serving the catdom. Simon saw the palace and the villages as his community, and Diamon meshed with the less civilized forest clans. The drive to leadership compelled the kitlings. Simon lusted for the power of the throne. And Diamon? He desired freedom from those responsibilities.

The image of his mother faded, but her pledge rang in his mind and heart. *I didn't ask her to sacrifice her fae bonds. I would never.*

A blind kitten couldn't make such a decision, though. The queen had done what she could to protect him from the sword. His father loved both his sons, but he was the Tomcat of Furlined Catdom, practiced in making hard choices, choices that were paid for with blood.

Diamon's blood.

"What must I do?" The question hissed from him, barely audible.

The frenetic wind and waves calmed. Silence seeped from every element.

"You would forfeit your place in the royal family?"

Was he willing to never show his face in public again? He'd spent time with both his parents and his brother outside of public view during his months of Manx life. Wouldn't it be more of the same?

"You will be an outcast." Her eyes bored into him, sifting through his soul.

"The tail is a chain."

Simon growled. "Because you don't deserve it."

"Careful, kitling." An angry spray of water buffeted against Simon's wind barrier. "The immortals may decide to judge what you do or do not deserve."

Simon cringed, and the hair on his back stiffened.

"I forfeit my place in line to the throne." Diamon had never wanted it anyway.

Simon glared at him through narrowed eyes. He'd come with betrayal in his heart and mind, so he must assume Diamon was trying to turn the tables on him.

"I will pay nothing to keep the tail." Simon meant to sound like the Tomcat, but his so-called proclamation came out with questioning inflection.

"The price is paid." Water spun around the spirit, hiding her from view.

Pain poked into Diamon's hindquarters. *No.* He'd given up the tail and exchanged the scorn for freedom to live the life he wanted. He hissed, nipping at the spot of scar tissue on his rump.

A yowl burst from jaws he tried to clench, and he curled into a ball on the rocks. Red fur ruffled the air beside him. One of the foxes.

Diamon writhed on the stones. Crackles and tremors from his fae bonds barely registered through the darkening haze around his senses. This was worse than any transfer he'd suffered in his nineteen years of life.

What was the Mystic Lady doing to him? What price was his vow costing?

The torture ground his bones to dust. Muscles stretched and snapped. Surely, he would never move again once this bargain was completed.

Maybe that was his brother's plan all along.

His mind escaped the relentless agony and revisited years chasing Simon around their expansive play yard. They prowled, pounced, and played until the nanny drove them inside, teaching them the art of grooming.

His mother cuddled them as both kits nuzzled into her side. She purred out a lullaby or a story. She groomed each kitling with equal care and listened to their childish fantasies.

His father taught them to stalk and slash. After their sixth birthday, things changed. The tailless one spent six months exiled to a hunting cabin, where quality interactions with other family members became less each passing year. Diamon loved the woods and befriended even the canine species that resided there. Simon leapt to the lake on their birthday, glad to be restored to the tail and proper society.

The images blurred and faded. Diamon blinked. His body ached, and his hindquarters burned. Both foxes and the bobcat circled him, staring down with worry and panic warring in their expressions.

"That was horrible." The words came out with a groan, not at all the sarcastic rejoinder Diamon planned.

His muscles trembled like foliage under wind fae attack. Whirring fae sped around his ears, and he snapped at them like pesky insects. With shaking limbs, he pushed to his feet.

The group surrounding his brother gasped. Guardsmen sidled backward, distancing themselves from Simon. The steward, still prostrate, gaped.

The tail flicked instinctively. A fine mist cooled his sore muscles. The water spirit hovered ever closer, the zing of her magic still tainting the air.

Tail?

Diamon glimpsed toward his back. A long, fluffy black tail with only a faint silver tip switched the air. Several wind fae buzzed around it.

A glorious tail. Their voices chimed in his ear, as if they were bonded to him. *A most royal tail.*

"What have you done?" Diamon stared at Mystic. She'd given him the tail anyway. His brother would murder him for sure.

"Why? Why should he get a tail?" Simon's whine reminded him of their childhood years.

Diamon glared toward his brother. The tail they'd been born with twitched to and fro in agitation behind Simon. Its pair of silver rings marked it as unique.

"Will you never learn?" The spirit's voice stormed over them. "The selfless heart reaps rewards. Your mother taught you that truth in deed and word."

Simon sputtered, hissing and growling out a meaningless string of garble.

"I don't want the tail." Diamon straightened into soldierly stiffness, muscles moaning at the movement.

"This is not the cursed tail." Sea-green eyes softened and warmed.

A bevvy of wind fae smoothed along his back. Diamon shook his head. "My life without a tail is fulfilling."

"You wish a compromise?"

Warnings buzzed at him from every side. Immortals never compromised. There was always a price to be paid.

"I never asked for anything."

Wind and water buffeted him. The tail bent. Diamon hissed and yowled as pain ripped through the new appendage.

When the air cleared, the spirit loomed over him. He panted, and his legs trembled as he stood again. Fire buzzed up his back legs and along his tail.

Diamon blinked. The end of the tail curled, making it appear short and thick. The silver end bobbed as he twitched it.

"Neither Manx nor Royal." The spirit withdrew toward the lake. "Your brother will bear the cursed one—alone."

"Cursed? If I don't have to share it with him, there's no curse." Simon licked his lips with slow approval, as if tasting a sweet treat. "My bargain is accepted."

The spirit shook her head and slid into the water. A tear rolled down her translucent cheek.

"Wait! The wind fae." Why could he hear them?

"Your mother is beyond my reach. They were hers." The voice faded to a whisper. "Your pure heart caused the fae to bond with you in her stead."

Water frothed and whirled until the lake returned to its glassy norm. Without the mist, the far shore offered its verdant beauty.

"He has wind fae?" The steward's awe was apparent. "No feline bonds with three elements."

"A fluke. Or maybe a lie." Simon raised his chin and glowered down his nose at his brother. "Don't think that...stubby...thing...gives you right to the throne."

Diamon blinked. Had his brother heard nothing? Were his ears stopped by his own drive for power and prestige?

"I will stay in the forest." Diamon straightened and battered his fox companions with his flinching tail. "After I visit Father."

Fire smoldered in Simon's hateful gaze, which focused on the unique tail gracing Diamon's backside. Diamon's tail.

"The silver looks foolish on such a stump." Simon twitched the end of the tail they'd shared for a lifetime.

A tail with a different-colored tip marked Diamon as immortal-touched. It would inspire as much awe as his taillessness had gained spite.

The steward rose, his expression wistful as he stared at Diamon. With a toss of his royal blue cape, he dusted off his soiled limbs and marched toward Simon.

"You possess the tail, Milord. Your task is accomplished."

42

The ire remained in the ice-fire blue eyes staring at Diamon. His brother had expected Diamon to pay for the tail with his life.

Diamon's chest ached.

"It is your tail, Sie." He barely uttered the words, hoping the guards would not hear. "Be at peace."

His brother's strangled growl refused the advice. The tomkit stomped away, tail lofty and stiff. Several guards nodded to Diamon, and others ducked in a bow befitting the tomkit station. Diamon nodded in return.

The entourage disappeared in a slash of swinging branches and jangling mail.

The woods came alive around them. Chattering tree dogs and limb cats woke from the befuddled state the spirit's presence had cast over them.

Diamon stared at the faithful friends surrounding him. The bobcat, its own stubby tail pressed flat, bowed before slinking back into the brush.

Diamon flicked his tail and swung toward the mountain.

"We have an eagle to address."

The fox brothers yipped with delight, and the trio melted into the line of evergreens, oaks, and pines.

And for many full moons, they lived happily.

Sharon Hughson loves magical stories and cats, so it wasn't a stretch for her muse to dream up a tale about an island ruled by magical cats. In real life, her three cats assist her writing by jumping on her keyboard or demanding attention at inopportune moments. If not for her husband, she would be a crazy cat lady (and she doesn't think that's a bad thing). While she dreams in multicolor fantasy, most of her published works involve more romance and fewer feline characters, but always the same positive outlook and hope-filled resolution.

http://sharonleehughson.com/

Black Knight

LAURA L. ZIMMERMAN

*I*t begins on a night like any other, in a shadowed second-floor hallway of the typical middle-class American home. On the loft landing, the supercat, Black Knight, keeps a protective watch over his domain, muscles taut. The job is a dirty one, but somecat has to do it. A white-and-gray-spotted female kitten watches from below, her twitchy twin brother close by.

In the silence of the dark, Black Knight's distress signal shines from below, a pinpoint red dot jetting across the floor. It zigzags along the carpet, catching the supercat's attention. His pupils grow large with excitement.

The feline springs through the air, glossy black fur reflecting the luminescent light of the moon streaming from the window. He softly alights on the mud brown sofa covered in cat fur.

Black Knight's yellow eyes roam the living room for danger, finally settling on the familiar sibling kittens. "What seems to be the problem?" he asks in a raspy voice. With a lurch, his body convulses as he hacks up a hairball. "Ahem. Sorry about that." His voice is now low and deep.

"It's my ball," the female says. "The one with the jingly bell inside?" Her ears droop. "I've lost it. I was going to search for the blasted thing, but—"

Black Knight clears his throat again. "It's best to leave crime-solving to the professionals, miss. Can you describe this ball? The one with the jingly bell inside?"

The gray male kitten scoffs at his sister. "Give it a rest, Tink. You know where it is. It's in...The Bedroom." He shifts his gaze down the gloomy hallway, his ears twitching wildly.

"But, Tank, I'm scared." Tink cowers against the sofa, her gaze pleading with her brother.

"It's going to be all right, miss." Black Knight's whiskers spasm dramatically. "Sometimes the worst crimes smell like catnip."

"What are you talking about?" Tank shakes his head in confusion.

"It's a crime-fighter thing. You wouldn't understand." Black Knight looks to the side, aloof yet fully invested.

Tink shivers. "But, Tank, you know I won't go in there as long as the lights are out." She turns to the supercat and bats her eyelashes.

"Whoa, whoa." Black Knight raises a paw. "You want me to go into a dark room?" His eyes narrow as he glances toward the room in question. "Sorry. I don't do dark rooms. Too many...bad memories." He stares at the wall, a hidden recollection clearly not far from his mind.

"Oh." Tink frowns, casting a longing look in the direction of her lost toy.

"Well, what if we push the door open for you? So there's plenty of light from the hallway shining in?" Tank bounces on his back paws, mischief in his eyes.

"The Bedroom?" Black Knight asks. "Isn't that where The Boss lives?"

"Sure thing, but—"

Black Knight attempts to hack another hairball but comes up short. "Sorry, kids. That's off the plate, too. I don't tangle with The Boss directly. His network runs deep in these parts. It would take weeks of planning to take him down for good." He glances around with narrowed eyes.

A rumble comes from outside. Black Knight jumps three feet in the air, hackles raised, and races to hide under the closest chair.

"BK? You all right?" Tank trots over to check on the supercat.

"W-was that thunder?" A strange whine echoes from the back of the supercat's throat.

"Nah. That's just the smelly old truck from the neighbor." Tank's easy smile fades, his brow pulled tight. "Hey, you okay?"

Black Knight exhales. "Right. Yes." Slowly, he creeps from the security of his hiding place, chin tilted high once more.

Tank's ears flatten against his head. "Um, what exactly are you good at?"

"Excuse me?" Black Knight licks his paw, wrapping his tail around his body.

"Well, if you're afraid of the dark and of The Boss—"

"And of thunderstorms," Tink adds as she bats her eyelashes at the supercat once again.

"Don't forget loud noises." Black Knight nods in agreement.

Tank blinks rapidly but recovers. "Then, what is it exactly that you do?"

"I fight crime. My identity is secret, so I'll never have fame, true, but...somecat's got to do it." The supercat prances back and forth as he boasts.

Tank rolls his eyes. "What I mean is, if you're so afraid of everything, then what are you a supercat *of*?"

Black Knight bounds across the living room, coming to rest beside a ceramic lamp with visible cracks, small clumps of glue residue plastered

46

throughout. He squints at the twins with a smug expression. "Allow me to show you." He swishes his tail. "You might want to take cover."

Before either kitten can question him, he swipes his paw in a karate chop action. The lamp tumbles to the ground with a crash. Black Knight disappears into the shadows, the spot where he stood now void of cat or lighting fixture.

"What in the world?" a deep voice booms from The Bedroom, followed by heavy footsteps.

Black Knight's claws dig into the carpet from his spot beneath the sofa. He gives a curt nod to the kittens where he spies them hiding under the dining table. With a sniff, he braces himself.

Then the supercat is gone.

The Boss mumbles as he sifts through the carnage that once was the lamp. "Not again!" Minutes pass while he fills a garbage bag with shards of glass and grumbles, "I'll deal with the rest of this mess in the morning." He stomps off to The Bedroom.

In the shadows of the night, a dark figure creeps into the living room once more, something round and jingly between his teeth. Tink and Tank emerge from the safety of their position, curious looks on their faces.

Black Knight drops Tink's jingly ball at her feet. He stretches, a chuckle barely contained. "Mission accomplished."

Tink sighs, gazing longingly at the brave supercat. "My ball," she purrs.

"So, you just...retrieve lost balls?" Tank asks, doubt lacing his voice.

Black Knight bounds onto the sofa, head stretched high with pride. "No, my young feline. I'm a supercat. *A supercat of distraction.*"

Without another meow, he takes his post at the top of the stairs, his keen eye back on the job of protecting his beloved domain.

Another crime has been solved by the mysterious supercat. The house is quiet, the halls safe for felines to roam, the distress signal silent. Silent until Black Knight is summoned again, called to bring peace and harmony to the halls of his home once more.

Laura L. Zimmerman is a homeschooling mom to three daughters and a doting wife to one husband. She currently resides in a suburb of Charlotte, North Carolina. Besides writing, she is passionate about loving Jesus, singing loudly, drinking coffee, and pretending to do yoga. You can connect with her on Instagram (@lauralzimmauthor) and Twitter (@lauralzimm).

www.lauralzimmerman.com

Sulphur & Sunshine

GRACE BRIDGES

As if the summer day wasn't warm enough already, steam rose lazily from the drains and gutters of Rotorua. Somewhere far below, a hot spring's emergence had broken through the manmade pipes again and now found its way up, up to the world of light, *te ao marama*.

A lanky yellow street cat dodged a plume of steam where it split into hazy stripes over a metal grille, then she loped on through the back alleys and parks. For her, safety lay away from the busy central city. Instinct and hunger called her to watch the seagulls at the shoreline; perhaps one would be slow enough for her to catch today.

Besides, she remembered—with some yearning—a person who often sat on the boardwalk at lake's edge, surveying the cloudy water of Sulphur Bay. A person of indeterminate appearance but reasonably advanced age; a person who had smiled at her and shared bits of a picnic on occasion.

The cat made her way down one final block toward the shore, passing a couple of hotels. She dodged the door of the last one as a crowd of oddly-dressed humans tumbled out, laughing; some wore jingly metallic accessories, others strange headgear, while some carried gnarled sticks and one even looked like he had pointed ears. The cat cocked one of her own ears at this; humans were not supposed to look like that!

She skirted the crowd and trotted off toward the boardwalk, tail held high. Was her friend here? She sniffed the air, laden with the aromas of warm sulphur and seagull guano. The birds wheeled above, eyeing her closely but keeping their distance.

Yes—that hint of a scent—it was her person. She approached the wooden bench from behind and curled around the stubby legs before it. The person greeted her with soft and friendly tones, but spread empty hands, looking along the shore to the south. *Yes, yes,* said the cat's stomach. *That's where the great yellow house of food is.* She was pleased when the person creaked upright, patted her goodbye, and set off in that direction; perhaps there would be food in a little while, if she just waited.

Well, waited nearby, at least. The cat pushed through the gap in the boardwalk's railings and paced out over the sulphurous rock. Gulls shrieked when she got too near a nest, so she detoured toward the waterline, but kept watch anyway, seating her thin hips on the thermally warmed stone.

The sun burst out from behind a cloud, and the cat half-closed her eyes for a moment, basking in the heat from above and below. Before she could stretch and relax her muscles, something huffed nearby, and she became fully alert in an instant. Her head turned toward the odd disturbance.

Fire. She did not know its name, but she knew what it was. A small clump of powdery sulphur burned all by itself not two feet from her nose. Hair rose along her back and her tail puffed up.

She backed away, afraid; her back paw sploshed into the edge of the lakewater.

Now, we all have a fairly good idea what a cat might do when suddenly becoming wet. That's right—fire or not, she marched back up the rocks, shaking her paw then sitting down to give it a good lick. And that's when it happened.

Who left a great ruddy lake just exactly there, anyway? How inconvenient of them.

The cat blinked. *What's all this then—I'm stringing words together in my head. I know what they mean. I think, therefore...*

She remembered just a few moments ago, when she had lived on instinct alone, nothing more. Of course, it was adequate, it was how all cats existed. But now that she was discovering the power of actual thought, her prior awareness seemed much inferior.

Lick, lick. The foot was mostly dry. She set it down and eyed the glowing sulphur with rather more consideration than before. The flame was only just visible, a blueness engulfing the stone that now melted into a puddle of viscous red. *Sulphur deposits are liable to spontaneous combustion if the sunshine is strong enough.* She flicked an ear, shook her head. *How do I know these things?*

She turned her head, and her gaze fell on the row of hotels, suddenly understanding that the pointy-eared human was just dressing up for fun, the same as the others with him. *Fake ears. I know about cosplay, a lot of it goes on here, after all. I just never had a name for it before.* She shook herself, but the strange feeling did not dissipate. Her eyes panned and took in the view of the bay, the noisy gulls in their animal instincts, the milky water where the thermal springs lurked below. The panorama was familiar, but now she regarded it with a sharpness that was clearly unrelated to her magnificent feline vision.

Oh. That's new, too. Well, she had always had her rightful share of catitude, the non-verbal kind. This *wordy* attitude was a whole other level. Her eyelids drooped in a smile. She could get used to this.

The sulphur fire flared up, blue-white and transparent, and she thought it must be going out. Such a little pebble to burn so long alone! But as she watched, the shape of the flame extended and spread, gaining clear edges and a shape that remained stable even as it flickered.

That's not normal. Neither was thinking in words, but fires certainly weren't supposed to behave like that, even weird mineral fires on thermally heated shores.

The shape morphed into something resembling a cat's head. Suddenly the street moggy had thoughts of Bast or perhaps some other feline deity—how *could* she know of these things?—an entity from the unseen world grew solid before her, though made of delicate fire.

All of her thoughts were impossible, including *having* thoughts in the first place. But she kept her perfect poise, observing the creature before her and no doubt likewise being observed.

Not a cat. A dragon. The difference was delicate, and she looked away. Not Bast, then.

The body made of flames rose farther out of the ground until finally it stood before her, four sinewed legs, a pair of strong wings, a fierce kind of face she thought couldn't be entirely non-feline in nature. The sulphur pebble burned on, a small flicker against the horse-sized being who now paced a small circle around the immediate area.

The cawing of gulls had stopped entirely, and a glance told the cat they had all vanished away. Had they seen what was happening? Could they? People walking by on the boardwalk not twenty feet away paid no attention, leading her to believe they were unable to perceive the dragon.

A sound brought her attention back to the dragon. It was a rustling, burning sort of voice, and to her surprise, she understood it.

"Kua karanga koe i ahau."

The cat comprehended at once that the creature was speaking Māori and also that she could understand it without translating. *A language of the heart. Wait, so that means my head speaks a different language…* Her brain lit up more with every moment. It would hurt if it wasn't so beautiful.

The dragon went on smoothly in Māori. "You called me here, to the burning stone. Why?"

Sunshine called you here, then. The stone burns of its own self in the sun.

The dragon frowned down at her. Had it heard her thoughts? Apparently so, for it replied. "You are sunshine, then."

Am I? She glanced down at her golden self and spared a self-conscious lick to her shoulder. *I'm certainly the right shade of yellow.*

The dragon blinked slowly, a friendly gesture. "Hello, Sunshine. Why did you call me?"

I don't think I did. You know, around here sometimes things burn without help.

"I do have a certain...connection to the sun, myself. But I am here now."

What are you going to do? Sunshine watched as the creature stopped its pacing and looked at her.

"I do not know. No human has called me. You have no request yourself."

Is this a problem for you?

"Only because it should not happen. I come when the humans call in the right way. The proper call has been made...without humans."

Sunshine sauntered over to the burning sulphur pebble. Beside it, a patch of yellow gleamed among the other, dimmer rocks. *That'll be why. Some seagull has scratched the top off this sulphur deposit, so the sunshine can set it alight. It's exposed.*

"Kei te manea koe, e ngeru," said the dragon.

Sunshine restrained a snort. Of course she was clever. *No need to state the obvious, friend taniwha.*

Taniwha, of course. More brand-new puzzle pieces fell into place behind Sunshine's sharp eyes. *Rotorua is famous for its taniwha. I am pleased to meet you.*

The dragon chuckled softly, a deep rumbling crackle of fire. "In any case, you are right. These birds have exposed the sulphur to the heat of the sun, and that means I can be called...by accident."

Something's wrong with this picture.

The taniwha nodded its enormous head. "Can you help me?"

Me? Help you? Surely, Mr. Taniwha, you are the stronger of us two.

"Kaore he tāne."

Not a mister. Okay, fine. Miss? Mrs.?

"Not that either. It doesn't matter. Back to the point. Will you help?"

Depends what it is you want done. I'm just a cat, even though I'm so fabulous.

"Ko te mea nui... The important thing is, I am not a physical form. I can take on a physical shape with great effort, but this is not an emergency."

Sunshine thought she could tell where he—she?—was going with this. *You want me to do something physical for you.*

"Ae, little Sunshine. You said the birds uncovered that patch of sulphur. Do you think you could cover it again?"

Things became clear. Sunshine pointed her nose in the air. *You want me to DIG?*

"I cannot do it. But if it is not done, that patch or others like it will burn up in the sun, and I will be called from my rest without reason again."

With this, Sunshine experienced deep empathy. She didn't like being woken up for nothing either. *If I cover this patch, what will you do for me?*

"You don't know what I have done for you already? Think about it."

Sunshine did so, and the answer was clear as day. *It's you! This is your power that—somehow turned my brain on.* She bared her long front teeth ever so slightly. *Will this...thinking...remain after you return to your bed?*

"I will see if I can make it so. I need you to make sure none of this sulphur burns needlessly."

Makes sense. Sunshine even nodded, just as she'd seen humans do often. Now she knew what it meant. *If my thinking sleeps as before, I will not know to keep the sulphur buried.*

"True enough. Let me touch your mind, to keep it sharp if I can."

Sunshine flattened her ears against her head. *I don't like it. But I suppose you must.* This day was just an enormous pile of impossible things so far. One more made little difference at this point.

The dragon nodded and reached out a fiery wingtip. It brushed the top of Sunshine's head, and she shivered despite the blaze of heat.

"Ngā mihi," said the taniwha. Thank you.

You're welcome, I'm sure. Thank you for a most enlightening day. I do have one other request...

"Nō reira, kōrero mai." Therefore, speak it to me.

Tell my person my new name. Sunshine glanced over her shoulder at the hunched figure even now hurrying back from the shop in the next block over.

The taniwha followed her gaze and laughed. "Your person has a name, too, you know. That's Harley, who has also received gifts from my kind."

How do you know Harley's name?

Another laugh. "Harley is my person, too."

Sunshine clambered over the boulders to the patch of sulphur, where she scratched at inert sandstones and loose pumice until only a glimmer of yellow remained. Easy enough. Before she swiped a paw over the last of it, she looked up at the dragon again and saw that the original pebble was about to go out. She and the dragon exchanged another slow blink, and she turned back to her task. A swipe, a kick, and it was done—thankfully there were no other bits of naked sulphur in sight. *But who knows what the birds will get up to, I'll have to keep an eye out—*

"I'm sorry. It's not working," said the taniwha, fading right alongside the last of the sulphur flame and Sunshine's clarity of thought. "I may yet call on you to awaken again..."

The cat found herself alone on the lakeshore, contemplating her very dusty paws. She set about cleaning them.

Harley rushed back from the supermarket, clutching a packet of cat treats and a little slice of fresh fish. But the boardwalk was empty. *Just my luck, that cat's gone and vanished again even though I asked it to stay.*

Sigh. Harley leaned on the railing and surveyed the expanse of sulphur-filled rock where the gulls nested. Such a familiar sight; the sight of home, really. *Wait, what's that?* Harley's eyes narrowed. Sure enough, way out there on the rocks, the golden cat licked at her paws like she hadn't a care in the world.

"Oi!" said Harley. *Blimmin' cat needs a name. I see her around often enough.*

The cat looked up, and Harley thought there was a trace of feline smile around her eyes, but she kept right on licking that paw. "Don't make me come over there."

Harley waited a bare minute. The cat remained planted where she was. "Fine. I'm coming." Around the end of the railing, across the pale rough stone and some larger rocky outcrops. Harley peered at the ground, suspicious. Was that the scent of burning?

Finally, Harley approached the cat. "You'll be wanting some of this, little missy."

The cat smelled fish at last and approached, sniffing at the package while Harley tore it open.

Some moments later, Harley's eye fell upon a disturbed patch of ground. A burnt-out pebble rested beside a series of burn marks...that strongly resembled...*letters?*

Harley stepped closer to examine the markings, sounding out the word hidden in plain sight. "Tama-nui-te-rā." A long, low whistle caught the cat's attention, but she returned immediately to her fish. Harley stared at the ground a little longer, then at the sky, and the cat. "The name of the sun himself, eh? I guess he set the sulphur on fire again. Hope there's no more while I'm standing here."

The cat finished the fish and came seeking the other treats, her purr a sudden loud rumble. Harley opened the bag and spilled some out, and the cat allowed herself to be patted as she ate.

"Little golden missy," said Harley. "I think your name will have to be Sunshine."

Grace Bridges is a geyser hunter, cat herder, professional editor, and translator. She has edited and co-edited a number of short story collections including *Avenir Eclectia*, *To Speak of the Home Fires Burning*, and *Timegate to Tomorrow*. Her novels encompass space opera, Irish cyberpunk, and the *Earthcore* urban fantasy series, of which "Sulphur & Sunshine" is a part. Several of her works and edited collections have been shortlisted for the Sir Julius Vogel Award from the Science Fiction & Fantasy Association of New Zealand, and *Mariah's Prologues* won Best Collection in 2018. Read another *Earthcore* story for free at www.gracebridges.kiwi.

The Magic of Catnip

A. J. Bakke

The automatic doors swished closed behind her as Julia walked out of the pet store. Rain fell sideways beyond the awning protecting the entryway, and a waterfall noisily splattered on the pavement.

She reached for her hood to pull it up but paused when she caught movement in her peripheral.

A young girl approached her. Her cat-themed onesie was cute, if a little out of place in this kind of weather. She held out a plastic baggy of what Julia hoped was something innocuous.

"Fresh ground catnip?" the girl asked beseechingly. "It's only a dollar."

"Um…" Julia didn't exactly need more catnip, but how could she say no? Something about the child's gaze compelled her. "Is this a new fundraiser thing?" she asked as she fished a dollar from her purse.

The girl smiled and handed her the baggie in return. "Oh no, I just like to entertain cats. Catnip is magic to them."

"That it is," Julia warmly agreed. "Thanks!"

"Have a good day, ma'am," the girl responded brightly before walking back to her post by the door to await more potential customers.

"Funny," Julia mumbled to herself as she scurried out under the rain. "She wasn't there when I came in."

Once safe in her car, misgivings suddenly hit her as she put her bag of purchases in the otherwise empty passenger's seat.

She brushed blond bangs from her face and looked at the baggie. "I really hope this is catnip." Opening it, she gave it a wary sniff. "It smells like catnip and not skunk." Whew. Looking toward the store, she noticed that the girl was gone. Most likely the "lovely" spring weather had driven her inside.

At home, Julia dodged around three cats to carry her bags to the kitchen counter.

"All right, all right, I'll feed you. Just wait a second."

Tapioca, a white short-hair, meowed pitifully, trying to rub against her legs.

Julia stumbled as she attempted to avoid her and not step on the calico Ginger who had stealthed behind her.

"You guys are gonna be the death of me!" Julia exclaimed. She unpacked the bag and cut a mouse toy free from its packaging.

"Here!" She threw it toward the living room. All three cats raced after it. Macchiato got to it first, plowing into it and rolling with it. He was the biggest of the three. Almost all black fluffy fur. He had a little white mustache and one white paw.

"You guys will be bored with it in three seconds anyway," Julia mumbled. Annoyed with herself, she added, "I forgot to lock the door again. Why do I do that?" She went back and clicked the knob lock before turning the deadbolt into place. Someone had recently "broken" into her house by walking right in the front door while she was at work. This wasn't the greatest neighborhood, so she needed to be more careful.

Other homes in the area had also suffered the same fate lately: someone walking in or breaking in. According to the news, they hadn't caught the perpetrator yet.

"I hate thieves," she muttered on her way back to the kitchen. She got down on hands and knees to reach under a table and retrieve an "old" toy. "Old" meaning she had bought it maybe a month ago.

It looked like some kind of weird fuzzy weasel thing to her, so that's what she called it: the fuzzy-weasel-thing.

"This should renew interest." She put it in a plastic container that used to hold peanuts. She now used it for revitalizing cat toys with catnip. She sprinkled some of the new catnip in with the toy and then put the lid on. After giving it a good shake, she set it down on the counter and moved on to feed the cats before leaving for work.

She returned late that evening, dragging from a long shift of janitorial duty. It wasn't anything amazing, but it sort of paid the bills. The best thing about the job was that there weren't a lot of people involved.

She locked the door and then gave the cats a quizzical look.

All three crouched by the couch, tails twitching, staring under it.

Julia paused. "Lose it already?" No doubt the toy mouse she had bought that morning was underneath the couch with a graveyard of other lost toys. She stopped to run a hand along Ginger's back, but none of the cats really paid attention to her. They were very focused on that mouse for some reason.

"Well, okay." She yawned, ready to settle down and read with cats piled on her before bed.

Her plans to pass the kitchen were foiled when she noticed the container she had put the fuzzy-weasel-thing in lay on its side on the counter, open, the lid on the floor.

"Huh. You guys must have really wanted that toy." She stooped down and picked the lid up. She didn't feel like putting another toy in it, so she put the lid on the container and brushed scattered catnip off the counter.

The cats would happily roll in it later.

Grabbing a book, she reclined on the couch with plenty of lap room for kitties. One by one, they abandoned their post and gathered on her legs, purring and grooming each other.

As Julia became happily lost in the story, a skittering sound drew her out of it. She looked up and around. The cats also went on alert, ears pricked.

"What was that?" Julia asked, listening intently.

The sound happened again, running from the back of the room to another part. Julia looked down at the floor. Nothing. She looked around at the walls. Nothing. She looked at the ceiling—

The fuzzy-weasel-thing was up there, stuck to the ceiling.

She put the book down. "What...the...?"

The cats grudgingly moved as she scooted to stand.

Peering up at the toy, Julia wondered how it had even gotten up there. "Was it you, Macchiato?" He was the only cat she could think of that could throw something that high.

Grabbing a handy backscratcher lying on a nearby table, she poked at the toy to dislodge it.

What happened next was not what she expected in good ol' solid reality.

It moved! Clinging to the ceiling, it slithered along with a faint pattering sound like many tiny feet. That didn't make sense. It didn't even *have* feet!

Julia jumped and screamed as it shot down the wall and then took off across the floor.

The cats dashed after it in a heartbeat.

It ran under the couch, but Macchiato snagged it with a paw, dragging it out and flipping it in the air. It twisted about and then darted away as soon as it hit the floor.

Its trajectory took it toward Julia's feet. She shrieked and jumped backward to get out of its way. It abruptly changed direction and ran for a wall, skittering up as if it were a spider-fuzzy-weasel-thing.

Ginger leapt for it, caught it, and brought it back down. It squirmed in her grasp.

Julia backed into the wall by the door. She felt around for the doorknob she knew was nearby but didn't dare look to check because she was too busy watching the horror play out before her.

The toy escaped Ginger's clutches and slipped under the couch.

The cats gathered to stare, waiting for it to emerge, ready to pounce.

Hand on the doorknob, Julia reminded herself to breathe. "This isn't real. This isn't happening. I must be dreaming."

She pinched herself.

"Ow!" Well, that hurt. Was she awake then?

She edged around the room, giving the couch a wide berth. Creeping into the kitchen, she grabbed a butterfly net she kept in the corner niche with the garbage can, mop, vacuum cleaner, and broom. She generally used the net to catch bugs outside and bring them in for the cats to chase. That wasn't weird at all, right? No stranger than a live cat toy running around the house.

Heart pounding, she stalked toward the couch, holding the net ready. Macchiato lay on his side, reaching under the couch with a paw, but he couldn't seem to reach the animated toy.

They all waited. And waited. And waited.

Nothing happened.

Finally, Julia became too impatient to be afraid anymore. "I can't handle this kind of suspense." Net in one hand, she tiptoed to the couch and then squatted to grab the front end and lift it up.

"Oh, what am I doing?" she exclaimed. She gently set the couch back down then grabbed a flashlight before returning to lift it again. Once it was high enough, she slipped a knee under the front to brace it.

Among a million coffee drink stoppers, hairbands, milk jug rings, and other random cat toys, she finally spotted the fuzzy-weasel-thing.

Its beady eyes glinted with malice as the flashlight hit it.

Julia froze, heart in her throat.

The toy didn't move.

But the cats did! They wiggled underneath and began to explore, sniffing at all their long lost toys.

"You guys!" Julia exclaimed in dismay. "I can't hold the couch up forever."

She tried to shoo the cats out, but they wouldn't leave. Her arm and leg shook with fatigue. "Ow..." Carefully, she lifted the couch higher until it leaned against the wall behind it.

Tapioca patted at a hairband until she could flip it up enough to catch it in her mouth. She bounded away with her favorite treasure.

Letting the cats do their thing, Julia crept toward the miscreant toy and poked at it with the handle of the net.

Nothing happened.

She poked it a few more times before catching it in the net and twining the fabric around it to keep it there.

"I'm crazy," she mumbled as she carried it to the kitchen to find something to put it in. For lack of anything better, she put it in the container it had been in originally to soak up catnip.

Then she shook a bag of cat treats to lure the cats from under the couch so she could put it back down without squishing anyone.

Sleep wasn't even on the menu after something like that. Julia tried to relax and read for a while, but she couldn't settle the restless fear thrumming through her veins.

"Sorry, guys." She gently pushed the cats off of her and went back to the toy in the container. She gave the container a shake, shifting toy and residual catnip around inside it.

The toy jumped at the side, thunking into it.

Julia shrieked and dropped it on the floor.

The toy hit the sides, making the container shift around.

"Oh no! Oh no! It's real!" She ran and grabbed her phone to start recording it. That way she would have a record of it doing this that she could watch later to assure herself that it was really happening.

"I could get famous," she mumbled but then said, "Naw. People would just think it's special effects."

The cats came running to bat at the container, sending it sliding across the kitchen floor. The toy continued its fight for freedom. All the jostling started to wiggle the lid loose.

"Oh no, you don't!" Julia set her phone aside and scrambled to grab the container. She tightened the lid and set the container down on the floor.

After watching the toy bounce, skitter, and slither around in confinement for half an hour or so, it abruptly stopped, falling limp and motionless.

Macchiato batted the side of the container as if hoping to make the toy move some more.

Tapioca turned a pleading gaze on Julia and meowed, disappointed that their fun was over.

Ginger merely wandered off with her fluffy tail curved in the air.

"Is this a trick?" Julia examined the toy warily, turning the container around in her hands. She gave it a shake, but the toy didn't react.

Fearing for her fingers' lives, she undid the lid and cautiously took the toy out. It hung in her hand, appearing to be perfectly normal.

Since she had successfully caught it before, she braved throwing it out on the floor. All three cats dove for it and started playing around with it. Macchiato used his bulk to push the other two away so he could monopolize the toy. He rolled around, throwing it, licking the deliciousness of catnip, and hugging it with his forelegs to claw at it with his back legs.

Ginger huffed and turned away in offense while Tapioca lurked, waiting for her moment to snag the toy.

Julia looked at the container, then the cats and the toy, then the container, then the cats and the toy. "Hmm. Who needs sleep anyway?" She made herself a pot of coffee. While it brewed, she put more catnip in the container and then dropped a little white fluffy mouse toy in it. The tail had long since been chewed off and eaten by Ginger.

She shook the container and then waited while sipping her coffee. She was soon rewarded when the toy bounced to life and began trying to escape. Smaller and weaker than the fuzzy-weasel-thing, it didn't move the container nearly as much.

Fascinated, Julia picked the container up and watched it. "That must be some interesting catnip." Did she dare call it "magic?"

Tapioca, Macchiato, and Ginger gathered around her legs, bright eyes staring up at the toy with playful hope.

Julia couldn't think of anyone she dared tell. She wasn't so sure about the reality of it all, herself. She decided to keep this weirdness close to the chest for the time being.

She took the lid off and dumped the mouse on the floor. It dashed away, the cats hot on its lack of tail. The toy managed to outlast the cats since they had already spent a lot of time chasing the prior one.

Macchiato gave up first, lying down, tail flicking as he panted for breath.

Ginger and Tapioca soon followed suit, idly watching as the mouse toy skittered back and forth along the base of a wall. There didn't seem to be any rhyme or reason to its choice of direction.

The next day, Julia tried a different toy.

"This stick is annoying," she remarked as she shook a feather toy inside the container. The toy was attached to a string which in turn was attached to a stick that clattered and bumped with the jostling.

Once the toy burst to life, she set it free. The cats raced after it.

"It flies!" Julia exclaimed in delight.

The stick wavered out behind as the toy flew around the house, feathers spinning.

Macchiato got bopped on the nose by the swinging stick. He skidded to a halt, shaking his head in surprise.

Concerned, Julia joined the chase, catching the stick. "I'm sorry, Macchiato. That wasn't well-thought-out."

The feather toy fluttered around on its tether, seeking freedom while Julia took it back into the kitchen. The toy changed direction often, tugging the stick. She held it tightly as she grabbed scissors.

She didn't want to risk the cats being strangled by the string, so she pinned the feathers down and snipped the string off at the base of the toy.

Lifting her hand, she set it free.

Another problem soon presented itself as the toy ran into pictures on the walls. All of the collectibles were safe behind glass, but Julia worried it might destroy a painting.

The cats enthusiastically chased it around as it dipped and whirled, almost as if it were teasing them on purpose. While the toy kept the cats entertained, Julia took all of her framed pictures and paintings down and squirreled them away in the extra room she used to store random stuff in.

After that, she stuck to toys that mostly stayed on the floor. Every day, before and after work, she let a toy or two loose for the cats to chase.

She used the catnip sparingly to make it last. She had a funny feeling that she would never see that little girl again. Still, she cruised by the pet store now and then to check.

Each toy remained "alive" depending on how long they had been exposed to the catnip.

A couple of weeks later, Julia put the last of the catnip in the container with a sigh.

She heard the telltale thump and rustle of excited kitties dashing toward the kitchen.

"This is the last of it, guys," she said as she dropped five sparkle balls inside and shook them around with the catnip. She set it down while they soaked up the magic.

She turned toward the living room.

The sound she had thought was the cats—

—had not been her furry little family.

Where there should have been cats, a man stood with a bandana around his face to hide most of his features except malicious eyes.

Julia froze, staring at him in shock. Where had he come from? She must have left that stupid door unlocked.

"Hey there, sweetie," he said, brandishing a crowbar.

Julia mentally ran through a quick list of nearby weapons and drew a blank, unless she wanted to try fending him off with a spatula. All of her knives were in a lower cupboard. She wasn't going to get to them before he got to her.

Heart pounding painfully in her chest, she grabbed the container of sparkle balls. They weren't moving yet.

The man laughed. "Seriously? You think cat toys are going to hurt me? You're crazy!"

Nothing new, she intended to say, but the words stuck in her throat. She backed away, but the counter soon stopped her from going any farther.

The intruder seemed to enjoy her fear and helplessness as he slowly walked toward her, taking his time. Where would she go? It wasn't like she had a lot of options.

She shakily unscrewed the lid, inwardly praying like mad that she hadn't been delusional all this time. Her life depended on it.

He raised the crowbar. "This can go painful or extremely painful for you. Your choice."

"I choose neither," she gasped in a trembling voice. She had meant for it to be firm and brave.

He laughed.

She launched the sparkle balls at his face.

The timing couldn't have been more perfect.

They burst to life as he yelled in surprise, swinging the crowbar around. He accidentally bopped himself on the head with it as the glittering toys assaulted his face, bouncing around and trying to cling to his eyeballs.

Julia watched, eyes wide. She could barely believe this was happening.

Screaming, the intruder flailed and stumbled around. He dropped the crowbar and fled the house, leaving through the front door. He didn't bother to close it behind him.

Julia *had* left the door unlocked! Grrr!

Vaguely, she hoped none of the cats had run outside as she dashed to close the door and lock it. She peeked through the trio of partitioned mini-windows.

The man ran down the lamplit street, sparkly cat toys bouncing around on his head.

Julia double- and triple-checked the lock. Her pulse raced, and her knees turned to rubber. She sank to the floor, leaning back against the door, trying to calm herself down.

It had all happened so fast. Should she call the police? How would she explain the killer attack cat toys?

Slowly, all three of her cats ventured out of hiding to join her, cuddling around her and purring.

She had all of her cats. She was alive. Everything would be okay.

Thanks to the magic of catnip.

A. J. Bakke writes goofy, quirky stories full of magic and adventure. One of her favorite themes throughout her books is that cats are attracted to magical people, which explains why she ends up with as many as five cats piled on her while reading a good book.

https://www.facebook.com/ajbakke/

The Secret Treasons of the World

J. L. ROWAN

With a laugh, Braelin flipped her long braid over her shoulder, out of reach of her gelding's curious nips. She kissed his velvety nose and ran her hands down his neck and over his withers before adjusting his blanket and centering his saddle on his back. It was a glorious summer day, and Blaze was as eager as she to be in the sun after the heavy rains of the past fortnight. He stamped his hoof impatiently as she tacked him up.

"Be back in time for evenmeal, Filly," came her father's voice, and she looked up to see him standing at the stall door.

She lifted an eyebrow, even as her lips twitched in an effort to hold back a smile. "Papa, I'm sixteen now." She had fallen asleep last night a child and woken this morning an adult, at least according to Crown law.

A smile crinkled the corners of his eyes. "I don't care if you're sixteen or twenty-five. You will always be my Filly."

She shook her head and surrendered to her grin. What would life be like, after all, if she weren't?

"Lord Dalton!"

Braelin ducked under Blaze's head and glanced out of the stall to find her father's huntsman striding toward them, trailed by three of his bay hounds. She lifted one of the saddlebags hanging from the open stall door and returned to her task.

"What is it, Kyrith?"

"Tracks, my lord. Large ones and strange."

"Where?"

Braelin came around to fetch a second saddlebag and paused in the doorframe to listen.

"At the edge of the forest, near the northernmost fallow field." He nodded respectfully to her. "A happy day to you, my lady."

She murmured a polite greeting but glanced out a stable window to the forest in the distance. It was home to any manner of arcane spirits—or so sang the bards and minstrels—and she planned on riding there alone that afternoon.

Her father frowned. "The edge of the forest? What do you think it is?"

Kyrith shrugged. "The rains muddied most of the tracks, but if I were pressed, I'd say—well, I'd say snowcat, but it's not."

The hounds loped over to her, and she petted their heads. "Snowcats keep to the mountains in summer."

"Indeed, my lady, and the tracks are too big. Whatever this is, it isn't a snowcat." His gaze shifted to include Dalton. "It has a broken leg. I searched an arrowshot into the forest but have found nothing."

"A broken leg, and you can't find it?" Dalton stroked his trimmed, graying beard. "What is this, a phantom?"

Kyrith offered a rueful smile. "We may jest, my lord, but the forest is a strange place. Best to avoid it, at least for now."

"Is the stock safe?"

"Aye, I've checked the stables and pens. It didn't stray far from the forest line." He let the hounds lick his hands. "I can't imagine why I haven't found it."

Dalton caught Braelin in his gaze. "Be careful. Bring your bow with you."

"I have it," she said. "And my dagger." Behind her, Blaze huffed and stamped another hoof, and she picked up the second saddlebag.

Kyrith shot her a sharp glance. "Keep to the meadows."

She tightened her grip on the bag. Surely he couldn't know her plans. "You think it's that serious?"

"The dogs shied away from the tracks, and they've stood their ground against wounded boars before."

More than strange. She met her father's gaze and saw the concern in his eyes. "Blaze needs the exercise. I'll be careful, Father. I promise."

"I know you will." He kissed her forehead. "Don't be late for evenmeal. Your mother is planning a small feast for you." He started for the stable doors, and Kyrith fell into step with him, whistling for the hounds. Their conversation shifted to other matters, and she returned to Blaze to tie on the other saddlebag.

Fears of phantom cats and the arcane unknown vanished in the sheer joy of riding. She cantered about the meadows until the sun was high in the sky and hunger turned aside her thoughts. She'd trained Blaze to be ground tethered, so once she retrieved her noonmeal from a saddlebag, she dropped the reins and let him graze to his heart's content. After she ate, she dozed in the soft grasses for a time, content with the day, with life and the promise it held.

She roused herself mid-afternoon and whistled for Blaze. She intended to hunt in the forest, but Kyrith's tidings gave her pause. She stared at the dark tree line, caught in the grip of the minstrels' songs.

"Foolish girl!" she whispered harshly, shaking off the disquiet that crept up the back of her neck. She'd ridden in the forest dozens of times with her father and seen nothing stranger than a bird and a squirrel fighting over the same nut. Riding alone would be no different. For that matter, Kyrith rode almost daily in the forest and had never reported anything odd, however strange a place he claimed it was.

Until now, her mind whispered.

"Nonsense!" she snapped, startling Blaze as he trotted up. After all, she was no longer a child, and whatever this creature was that Kyrith feared, it had shown no interest in easy prey, so why should it hunt her—assuming it even could with its broken leg? With forced determination, she mounted and trotted into the forest. But she kept one hand on her bow.

Cheerful birdsong and the antics of chipmunks soon drove all minstrel songs and well-meaning admonitions from her mind. She slowed Blaze to a walk, narrowing her gaze as she spied the spaces between the trees. A young deer would be a welcome addition to the table, its hide an added boon, for her favorite winter slippers were wearing thin.

Her gaze froze as she sighted something in the distance. She tensed, stopping Blaze and staring hard at the large, fallen mound of black fur half an arrowshot ahead of her. A boar perhaps. It didn't stir, so she nudged Blaze forward one step at a time. If it were a boar, he would scent it in time to warn her. Step by step, they drew closer, and she held her breath. She squinted and nocked an arrow in defense, for she could not determine what lay amidst the fallen leaves of yesteryear.

At last, the mound of fur took shape, and she gasped. There before her lay a cat, an enormous snowcat. It must have died, for Blaze showed no signs of fear. She lowered her bow and dismounted, glancing at its extended hind leg. The lower half jutted out at an unnatural angle, broken.

Kyrith's phantom.

She gave it a wide berth, studying it as she walked around it. Kyrith was right—this was no snowcat. It was far too large and muscular, had more rounded ears, and the tail was itself longer than most snowcats she'd seen.

She stopped by its head and knelt before it. It weighed as much as four or five of Kyrith's largest hounds, she guessed, and would stand as tall as her waist. Its pelt would make a lovely midwinter gift for her father. "However shall I get you home?"

It opened its eyes and lifted its head.

With a shriek, she scrambled backward, her heart pounding. She stumbled into a tree and reached behind her back to grip it and awkwardly clamber to her feet. Blaze still showed no fear, and when she whistled for him, he only whickered in response. She inched her way around the tree. The cat lay between them, and she eyed Blaze, calculating the risk of dashing for him and the likelihood of escaping with her life.

She studied the cat, gauging the severity of its injury and its potential reflexes, but as she met its gaze, curious and intelligent, her designs were scattered to the winds. Its eyes were a luminous silver that made her breath catch in her throat. She couldn't look away, and only in that moment did she realize it had made no move to attack her. "What are you?"

I am a Guardian. He rolled from his side to lie on his stomach.

She started at the sound of a voice in her head, gasping. She glanced again at Blaze. He remained at ease. She stayed behind the tree and turned her gaze to the cat. "Did you speak to me?"

Yes. He inclined his head to her. *My name is Valamir.*

"I—my name is Braelin." She swallowed hard. "Are you—are you going to kill me?"

If I wanted to kill you, child, you would already be dead. He yawned, displaying sharp teeth as if to prove his statement.

She moved with cautious steps around the tree and sank to her knees, keeping out of reach of his paws. "You're a Guardian?"

Yes.

"Impossible," she whispered but shifted backward all the same. "You're dead. You're all dead." Fifty years ago, King Shansor had led the people of Talithia in a glorious revolt against the oppressive rule of the Guardians, who held them back from trade and commerce with other kingdoms, wanting to keep them isolated and ignorant of the wonders around them. The Guardians had been destroyed and the kingdom of Shansor firmly established.

Obviously not.

"I—" She stared at him for a long moment. "I didn't know you were cats."

Of course not. Our memory is outlawed.

Indeed it was. "Even to speak of you is tantamount to treason. You—" She bit her lower lip, hesitating. "You oppressed our people."

Valamir's tail lashed against the ground like a whip, startling her. *No, we did not.*

"But King Shansor—"

Shansor was a blood mage and we opposed his use of dark magic.

Dark magic. The words washed over her like a spray of icy water. She hardly breathed as long-ago whispers resurfaced—whispers that her grandfather, a close confidante of Shansor, had been a mage and that their manor and lands were reward for his service to the king. She hadn't listened to them, had always dismissed them as foolish, but now—

He turned the people against us and made himself king, he continued. *We couldn't defeat him. Those who opposed him fled north under the leadership of Arnon and founded a new kingdom in untamed lands.*

"I know," she murmured, though she'd been taught a different version of events. The border between the eponymous kingdoms lay on the northern edge of the forest and was heavily guarded on both sides. "Are you alone? Are there more of you?"

We were thirty-two. Twelve of us remain.

She really shouldn't be there. He was a *Guardian*, after all. But her gaze dropped to his leg. "You're hurt." She stretched out her hand as if to touch him.

His silver eyes followed her gaze. *My leg is broken. The ground gave way beneath me during the rains and I fell.*

She winced at the thought. "Can the other Guardians help you?"

The others have left for Cairna. Arnon has died, and they have gone to the palace to honor him. I stayed behind to care for things. They are too far away now to hear my call for help.

She glanced up at the sky. She should start for home soon, though she hated to leave him, Guardian or not. But what could she do? She wasn't trained to set breaks and knew very little of wortcunning. "Are you hungry? I could return with food later this evening."

More thirsty than hungry, but thank you, yes. I would welcome food.

She climbed to her feet. "I have some water with me." She stepped to Blaze's side and untied her waterskin from the saddle. But away from Valamir now, she hesitated, glancing at his lethal paws. A shiver stole over her. Could she trust him? Perhaps she should flee while she still breathed.

I'm not going to hurt you.

She gasped and met his gaze. "You—how did—?"

I can read your thoughts. He straightened to sit upright, his broken

71

5

leg trailing to the side. *I have no desire to hurt you, Braelin.*

Heat stained her cheeks, and she looked away, focusing on opening her waterskin. "I'm sorry."

I don't blame you for being afraid. It's all you know of me.

She returned and knelt before him. She poured some water into her cupped hand and held it out to him. He lapped it, his rough tongue brushing her palm. She longed to know if his coat was as soft as she imagined but didn't dare touch him. He drank until she had emptied the waterskin.

Thank you. You are most kind.

She fell captive to his silver eyes, to the genuine gratitude within them. "I'll return with food and more water. I promise."

As she cantered home, her thoughts tumbled about her head and her heart beat fast. She hadn't thought of the Guardians in years, assumed them all dead as she'd been taught. In truth, she should have fled Valamir's presence when he identified himself, but his words had stirred to life in her soul both curiosity and fear. Of course, it would be easier to cling to the belief that the Guardians were cruel and oppressive, but he hadn't displayed any cruelty toward her. He could have easily killed her to ensure her silence and his own safety. Perhaps everything she had been taught was a lie.

She hurriedly groomed and fed Blaze before dashing to the house for a quick bath and a change into one of her best gowns. She arrived in the great hall as the servants were bringing in the first dishes of her birthday feast from the kitchens.

The food was delicious, of course, and she enjoyed her gifts—a new saddle for Blaze, a pearl necklace and ring, silk and velvet fabrics—but her thoughts turned once and again to Valamir. He had to be in pain. Was he safe? Wild boars roamed the forest—could he protect himself, injured as he was? What if—

"Braelin!"

She started and came to herself to find her mother staring at her. "I'm sorry, Mother. What is it?"

"Your father asked you a question."

She blushed and glanced at Lord Dalton. "Yes, Father?"

"I asked you how your ride today was," he said, cutting into a slice of his cheese and elderflower tart with a fork.

"Oh, it was nice." She took a bite of her own tart. "Blaze really enjoyed it."

Her parents exchanged a glance she could not interpret.

Her father drank from his goblet. "I haven't seen young Lord Esterlin about lately."

She blushed again, but for a different reason. Lord Esterlin, seventeen, lived on the neighboring manor to the west. He was charming and handsome and made the silliest of excuses to ride over to visit her father—visits that would often end with him spending time with her. When last he came, she was certain he would kiss her, but he fumbled his words and tripped over his feet until he grew so flustered he mounted his horse and rode away without even taking his leave of her. "I'm sure he is busy with manor duties. King Gradik summoned his father to the palace in Atalar."

"Yes, I think I remember him telling me that." He exchanged another glance with Lady Brenna. "He's a very capable young man. We should invite him to dine with us some evening. Perhaps you could mention it to him when you see him next."

Wait—had they thought she spent the day with Esterlin? Her blush deepened, and she stammered something incoherent.

Lady Brenna hid a smile as she stood, one arm cradling her swollen abdomen. "If you will excuse me, I think I'll lie down." The babe, a joyous surprise to all, would arrive in autumn, and the whole manor fairly hummed in anticipation.

Lord Dalton stood to kiss her and murmured something Braelin could not hear.

Braelin's thoughts returned to Valamir, and she pushed her tart about her plate with her fork until her mother was out of earshot. "Father, I want to ask you something."

"What is it?" He resumed his seat and his eyes twinkled, as if he knew what her question would be.

She nibbled a bit of her tart as she weighed her words and the wisdom of speaking them. Perhaps she should pretend she hadn't ridden in the forest that day. But no. She needed the truth. "Grandfather Falkrith—was he a mage?"

He instantly sobered, a deep frown overshadowing his features. "What kind of a question is that?"

"Papa, I'm not a child." She laid down her fork. "I've heard the rumors. I want to know if they're true."

"Magecraft is outlawed."

"I know, but it wasn't when Shansor was king, and Grandfather helped him become king, didn't he?" Shansor had been young when he overthrew the Guardians—twenty-five—but he survived only another twenty years before passing. His son, Andreth, was crowned but died five years later in a hunting accident. King Gradik, Shansor's grandson, had ruled for the past twenty-five years. One of his first acts as king had been to outlaw magecraft.

Lord Dalton drained his goblet and sighed heavily. "Yes, he did. Your grandfather was close friends with Shansor and helped him with his spellcasting, but he was *not* a mage. Shansor feared for his power and his position and wouldn't allow any other mages. He rewarded your grandfather's service by giving him our lands and the gold needed to build this house. Your grandfather would not have risked what he had gained, to say nothing of risking his life, by giving himself over to magecraft."

She didn't understand how he could have helped with spellcasting and not have been a mage, but she felt a little better knowing that he wasn't. "Was Shansor a good king?"

"I was only ten when he died." He glanced away, looking past her with unfocused eyes, as if caught in a memory impossible to escape. "It was a different time then."

"What were the Guardians like?"

His gaze snapped back to hers, his eyes widening even as his countenance darkened. "What did you say?" His tone frosted the air between them.

She shrank into herself a little. "I only meant—"

"They are as outlawed as magecraft," he said, his voice hard. "They died a long time ago. Do *not* speak of them again. Do you understand?"

"Yes," she said in a small voice. But they hadn't died. Did he know that, or was he merely repeating the lies of the Crown? She glanced out the window. The sun was making its descent into the west. Valamir must be hungry. She was anxious to keep her promise, but it was midsummer and would stay light for several hours more. She couldn't leave the house until her parents had retired to their suites.

"Braelin."

She met her father's gaze. Concern now eclipsed the anger in his eyes.

"You've been very distracted this evening. Is everything well?"

She nodded. She had thought he might have helped Valamir, but she could hardly tell him about the Guardian now.

"Then let's not discuss these matters again. They're over and done with, long ago." He pushed back from the table. "I trust your thoughts are better occupied." The twinkle returned to his eyes. "Perhaps young Lord Esterlin is the reason for your distraction."

Her cheeks warmed, and she rose. "I'm sure Lord Esterlin has more important things to think about right now than me." She started for the door.

"If he does," he said, "he's not worth your time."

She couldn't help but smile. "Thank you, Papa." She paused to kiss his cheek. "I'm going to check on Blaze."

At sunset, she returned to her suites to dress in her riding clothes and pace the length of her bedchamber while waiting for night to fall. When at last it grew dark, she crept through the house with nervous anticipation, a sack slung over her shoulder. Her parents had retired, as had the servants, and all was quiet. She made her way to the kitchens, where she claimed a meat pie and some roast from the feast. She tucked them into her sack along with a bowl, slipped out the door, and hurried to the stables.

She fitted Blaze with his bridle, put on his saddle blanket, and led him from his stall. After filling two waterskins, she mounted bareback and nudged him into a walk. Once free of the stables, she kicked him into a canter.

The full moon illuminated her return to the forest. Valamir lay where she had left him, and she dismounted beside him. "I brought food," she said without preamble, and she retrieved it from her saddlebags and set it before him.

Thank you.

She filled the bowl she had brought with water and set it down next to the roast and meat pie. He made short work of both, and as he ate, she spread out Blaze's saddle blanket atop the leaves and sat.

"I spoke to my father this evening," she said once he had finished. She related their conversation.

Your grandfather was not a mage, Valamir said.

She frowned. "How could you know that?"

I was there. I am a hundred and seven years old but young still for a Guardian. Your father was correct about Shansor as well. He suffered no one else to be a mage, not wishing to share his power.

"Then how did Grandfather help him if he wasn't a mage himself?"

Dark magic requires the spilling of blood to effect its spells. Your grandfather offered his blood on many occasions to help Shansor spellcast.

The weight of his words settled into her heart. "Grandfather helped destroy you."

Valamir made no reply.

Sudden tears stung her eyes, and she toyed with the edge of the blanket, unable to meet his silvery gaze. "I—" She should apologize for what he had done, but the words sounded trite in her head and more than a little meaningless now. She glanced up at him. "What really happened fifty years ago?" And how much of what she had been taught was a lie?

Ten years before the revolt, the people of Talithia settled this land, having sailed across the sea after being driven from their own

75

land by an invading queen and her army. King Orontes, an ally, gave us the ships we needed to flee, on the condition that we take his bastard son, Shansor, with us. Shansor had attempted to kill the heir, his half-brother, and would have been executed if not for his father's intervention.

Upon settling here, it did not take him long to make allies among the neighboring kingdoms and sow dissension among our people. The Lady created the Guardians to rule over her people, but he could never accept our authority. He wished to be king. He turned the people's hearts from us and, with dark magic and assassination, rid the land of most of the Guardians, and then he did all he could to destroy our memory.

"You were chosen to rule over us?" She stared at him, the hair on her arms prickling as it had the day she had visited the Temple in Atalar, as it did sometimes when she worshiped in the manor Sanctuary. "How did she—why would she let such a revolt happen?"

It is not the way of the Lady to force herself on anyone. The people rejected us in favor of a king; therefore, a king they have. He shifted his position, and she winced at the sight of his leg, a far more pressing concern than history or theology.

"You are badly injured, Valamir. You cannot continue like this." Even in the moonlight, pale and filtered through the trees, she could discern his waning strength in his matted fur and dulling eyes. She reached for him but still dared not touch him. "Our huntsman has been looking for you. I don't want him to find you."

I know. I've been able to avoid him.

"How?"

Without reply, he vanished from her sight.

"Wait!" She stretched her hand farther and encountered the warmth of his bulk, even as he remained invisible to her eyes. She jerked back her hand as if stung. "Valamir?"

He reappeared. *Our own version of magic, but it takes energy to maintain.*

Energy she was certain he no longer possessed. He probably hadn't intended for *her* to find him. She laid a hand on his paw. "I don't know what to do. I don't know how to help you."

There is nothing you can do.

"I don't believe that. You need help. Surely there is someone, somewhere—"

The only help you could bring would come at great risk to yourself.

76

A chill stole over her, but she didn't flinch. "Tell me."

There is a Healer stationed at Terfalls Keep.

Terfalls Keep and its castle were built upon one of the cliffs of the Ashlyn mountains that bordered the forest to the east and north. On a clear day, she could see it high in the distance from atop the manor walls. She drew back her hand. "I would have to cross the border." It would be an act of treason that would render speaking of the Guardians a mere trifle by comparison.

Yes.

She glanced away, twisting her fingers in the hem of her tunic. "It is a warm night, but I will leave you my blanket, if you like."

That won't be necessary, but thank you.

She rose. "I don't know if I can do what you ask, but I will consider your request and return in the morning with an answer."

You are very kind, Braelin. Thank you.

She gathered her things and rode home, letting Blaze find his way back to the stables as she wrestled with Valamir's request.

Treason.

If caught, she would die. Crown law was explicit in this matter. No Shansorian could cross the border or otherwise have contact with an Arnoni citizen. But only a Healer, who treated illness and injury with a divine power, would be able to save Valamir. If she did nothing, he would die, and soon.

And the border... Even if she wanted to help Valamir, the border was sewn so thick with guards on either side, she didn't know how crossing unseen into Arnon would be possible.

Her stomach knotted as she dismounted in the stable yard. What kind of a choice had she been given? She led Blaze into his stall and pulled the saddle blanket from his back.

She turned to hang it over the door and started back with a gasp. "Kyrith!" He stood on the other side of the door. "I didn't hear you." She took a deep breath to calm her startled nerves.

"My apologies, my lady. I didn't mean to frighten you."

She draped the blanket over the stall door. "You're up late."

His eyes sparkled as he pulled open the stall door. "As are you."

A warmth spread across her face, one she hoped the dim light of the stables hid. "I didn't mean to stay out so long."

"Give it no thought, my lady," he said with a laugh. "When I turned sixteen, I spent the night in the forest, determined to hunt a boar on my own."

"Did you succeed?" she asked, removing Blaze's bridle.

He nodded. "And I have a scar on my thigh to prove it." He crossed his arms and leaned against the doorframe with a sigh. "Ah, the folly of youth. That said, I'd have come looking for you if you'd stayed out much later."

She shot him a knowing look as she hung up the bridle. "Did Father put you up to this?"

Kyrith grinned. "He was sixteen once, too."

Braelin laughed and claimed Blaze's brush. "And how old are you now, Master Kyrith?"

"Seventy-four, my lady." He pushed away from the door and retrieved a hoof pick.

Seventy-four. He would have been well of-age when Shansor revolted against Valamir and the Guardians. Her smile faded, and her hand trembled as she brushed Blaze's nearside in slow strokes. Surely he had witnessed the things Valamir had spoken of. "You've seen a lot, I suppose."

He slid around to Blaze's offside. "Aye, my lady, I have." He pulled up Blaze's hind hoof.

She listened to him pick Blaze's hoof free of stones and dirt as she brushed. Questions she had no business asking made her heart beat fast, but she could not stay her tongue. "Kyrith, where were you born?"

Something flickered in his eyes as he moved toward Blaze's head. "That's a curious question." He bent to pull up Blaze's forehoof.

"Were you born across the sea?"

He straightened, and their eyes met over Blaze's withers. "And that's a dangerous question, my lady. *Very* dangerous."

Her mouth dried. She swallowed twice, but still her voice was a scant whisper when at last she asked, "Kyrith, were you there when King Shansor destroyed the Guardians?"

His eyes widened, and he glanced beyond her, past the stable door. She turned to follow his gaze. "We're alone," she said, turning back to find him pacing the short length of the stall in quick turns. "Kyrith—"

"Foolish girl! If your father knew—if anyone heard—"

Her heart sank. "Please don't tell him!" She threw Blaze's brush back in his curry box and ducked under his head to face Kyrith. "He was quite displeased with me when I mentioned them at evenmeal."

Kyrith froze and glared at her. "Of course he was! You must not speak of them. You *know* this, Braelin."

"I'm sorry, I—" She shook her head. "I have questions, and I thought now I'm sixteen..." She trailed off under his stare.

"Now you're sixteen, your head can be placed on the block," he said. He jerked his chin toward the house. "Get you to bed. I'll finish with Blaze.

And I'll say nothing of this to your father. See that you do the same."

She glanced down at her hands. "Yes, Master Kyrith."

The full moon illuminated the way to the manor house, but as she approached the door to the kitchens, she paused. Apart from the house, in the midst of the gardens, stood the small, cylindrical stone Sanctuary, an island in the silvery moonlight. It beckoned to her, and she twisted her way through the garden footpaths to its door and slipped inside. In the daylight, the stained glass windows that encircled the Sanctuary were alight with colored fire, telling tales from the sacred texts, but in the moonlight, all lay dark and quiet.

She lit a candle at the altar and gazed upon the statue of the Lady Warrior. She wanted to help Valamir, but the danger held her back. Already, she had committed crimes that would demand her life. Was she to make it worse?

"I don't know what to do," she whispered.

At once, her conscience pricked her. Didn't she? Valamir was hurt—was dying, in fact—and she had nowhere to turn. Her father would not help, nor would Kyrith. She dared not seek assistance outside the manor. Where else did the burden fall, but upon her? And how could she *not* help? Valamir was goddess-sent. To abandon him was to abandon the Lady.

And yet...

She stared into the candle flame, flickering with her breaths, and let the doubts and certainties wrestle for rule of her heart.

Finally, she sighed and closed her eyes. "Very well." With her concession, the weight about her heart lifted as plans and ideas of plans coalesced in her mind. The border would be the greatest challenge, of course, but surely there must be *someplace* where she might cross. Valamir would know. She blew out the candle and hurried from the Sanctuary. She would pack now and leave before dawn to be back in time for noonmeal. She glanced at the sky. The moon had started her descent to the west, but morning seemed years away.

The sun had barely kissed the tips of the meadow grasses when she dismounted beside Valamir, waking him. His silver eyes had a new, glassy sheen to them that frightened her, and his breathing seemed labored. She knelt beside him. "Tell me where to go. How do I cross the border unseen?"

Braelin—

"I'm going, Valamir. Tell me where to cross."

He blinked once, slowly. ***In the heart of the forest is a valley. At its northeast edge, you will find a path that leads toward the cliffs. Follow it. It will take you to Terfalls Keep. Magden is the Healer there.*** He closed his eyes, his head dipping.

She touched his head with trembling fingers. "I have water." She filled his bowl and drew it close. "I will return soon."

He said nothing.

She bit her lower lip. Spying some fallen branches, she dragged them over and placed them around him. Perhaps they would provide some cover. She mounted Blaze and set off.

She found the valley with relative ease, and even the path, but navigating it proved more of a challenge as it ascended into the cliffs, wending narrow and treacherous in places. Twice, Blaze nearly lost his footing. At last, it leveled out as she approached the castle, its Keep rising high behind the tall stone walls. She rode up to the gates, catching the attention of the two guards stationed there.

The taller one looked her over. "Your business, milady?"

"It is imperative I see Healer Magden. Someone is gravely injured."

With a curt nod, the guard turned to his companion. "Fetch the Healer."

"It is a matter of great urgency," she called to the second soldier as he slipped inside the gates.

She waited, gripping the reins. The dangers of the path had forced her to concentrate on her every step at times, but now in the silence of waiting, she tried not to think of what she had done, of how she must conceal it from her parents, of the consequences if she failed. She turned her thoughts to Valamir instead. His condition had deteriorated overnight much more than she'd have thought it would. Surely she was not too late. She *must* not be too late. Her hands ached, and she relaxed her grip. Where was the Healer? She stared at the gates as if she could will them open. Blaze snorted and pranced uneasily, reflecting her own unease and impatience. She reined him in, patting his neck and murmuring reassurances.

The gate scraped open, and she snapped her head up and dismounted as the Healer, of an age with her mother, emerged, a saddled horse trailing behind her.

"I am Magden," she said, approaching Braelin. "Someone is injured?"

"Yes," she said. "It's Valamir."

Magden froze, her eyes wide, and she examined Braelin with a wary eye. "And you are?"

"Braelin." Her heart beat fast, and she swallowed hard. "Braelin of Falkrith Manor."

The tall guard's hand slid to the hilt of his sword. "From Shansor?"

"Yes." She turned her gaze to Magden and stepped closer. "I found him in the forest. His leg is badly broken, and he—he is not well. Please. He told me how to find you, and I think he will die soon if you do not return with me." She gestured to the midmorning sky. "We must hurry. I know not what Arnon's laws are, but I have committed treason to find you. By midday, my absence will be noted."

"Then we will leave at once," Magden said, mounting her horse.

Braelin swung up into Blaze's saddle and cantered back the way she had come until the path narrowed as it had before. The women did not speak again until safe on the other side, and once clear of the trees, they galloped across the valley on swift hooves. Braelin led the way through the forest to where she had left Valamir.

He lay undisturbed and unmoving. With a cry, she jumped from the saddle and hastened to pull away the branches she had used to conceal him.

Magden knelt before him and placed her hands on his head. "He's not dead, but I'll have to put him in a light trance to keep him from moving while I heal him." She closed her eyes and sat as still as Valamir. Her hands glowed faintly as she used her healing power on him.

Braelin paced for a moment and glanced at the sky. The sun was nearly overhead. She should return to the manor. She started for Blaze, but as her gaze lingered on Valamir, she slowed her step and bit her lower lip. He and Magden were unprotected and vulnerable. She shouldn't leave them alone. And how could she leave without knowing his fate? She glanced again at the sky. Soon. She would return to the manor soon. She mounted Blaze and rode in a wide perimeter around Valamir, searching for any indication that others were near or that he had been discovered in her absence. She found none. When she returned, she dismounted and sat before him. He remained in trance, and Magden's hands had moved to his broken leg. "Will he recover?"

"He had internal injuries, and this is a rather complicated break," Magden said, her eyes still closed, "but he should be healed and walking soon."

Walking, Braelin realized, and gone from her life. Her shoulders sagged, and she ran a hand along his coat. He hadn't groomed in days. "I wish our kingdom didn't hate him so."

Magden shifted her hands lower on Valamir's leg. "Not all who live in Shansor hate the Guardians. The minstrels' songs about the forest have helped protect the Guardians from discovery."

"How? Oh, tell me more about them, please." Did the Guardians live in the forest—in Shansor? Might she see Valamir again? Magden told her tales and answered her questions, and so caught was she in the telling that she did not hear the soft approach of hooves on the fallen leaves until a whicker called her back.

She twisted to see her father and Lord Esterlin sitting on horseback behind her, and the blood drained from her face. "Oh, no," she breathed. No. How could she have been so careless? She shot to her feet as Magden opened her eyes. "Father—"

He stared beyond her to Valamir and Magden, his face an impassive mask.

Esterlin craned his neck to see past Braelin. "A Guardian?" He glanced at Dalton with a puzzled frown. "How is that possible, my lord?" He shifted his horse over a few steps to look at Valamir.

"Lord Esterlin," Dalton said, meeting Braelin's eyes, "would you kindly return to the manor and fetch Kyrith?"

"Yes, of course."

"Tell only him what you have seen, then ride to the nearest border post and summon the captain of the guard."

Braelin gasped. "No—Father—"

"When you have done that," Dalton said, turning to look at Esterlin, "ride straight to your manor and stay there. For your own sake, speak of this to no one. Do you understand?"

Esterlin glanced at Braelin, his curiosity giving way to a look of mingled horror and pity. For a moment, she thought he might have stood with her, but the pity in his eyes turned cold. "I understand, my lord." He tugged on the reins to turn his horse about and cantered away without a backward glance.

"Papa, please," Braelin whispered.

"What have you done?" he asked in a low tone that sent a chill down Braelin's spine. He dismounted from his horse.

"His leg was broken. He had internal injuries."

His face flushed red, the cold mask gone, and he clenched his fists. "What have you *done*, Braelin?"

She winced, blinking back tears. "I couldn't let him die, Papa."

"And so you risk us all?" he cried. He paced in long strides between the trees. "How could you be so foolish?"

"Papa—"

"And you," he said to Magden, "who are you?"

"I am a Healer." Now standing, she bowed to him. "My name is Magden."

He frowned, narrowing his gaze. "I know of no Healer by that name, and I doubt you are here by happenstance. From whence do you come?"

Braelin's breath caught in her throat, and she exchanged a quick glance with Magden. *Oh, Lady, please.* What would her father do if he knew Magden hailed from Arnon?

Magden didn't flinch, however. "From Terfalls Keep, my lord."

Dalton halted in mid-step, his eyes widening as he glanced from Magden to Braelin. "You didn't—did you *cross the border* to find her?" He stared at her, his jaw slack, and pointed northward. "Tell me you did *not* cross that border!"

Braelin couldn't find the words to answer him.

"I don't—I can't—" He pressed his face into his hands for a moment and then looked at her as though he had never seen her before.

I sent for Magden. Valamir rolled to his feet and stood, his leg no longer appearing broken. *If you wish to blame someone, blame me.*

"I do blame you!" he roared before turning his back to them, his hands on his hips.

Braelin slid forward to stand beside Valamir. "The Guardians aren't evil. You have to know that. It was King Shansor who—"

"It doesn't matter what I know!" He spun on his heel to face her. "The only thing that matters is Crown law! You have broken it, and I—" A sob choked him, and the anger in his countenance gave way to despair. "I will not be able to save you."

Kyrith's words from last night sounded anew in her ears. *Now you're sixteen...* Her hand flew to her throat.

His eyes grew misty with tears. "What were you thinking, Braelin?"

"I was thinking of Valamir. We have to help him, Papa."

Dalton brushed his hand across his eyes and faced the great cat. "When I was a child, my lord, living in our newly built manor house on the lands we'd been awarded by the king, my old nurse told me stories of the Guardians. Great stories. Stories of adventure and how they had sailed from far away to begin a new life after a wicked queen had tried to destroy them. My nurse was from the old lands. She was a good woman, but my father killed her with his own hands when he found out she had spoken of the Guardians." He drew in a shuddering breath. "Unjustly or not, you are outlawed. You have already taken my daughter. I will not risk losing everything else because of you."

"Taken me?" Braelin stepped forward, frowning. "Valamir hasn't taken me anywhere. I'm right here, Papa."

He said nothing but looked at her with eyes so mournful, her own filled with tears.

Muffled hoofbeats sounded behind them, and Kyrith cantered up. He pulled his horse to a stop and dismounted. "Esterlin is riding north for the guard." He inclined his head to Valamir, who returned the gesture.

Braelin tried to hold back a sob. "Why have you done this, Father? Valamir isn't going to hurt anyone!"

"My lady, we must send for the guard or we will fall under suspicion." Kyrith glanced at Dalton. "They won't be here until nightfall. It will give us enough time."

She wiped tears from her eyes. "Time for what?"

Kyrith unfastened two shovels from behind his saddle. "Time to save us all." He gave one to Dalton.

"Papa—"

"Braelin," her father said, "you have given aid to a Guardian. If only I had seen this, we could pretend it never happened. But Esterlin is most loyal to the Crown, as is his father, and for your mother's sake and the babe's sake, I must appear to be as well. Do you understand?"

Her eyes widened as Kyrith started to dig a hole. "What are you going to do?"

Her father stepped toward her, and she instinctively retreated. He winced and let the shovel drop from his hand. "I'm not going to hurt you, Filly."

Valamir paced forward, his whiskers twitching. **When the guards arrive, they will take her and execute her, I presume.**

Dalton's eyes filled with new tears. "Yes."

Magden stepped to Braelin's side. "Then she will return with us." She put an arm around her shoulders.

"What?" Exile—and in Arnon? She shrugged off Magden's embrace. "Papa, no! Hide me somewhere!"

"I cannot. If I am to protect you—" His voice broke and he swallowed. "If I am to protect your mother, I must convince the guard—and the king—that I am my father's son." The tears in his eyes spilled onto his cheeks as he glanced at the hole Kyrith dug.

Her grave.

Kyrith stopped digging. "My lady, you must flee Shansor. The guard will search the manor. Where would we hide you? And even if you weren't discovered, you could never again be seen by anyone, not even a servant. What kind of a life would that be for you?"

Her heart fell, and she could hardly breathe. She hadn't meant to put her family in danger. She hadn't thought it would be this way. She hadn't thought at all.

"I'm sorry," she whispered.

Kyrith retrieved a saddlebag from his horse and brought it to her. "I should have realized I was tracking a Guardian, but it's been so long. I would have assumed the risk myself had I known." He gave her the bag. "Coin and jewel. You will need them." He kissed her forehead. "I promise I will care well for Blaze."

She glanced at Blaze through tear-filled eyes. She must leave him behind, of course. She must leave everything behind. The weight of what she had done, of what must now take place, settled on her with a dreadful finality, and she began to weep. "What—what of Mother?" She would not even be able to say goodbye. And she would never see her new brother or sister.

Her father drew near. "I will tell your mother the truth."

She dropped her bag and threw herself into his arms. He held her tightly, his shoulders shaking with silent sobs.

The autumn winds teased free the few leaves that yet clung to their branches. From atop the walls of Terfalls Keep, with the sun overhead in a clear blue sky, Braelin gazed south over the forest to the clearing beyond its western edge. Falkrith Manor stood tall and strong.

She glanced at the letter in her hand, written by Kyrith and delivered that morning by Valamir, a laconic missive that left her with more questions than answers. Her father and Esterlin had been interrogated by the guard at the manor and then by the king in Atalar. After a fortnight, the king had closed the inquiry and awarded her father a royal accolade. What he had told them about Valamir and Magden, she did not know, nor did she know what excuse for her death her parents gave, since speaking of the Guardians was forbidden.

"How are you feeling?" Magden asked, stepping to her side.

She passed her the letter. "My family is safe."

"I'm glad to hear it." She perused the letter. "Braelin, do you regret helping Valamir?"

"No." She tore her gaze from home to look at Magden. "There was nothing else I could have done." Even after a season of reflection, she clung to that truth. She couldn't have let Valamir die. She did what was right, what was good.

But the price she paid felt like death.

Magden returned the letter and patted her shoulder. "Noonmeal is ready, if you wish."

"Thank you." But she remained standing, and only when Magden retreated did she turn her gaze back to the letter. Tears stung her eyes as she scanned the hastily scribbled postscript informing her of her brother's birth. She should have been there to help her mother. She should be there now. She folded the letter, tucked it in a pocket, and allowed a thread of hope to wrap around her heart. Perhaps it was not the last letter she would receive.

A skittering sounded behind her, and she glanced down as a small black ball tumbled against her feet. It uncurled, and she smiled as tiny claws shot out to grip her skirts. She held in a laugh until her stomach hurt as the kitten climbed her. A moment later, a second ball of fur pounced on her boots. She lifted them both by their scruffs and laughed as little silver eyes blinked owlishly at her. They were the first of a new generation of Guardians, a living testament to the Lady's grace in the face of arrant rejection. Someday, perhaps, Shansor would again embrace what it had rejected.

"Let's go find your parents, shall we?" She cradled them in her arms and, with a final glance at the manor, turned toward her new home.

J. L. Rowan dwells where her imagination takes her. The author of several short stories and a two-volume fantasy epic (all of which are set in, or touch upon, the world of Talithia), she has her MLS with a special study focus on rare books and illuminated manuscripts. When not writing, she enjoys practicing illumination and recreating authentic medieval recipes. Her website is www.jlrowan.co.

The Poor Miller and the Cat

Lelia Rose Foreman

Once upon a time, a poor miller was walking down the road. You might wonder how a miller could be poor. Easy enough, anybody with a father who drinks and gambles away his wealth can also inherit debt. The poor miller had also inherited a tumbledown house and a tumbledown mill. So he was walking down the road looking for wood to repair his tumbledown mill when he came upon some cruel children hitting a cat with sticks.

The poor miller snatched a stick from one of the children and waved it at them. "You should only pick on people your own size."

The boy whose stick he had taken shouted, "You are larger than us."

The poor miller said, "Why, so I am. If you hit that cat one more time, I will kill you."

The children ran away as fast as their legs could carry them.

The poor miller picked up the cat and carried her home. He tended her wounds and gave her the last of his food.

The next morning, the cat told the poor miller, "I will make you a wealthy man."

The poor miller told the cat, "I will be happy enough if you keep the mice away from my grain and flour."

The cat laid upon the doorstep a rabbit and some starlings. The miller made a stew of them and revived himself. The cat then showed the miller where a lord had stockpiled wood for a summer home which the lord abandoned when he was called away to a war and never returned. The miller used the wood to repair his mill, and the cat kept the mice away from the grain and flour.

Time went by as time does, and one day, the cat brought in a basketful of kittens.

The miller said, "Cat, you were supposed to make me a wealthy man, but here you have brought me more mouths to feed."

The cat said, "There is still time. You must buy the cow down the lane so my kittens will have enough milk."

The miller said, "Spending money is not making money." But he went and bought the cow down the lane. Soon they had enough milk and more than enough.

Time went by as time does, and the cow gave the miller milk and fertilizer and more cows.

The miller said, "Cat, you were supposed to make me a wealthy man. Instead, I am working from before the sun rises until after the sun sets."

The cat said, "There is still time. You must marry the sweet girl down the lane."

The miller said, "That will take money, not make money." But he was pleased with the advice and married the sweet girl down the lane.

Time went by as time does, and the sweet wife gave the miller a son, and then a daughter, and then another son.

The miller said, "Cat, you were supposed to make me a wealthy man, but here I am with more mouths to feed."

The cat said, "There is still time. You must buy the oxen down the lane and enlarge your fields."

The miller said, "That is spending money, not making money," but he bought the oxen and enlarged his fields. The cat and kittens kept his barns and fields free of rats and birds. The mice could not eat the miller's flour for the kittens ate the mice first. Soon they had enough food and more than enough.

Time went by as time does, and the day came when the miller sat upon a mill step to catch his breath, and the cat settled upon his lap. The miller said, "Old Cat, you were supposed to make me a wealthy man."

The old cat said, "You are a wealthy man."

The miller looked up at his barns and fields with his children working in them, his sweet wife churning butter on the porch, the mean children who had grown up to become his servants, and the house he had enlarged. "Why, Old Cat, so I am."

With that, the old cat purred once, twice, thrice and died.

The miller buried the old cat with honors and had much consolation from his sweet wife, his children, and multitudes of kittens.

Lelia Rose Foreman raised and released five children. Despite homeschooling three of them for fourteen years, everyone survived. She has written science fiction (*A Shattered World*) and been published in a number of anthologies. She is presently working on a science fantasy series with her oldest son.

Breatheoflifeart.com

Alex the Cat and Alex the Prince

Ace G. Pilkington

I will not marry that creature!" The princess was—as princesses usually are in stories but not so often in real life—beautiful. Her eyes were a remarkable blue, her hair what could only be called a royal chestnut, and her features so regular that they seemed unnatural. She wore a silver gown whose long, clingy lines emphasized her height and her figure. She was, in fact, so extraordinary that even something non-human could see it and be caught by it. Fortunately or unfortunately, her character was not as straight and regular as her body.

She said to her parents, "I don't care if you gave your word. I don't care if I gave mine. The money, the lands, and the palace are ours already. He can't take them back. There will be no marriage."

Her parents, who had been raised by the magical bargain to a wealth befitting their previously impoverished rank, looked at each other as they sat on their new and glittering thrones. They seemed pale and weak, almost too tired to fight or command. "You must marry him," her father said, "to avoid the curse and end any power he still has over us."

"Marrying him may end his power over you, the palace, and the royal lands, but it certainly won't do the same for me."

"Still," her mother said, "you must."

"And who or what will compel me?" the princess demanded.

"I will." In actuality, the gnome had done no more than step forward out of the shadows where he had been listening angrily and shifting from one foot to the other. To the princess and her parents, however, his sudden appearance seemed one more indication of his strange powers. He was just over three feet tall, his skin was gray, and his hair was silver. His eyes were a pale, icy blue, like the sky in midwinter. "We can have the wedding on the winter solstice, the shortest day of the year and, as you might expect, my birthday." He laughed, and the sound was like a saw whining as it cut wood. "No, you don't appreciate self-deprecating humor?"

The princess said, "Go away."

"You are," the gnome replied, "forgetting the curse that went with all your wealth. If you don't marry me, the man you do wed will die."

The princess did not become more beautiful when she got angry.

93

Instead, blood suffused her face, transforming her usually perfect complexion into something like the red hue of a blood moon, and indeed, it almost always heralded the eclipse of her reason and good sense. "I don't care," she said, "let him die, whoever he is."

The gnome seemed startled and upset in an entirely different way. "But you can't simply wave the curse away. Curses don't work like that. It's against the rules."

"I don't care. What if I never have a wedding? What good is your curse then?"

The gnome, who had certain magical powers but not much emotional control, sat on the stone floor of the palace and began to cry. "You must marry. You must marry. All princesses marry." And then slowly, he stood up and stopped crying, though he was still sniffling and wiping at his nose. "All right. I'll harm you in another way. Until you marry, this palace and the land of summer that surrounds it will enter another season. I give you winter. I give you snow and ice and a cold so biting it will burn your flesh. You will shiver and shake and slip on your frozen floors. You will not be so elegant and self-sufficient then." He turned and walked away, leaving the room quite normally.

The palace was made of stone and glass. It was vast as a wood, and, with all the doors and windows it had, nearly as open to the air and sky. As the gnome left, there was a breath of cold that soon became a wind. It was the first taste of the coming winter.

"You must marry him," her father said. "I do not care how ugly and eldritch he is; there is no other choice."

By this time, the princess had calmed down, and though she had many faults, stupidity was not among them. "He can't give us all the woes of winter immediately. His own spell of summer will fight against it. So perhaps I should marry after all. Some prince that nobody wants. Let his parents sell him to us for the dowry, just as you sold me. And when he dies, the curse and the winter will die with him. And we will live happily in this palace in the land of summer."

Her father and mother looked at each other. Her mother said, "I'm sure we could find someone suitable."

The princess declared, "Find someone soon. If the little gray man wants a wedding on the winter solstice, let's give him one. The longest night of the year will be a good time for my bridegroom to die."

The princess left the room, and her parents looked at each other. Her father sighed. "She's always reminded me of your side of the family, your Uncle Sigismond for choice."

Her mother said, "You know perfectly well that his name is Ruprecht, and yes, she's very like him, only she has perfect teeth."

The castle was old, battered by ancient sieges and tattered by winter storms of the usual variety. And it was rather small. It had a king, a queen, and a prince, but not much more than that. The fields were few and poor, and the peasants were friendly, but there weren't many of them. For years, the little kingdom had made a reasonable living by brewing beer. The king appointed a royal brewmaster, and the barrels rolled out to taverns and even to the occasional king and emperor, because it was very good beer, sweet, with just a suggestion of nutty flavor. And then something happened. The peasants called it a curse, and the king called it an economic downturn, but it meant that the beer tasted sour, and the barrels stayed home.

The king brooded, the queen worried, and the prince played with his cat. The prince might be forgiven because, first of all, no one had told him how bad things were, and second, it was a magnificent cat, and the two of them had been the closest of friends for years, ever since the prince had picked up a very small tom kitten who was alone in the snow, crying for warmth and food.

Now, the cat had a sizable ruff around his neck and weighed twenty pounds. He was brown with black stripes, and his paws were an inky black that extended halfway up his legs. "You shouldn't call them stockings," the cat said to the prince. "Think of them as camouflage. It makes it so much harder to see my paw coming in the dark."

Perhaps it was because they were such good friends that the cat could talk and the prince could hear him. Or perhaps as the cat said, all cats could talk, but ordinarily only magical creatures could hear them. So the cat asked the prince, "Are you sure there isn't at least a grain of magic somewhere in that big, awkward body of yours?"

And the prince replied, "You're mixing up your words again. 'Lithe' is what you meant to say, or 'limber,' not 'awkward.'"

They kept the fact that they could talk to each other a secret and so saved themselves much trouble, but in one instance, their chats caused difficulties for others. The kitten had insisted within minutes of their meeting that he was called Alex, and that happened to be the name of the prince as well, so from then on, everyone around them (except the king, who refused to use the short form of what would eventually be part of a royal title) struggled to distinguish between Alex the prince and Alex the cat, which, ridiculously easy as it was in real life, could be very tricky in conversation.

The prince first learned how truly bad things were when the king came to tell him that he was being married off to a very wealthy princess for the money her dowry would bring.

"It is large," his father said, "unusually, even suspiciously large, and we need every bit of it."

"Suspiciously?" said the prince.

"Well, you are reasonably attractive; you have your mother's green eyes, your grandfather's straight nose, and my dark hair, but otherwise, we won't be able to give you a thing. You're more a pauper than a prince, unless that cat of yours counts as great wealth."

"Alex is my brother, not my patrimony," the prince responded.

"I wish he *were* your brother, then I could sell him too. But let's not either of us say such things again until after the wedding. That cat adds more than a little to the mystery of why a princess with money and beauty would want you." Then, as he was about to leave the room, the king turned back, "I'm sorry to do this, Alexander. You can say 'no' if you must."

The prince shook his head "no," which in the circumstances meant "yes," and the wedding went forward at a speed previously unknown in royal nuptials. The queen said, with the sort of suspicion that mothers traditionally direct at the women who are about to marry their only sons, "Perhaps the princess has a deadline by which she absolutely has to have a husband in place."

The king, who had had suspicions on his son's behalf before and had been talked into fears for his dynasty now, made discreet inquiries. He found the princess to be a paragon of purity as far as anyone could or would tell. However, her family, though royal, had had nothing only a few years before.

"Those specially minted gold coins and that vast palace with seemingly limitless balconies and terraces," said the king, "all that is scarcely older than our last batch of undrinkable beer."

"Surely," said the queen, "the farms and forests..."

"Are reassuringly extensive and satisfyingly ancient, but they were purchased from neighboring estates to make up a royal holding."

It was precisely at this point that the princess sent a painting and several sketches of herself so that her bridegroom would recognize her at the ceremony, plus an elaborately embroidered handkerchief with a trace of her scent, and the courteous request that the prince would honor the custom of her family, which required newly married couples to spend the first nine months of married life in separate and celibate bedrooms. The king wondered if his inquiries had created this "custom," the queen was sure there would be something else to criticize soon, and the prince thought the princess must be breathtaking if she looked like her portraits. So everyone was satisfied for the time being or at least silenced—except the cat. He caught one whiff of the princess's perfume and began a great caterwauling that upset everyone, even those who could not understand what he was shouting.

The prince understood him to say, "It's magic, slippery, sickly magic, and you're meant to be the victim of it as surely as you will find that the princess is a monster in her head, no matter how she seems in paint and charcoal."

And the prince replied, "How do I refuse the marriage this close to the actual day in a sentence that begins, 'The cat told me...'?"

The cat said, "You're meant to be killed. I can feel it as surely as I feel the width of my whiskers in the dark."

"Then you'll have to warn me about what's coming in the dark." And when the cat looked unhappy and uncertain, the prince said, "There's nothing a cat like you can't do; you've told me so yourself."

And the cat asked, "Do you want me to quote back to you all the things you've told me? Go get a chess piece, and let's make your eye sharper and your hand faster."

What followed was what the prince called "playing with the cat." The prince tried to snatch a pawn before the cat could claw his right hand. It was not practice with a sword, but his sword arm and the hand attached to it were so much faster than they had been two years earlier that all his human opponents had given up even hoping to win.

"Ow," the prince said. "Can't you just whack me with your paw without claws?"

"No."

"All right. I'll show you who's faster. I can beat you even if you know when I'm going to strike. It's coming, it's coming, and it's here now! Oh, ow."

That night, the prince had a dream, or at least, it started as a dream. It rapidly became a nightmare of a winter storm, a fury of ice and snow, and somehow from out of the whiteness came a presence, not quite a shape, something monstrous and deadly, and the prince found himself unable to move or fight back, as happens often in dreams. But this felt real, as though he might truly die. When he awoke, he was shivering and afraid in a way he had not been since he had, at the age of ten, fallen into the castle moat and nearly drowned. The dream had been like that, a dark miasma that kept him from breathing, almost as though he was trying to move under water and failing, almost as though he was drowning in his sleep.

"How," the cat said when the prince told him about the nightmare, "can ice and snow be a black misty thing you drown in?"

"I don't know. It was unnatural but not like a dream is unnatural."

"It's the princess," the cat said. "It's that little touch of magic you have warning you to keep that great lumbering body of yours away from her."

"Maybe," the prince said, thinking back through the cold images and shivering while he did it, "but not the princess so much as something near her."

"Yes, well, anything that wanted to be near her would have to be a nightmare."

"I don't know about that," said the prince. "Do you ever have monsters in your dreams, Alex?"

"Yes, sometimes, but then they see me and run away screaming."

At that, finally, the prince laughed and remembered that it was, for a few more days at least, still St. Martin's Summer, with a last breath of warmth under a clear sky.

The time for the marriage came. The prince traveled in a special carriage the princess had sent for him, and Alex came with him.

"Why," the cat said, "is it winter here, with snow on the ground and icicles hanging from the trees, when it was much warmer when we left? How long have we been traveling?"

"Not that long, but it is the Winter Solstice. It has to get cold sometime."

"So why is the wedding on this day?"

"After this, the sun returns. It's a day of hope."

"And you think that's why?" the cat asked.

"No," the prince answered. "My father says it's because the Solstice is the traditional day when fermented beverages are ready to drink."

"Your father *would* say that."

Looking around, the prince declared, "I hate snow. Don't you?"

"Yes, let's go home before anything really bad happens. There's something odd about that snow."

The palace itself offered them another question. In a land of winter, it still seemed warm, its many doors and windows and its lovely terraces open to a friendlier season.

The cat said, "I hate snow, but I'd rather not go in there."

"Hush," the prince replied. "It's too late to run away."

The princess, dressed in silk and something that looked like gossamer spun by spiders, was astonishing, far more beautiful than her portraits. Still, from the look in her eyes during the ceremony, the prince thought he might have to admit that what the cat had said about her was true. Beyond that, she seemed nervous to be standing next to him, and once they were married, she said, angry and afraid at once, "I hope you have a good night," and vanished into the crowd at truly surprising speed.

The great ballroom, where the wedding took place, seemed too big to be enclosed by walls, and yet the crowd filled it and spilled through the many doors into open spaces and halls that were smaller than the ballroom itself but larger than seemed reasonable just the same.

The snow started inside the palace at the same time as the wedding ceremony. Tiny dots of white, almost too small to see, they might have been some tricky kind of confetti, specially designed for the celebration.

"Here it comes," the prince said, but he said it under his breath, and most of the guests pretended not to notice.

The princess's mother said to her father, "It's everywhere now. The summer spell is officially gone."

Gradually the flakes got bigger, until they were white and fluffy, floating peacefully like something from a painting of winter. And then, inevitably, there was a wind, a storm, and the snowflakes went whipping through the vast rooms, slashing the guests and making them put up their arms to defend their faces.

Prowling on the edges of the crowd, the cat hunted desperately for the source of the magic he could see and smell. It was in the princess's clothes, and it glittered on her face and hair. It was even scattered over the guests at the wedding, as though they would not have come without that secret persuasion. And when the snow arrived, that was magic too, the same and not the same, angrier, darker, and, of course, colder.

Finally, there it was—there he was—hidden as deeply in the shadows as the cat himself—a small, gnarled, nearly human shape but with gray skin and silver hair.

"Tell me," the cat said matter-of-factly, "about the curse."

"Which? No curse. Who's speaking?"

"Tell me. That's a wedding. Those are people with unearned wealth and unexplained magic. Not to mention a snowstorm inside a palace. You're a gnome with tears in your left eye. Tell me about the curse."

"Ah, I see you," said the little gray man, "a cat. Shouldn't give cats power of speech. I don't talk to cats. Go away, cat." He brushed at his left eye with a finger.

"Tell me," the cat said, still matter-of-factly, "or I'll jump on you and claw and bite you to death."

"Right, right," he snuffled. "What do I care if I tell you, stupid cat. Princess promised to marry *me*. Made the gold that bought all this from nothing, spun from dead stalks in the fields. Gave magic too. The curse came with the gifts—marry someone not me and he dies."

"More than once?"

"Which?"

"More than one husband?"

"No. One princess, one husband, one curse, stupid cat." His snuffling seemed to be limiting the number of words he could speak, that and the wind.

The cat reached up and swatted him in the face, though he kept his claws sheathed. "What if she marries again?"

The gnome looked confused, and the cat swatted him once more. "The prince there in front means nothing to her. You won't be getting revenge by killing him."

"Can't stop the curse. Won't stop the snow."

The cat raked his claws across the little man's gray face, and drops of red blood welled up. A snowflake landed on one of them and began to melt. "The prince is my brother. If he dies, I'll take a month to kill you."

"You won't."

"Why, because cats are known for treating the creatures they catch with such kindness? Or killing them quickly so they won't suffer?"

The gnome appeared to be very unhappy. "Won't find me," he snuffled.

"Yes, I will. There's always a cat around somewhere. Even in the snow."

The gnome shuddered, or maybe it was a shiver. "Can't stop the curse. It's a snake. Big, black, poisonous. It comes out of the storm, and it's cold, colder than the princess's heart. Soon. Unstoppable even by nasty cats. There, that's all I can tell." And he ran, slowly, limping slightly on his left leg. At one point, he slipped a little and almost fell; the snow on the floors was turning to ice.

The cat let him go. There was nothing more to do to him now. Now, he needed to find the snake and kill that—if in fact the idiot had been telling the truth. Was it a snake in the prince's dream?

When the wedding was over, the prince stood talking to his father. He had already hugged his mother, and she had said, "Be sure you come home for Christmas. Or if that's too soon, come for Twelfth Night. We can afford to celebrate. There will be real presents. Bring your wife if you must." Now, she was busy glaring at the mess in the great ballroom to which no one was attending. While his mother was complaining to people about the snow, taking it as a personal affront, his father was ignoring it in his best diplomatic manner, as if it were a quaint local custom to have a blizzard at weddings.

The prince said, "Her parents seemed as though they had been removed from a box and cleaned for the occasion."

His father said, "They've been poor for many years. Eventually, it shows on the face."

There was an unspoken worry in the words, and the prince wondered just how long the dowry would last.

"Where's that cat of yours," the king said, changing the subject abruptly. "I thought I saw him out of the corner of my eye during the ceremony."

"Yes, he's here somewhere. He hates the princess."

"I saw the way she looked at you, and more importantly, the way she didn't," the king said. "Maybe the cat has better sense than the rest of us." He paused for a moment, glancing at his son. "I think he'd die defending you if anyone tried to harm you."

"He should know," the prince said, raising his voice, "that's not his job. I'm the one with the sword," and he touched the not-so-ceremonial weapon that hung at his side.

"Ah, well," his father said, "cats don't care about such things. They don't believe in conventional behavior or treaties or doing what has to be done to keep the castle. They just know who they love."

The prince looked at his father, who suddenly seemed smaller and older. "What?"

"Just remember, Alexander, you can always gather up your cat and come home if, for any reason, the *climate* here doesn't suit you. We won't give the money back, no matter what." And the king walked away to find the queen, discreetly brushing off the snow that had settled on his arms and shoulders.

The prince didn't find the cat until he reached his separate and celibate room. Alex the cat was lying on the large bed. "At least," the prince said, "there's no snow in here."

"A servant lighted a fire, and it melted. I think there's snow in every room in this palace. I'm not entirely sure that it isn't falling from the ceilings as well as the sky."

"So that dream of mine may be coming?"

"Yes," the cat said, "and did you know that the doors on this room can't be locked or even effectively closed? The reason the princess isn't sleeping anywhere near you is because it's not safe. You'll be lucky to survive here for nine hours, let alone nine months. I have a story to tell you about a gnome, a princess, and a winter curse—and, oh yes, the prince that nobody wanted."

When the cat had finished, the prince said, "Just warn me when the snake is coming; I'll do the rest."

And the cat said, "If it's a snake. If that's all it is. Just be sure you wear your boots."

The prince not only kept his boots on but also the heavy uniform coat he had worn for the wedding, and even then, with extra wood on the fire and the cat lying across his legs, he shivered. From time to time, the doors blew open, the storm shrilled, and the strange snow swept in.

Not surprisingly, the prince found it hard to fall asleep. He told the cat, "You know, the princess and I have quite a lot in common."

"Oh yes? It's true you were both sold into marriage for money. Whom do *you* plan to have killed to get you out of your bargain?"

The prince was indignant. "I wouldn't do that."

"Of course not. You see how limited the similarities are?"

"Well, maybe," the prince suggested, "she does such things because she's a beauty trapped by horror."

"Or maybe," the cat responded, "she does such things because she's a horror wrapped in beauty."

"Maybe. You're too clever for me, Alex."

"Do you really believe you lost that argument because I'm clever and not because you're wrong?"

The prince sighed unhappily. "Calm down, Alex. We both know you're right."

After that, the prince closed his eyes and pretended to sleep, while the cat napped with his eyes half shut, as cats do. At three in the morning, the storm slowed and then almost stopped. There was even a break in the clouds and a line of moonlight trailing across the floor. The doors swung silently open in the sudden cold stillness. The cat came fully awake, watching the moonlight and shadows twist around each other. He rotated his ears and searched for what he knew he would hear if he listened carefully enough. There, there it was, the vanishingly small sound of scales on stone. It *was* a snake, and the snake was coming. Alex the cat ran forward at top speed; this was not going to be a battle of hide and pounce but of leap and strike.

The prince was suddenly sitting up wide awake in bed. Had he been asleep? He had heard the war cry of a tomcat, angry and fierce, but for him, far down underneath, there was still the sound of a lost kitten alone in the snow. The prince grabbed his sword and ran onto the terrace, out into the moonlight. He slipped and fell on a splotch of ice too small to see in the half dark, and he landed hard, the impact twisting his back and shaking the sword loose from his right hand.

"Get back, Alex," the cat shouted, "get back; it's the poisonous snake sent to kill you."

The prince gathered up his sword and stumbled to his feet, looking on helplessly as the cat leaped and fought with something the prince could not see. At times in the dark when the clouds swept away the moon, he could barely see the cat. "Where is it, Alex?"

And the cat said, "It's magical just as I told you; you can't see it."

"Then why can you?"

"Cats see everything. Get back and let me fight."

But the prince did not go away. He stood and watched, hopelessly at first, and then he began to see something in the snow and the wet on the terrace, even if it was not quite a snake. As the cat leaped in and slashed away at his foe with his forepaws, bloody scratches were appearing, seemingly from nowhere on nothing. The prince said, "There, I see where it is, Alex. I can see the blood."

The snow began to fall again, and the wind began to blow. The blood-streaked shape moved faster. The cat shouted, "Get out of the way, Alex, it's too dangerous."

And the prince shouted in his turn, "Get out of the way yourself, Alex, I have my sword, and you know how fast I am."

The snake, who, as a magical animal, was listening to all this, became understandably confused. Who was Alex and where was he, what could he see, and did he or did he not have a sword?

But the cat kept jumping in and slashing with his claws, and as the prince watched, he suddenly realized that in all those games he and Alex had played, the cat had been moving far more slowly than he could move when he really needed to. Still, the snake was fast, faster than the prince, and the blood was dark, almost too dark to see in the shadows. But how long could the cat keep jumping and slashing, how long would it be before he slipped and missed just one step or slowed just enough for the snake to strike home?

"Get back, Alex," the cat said. "This is my fight, not yours. This is no place for a human who trips over his own feet, even though he has only two of them."

The prince shouted back, "What, Alex, I'm sorry I fell, but it doesn't matter; I'm sorry I'm clumsy, but I don't care. Did the snake come to kill you or me? This is my fight too. Get ready, get ready; when I call, I can't have you in the way!"

The cat was fighting too hard to reply, and the prince said, "It's coming, it's coming, and it's here now!"

The cat leapt suddenly sideways, and Alex thought he might have skidded when he landed, but the prince's sword came down on what he hoped was the snake, striking sparks from the stone floor and partially shattering itself with the force of its own blow. The prince's right arm was suddenly numb almost to the shoulder, and the snake, visible now in death, was black shading into deep blue just like the early night sky but scarred with bloody scratches instead of stars. It had been cut in half, and it lay twitching and bleeding.

And then the storm screamed, and there was a black presence somehow in the white and swirling snow. This was the nightmare, not the snake. The monster was coming, and the prince suddenly knew it would be something with wings, something with poisoned talons, too fast to stop, too horrible to think about, and he fell backward onto the stone floor of the terrace. He could feel the cold and wet soaking into his back. He knew he had to get up, but he couldn't move; he could barely breathe. He seemed to be drowning.

It was then that something heavy landed on his chest, and just at that moment, he made out the bird shape coming toward him from the storm. If he had had the breath, he would have screamed.

"Put your legs up now," shouted the voice of Alex the cat, and Alex the prince, much to his own surprise, was able to obey. The monster smashed into his boots, nearly breaking his legs, and bounced off to land in a crumpled heap beside the snake. The prince was left gasping for air as if the attack had been successful and the poison was affecting his lungs.

"I knew that big, ungainly body had to be good for something," the cat said.

"What, Alex," the prince said, "how do you know I'm not dying?"

"Because I'm standing on your chest, and I can feel you breathing."

"What are you doing there," the prince asked accusingly. "You were planning to take the blow, weren't you?"

"I had a better idea at the last second. I don't think snow monsters are a very sturdy breed. Look what you did to the snake even if you did miss the head."

"I wasn't trying for the head. I barely had any idea where the head was. I knew I could hit the middle, and it kills just as well. Do you think I hit him too hard?"

"You broke your sword," the cat said, "and nearly broke your arm. What do you think?"

"Oh, shut up, the two of you." The small gray man stepped out of a shadow from where he had been watching the fight and glared at them both. "If I'd known you could talk to each other, I'd have known how much trouble I was in. My poor snake, my poor hawk, my poor snake, my poor broken hawk, never did anything bad to anybody."

"Not for lack of trying," said the prince. He moved the cat gently off his chest and managed at last to stand up. "Now," he said to the gnome, "why don't I demonstrate for you how much more painful it is to be stabbed by a broken and dull sword than by the usual intact, sharpened variety?"

"Is everybody," the gnome answered, "named Alex a cruel torturer?"

"Yes," said prince and cat together, and the cat added, "unlike those kind and considerate torturers you always hear about."

"There was one in Schleswig," the prince said.

"Really?"

"No."

The gnome went on as if he hadn't heard, "My poor snake, my poor hawk, and now I've lost, lost my revenge, lost everything, and I have to grant you a wish—a wish—just because you broke the curse—a wish for killing my beautiful snake and fierce bird and protecting these wicked, wicked people. I hate magic. It has too many rules. And I hate cats. They don't have any. So, kill me if you want, torture me until I scream louder than my storm. But if you do, you get no wish, and the snow will never stop. The princess thought it would stop immediately, but she's been wrong about so many things."

"Never?" the prince said, moving his sword back and forth and trying to restore the feeling in his arm.

"Probably never," said the gnome. "How can I tell when I'm dead?"

The prince and the cat looked at each other, and whether they were more stunned by the idea of a wish or the gnome's casual assumption that they had been protecting the people in the palace, it was difficult to say.

The little gray man, however, was not paying attention and didn't care. "All lost but what does it matter to anyone except me? Don't cry over spilt milk for the cat will lap it up." At which point, he gave a horrible laugh, like a saw cutting wood. The cat decided that full sentences and awful laughter were better than snuffling tears and a few halting, nearly unintelligible words, though not by much.

"I know what you want for your wish," the gnome continued. "Yes, it's always the same. Shall I say it first and save us all time? You want that despicable cat turned into a human being so you can truly be brothers, happy as kings or, in this case, princes together," and then he laughed again, while a tear glistened fitfully in his left eye, or perhaps it was just the snow melting on his face.

"No, no, no," said Alex the cat and Alex the prince together. And then the prince asked, "You'll take this?" And the cat said, "Absolutely."

"I," said Alex the cat, speaking alone, "would not want to be a human for anything or for anyone. Imagine not being able to see, hear, or detect smells properly. Imagine tripping and stumbling and moving like an arthritic mule. Imagine a lopsided face, a lumpen body, and a parti-colored, mostly bare hide. Imagine..."

But at that point, the gnome interrupted, "So, no, then. Just tell me what you want, and let's be done with it."

The prince had a thoughtful expression, and the cat, taking that as a warning sign, decided to speak quickly. "I've had this all figured out from the time I first smelled the stink of the princess's perfume."

"Oh, no, no, no," said the gnome in his turn. "The reason cats shouldn't have the power of speech is because they never shut up."

"Unlike gnomes," muttered the cat.

The little gray man went on as if he hadn't heard, "Say what wish you want—don't tell me its history."

"Very well. Here it is: Make it so the marriage never happened. Put everything back to the way it was before the wedding—with one exception. I want the princess and her parents in our castle, and I want us—every last peasant—in this palace. Well, I don't want the peasants in the palace, but you see what I mean. The gold, of course, stays here. And the snow stops. It stops now. In fact, with my wish, it will never have fallen."

"But you can," encouraged the prince, "feel free to visit the princess in her new residence. Make it cold. Make it snow. Freeze the moat solid if you like and skate on it to your heart's content. Take the kingdom of winter from here and put it there."

The little gray man stood with his mouth open. "That's a good wish, an excellent wish, a superb wish. I wish I had thought of it and wished it myself. It punishes those monsters far better than killing your prince."

"Which," the cat said to the gnome, "as I told you before, idiot, doesn't punish them at all. Why did you do such a thing?"

"He did it," the prince said, "because he loved the princess. If she married someone else, it must be because she loved that person, so the way to punish her was to deprive her of her love just as she..."

"Deprived me of mine," the gnome finished.

"That princess doesn't love anyone," the cat said.

"Well, she certainly doesn't love any of us. Strange, how different it is in the stories. If she'd loved me, you know, we might still have broken the curse and, as they always say, lived happily... But wait," the prince said, suddenly completing another thought than the one with which he had started, "Is the curse on the beer a curse on the castle or on my father?"

"No curse," the little gray man answered. "Just worn-out soil. The soil is much better here. No beer for the castle. Oh what a wish this is! Look, I'm smiling while I grant it, and I grant it with no tricks or reservations. My winter is going. Well, not so much going as moving, but soon it will be gone from here." He smiled a smile so big that his face seemed to have been divided in two, and indeed, the clouds were swept away, and the terrace was white with moonlight, not snow.

"I don't know if my father will like living here so suddenly and without warning, but being able to brew good beer again will make him happy."

"It will make the peasants happy too," muttered the cat.

And the prince said, "I guess I won't have to go home for Christmas. Home is coming here."

The gnome clapped his hands together and looked about him, still smiling. "Well, Alex the cat and Alex the prince, I don't hate you half as much as I did yesterday. In fact, I almost wish you well. And you, Alex the cat, I owe you a good turn for your tricky wish. Don't be shy; you can collect it any time you can find me." He ran off slowly, favoring his left leg.

The cat called after him, "Remember, there's always a cat around somewhere," and even at a distance, in the shadows, they could see a shudder pass through his body.

Alex the prince picked up Alex the cat and stood holding him in both arms. He felt remarkably light for a twenty-pound warrior who had just won two battles and a war. The prince managed to rub the cat's back and chest even while he was holding him, a skill he had learned long ago, and the cat, who might have said many things, including "I told you so," decided to purr instead.

Then, suddenly, the cat stiffened, and the prince almost dropped him. "Wait," the cat said, "I did it wrong. I wished it wrong. Of course, it wasn't for me to be a human, but you could have been a cat, and I never thought of it until now when it's too late!"

"No, no, don't worry, Alex," the prince said. "You got it exactly right. This is much better for my parents, and you and I both know that I'm not nearly clever enough to be a cat like you."

The castle was old, battered by ancient sieges and tattered by winter storms. And it was rather small. For the princess and her parents, it was an unfamiliar and uncomfortable place. Alex the prince could have given them a tour of what had been his home, but he was never likely to be there again.

The princess's mother said, "There's no room here at all. I think the only guests they entertained must have been enemy armies."

Her father said, "It smells of sour beer."

And the princess said, "I don't care what it smells like or how small it is or whether or not we're stuck here. I will not marry that creature."

Ace G. Pilkington has published articles, poems, and short stories in five countries. He is the author of *Screening Shakespeare from Richard II to Henry V, Science Fiction and Futurism: Their Terms and Ideas,* and *Our Lady Guenevere.* He is co-editor of *Lab Lit: Exploring Literary Fictions about Science, The Fantastic Made Visible,* and *Fairy Tales of the Russians and Other Slavs.* He is an active member of the SFWA, professor of English and history at Dixie State University, and Literary Seminar director at the Utah Shakespeare Festival. He has a D.Phil. in Shakespeare, history, and film from Oxford University.

https://www.facebook.com/profile.php?id=100009659826674

Whisker Width

H. L. BURKE

On the eve of her thirtieth birthday, Kara decided to bite the bullet and get a cat.

Kara had always liked cats but hadn't owned one since her senior cat, Einstein, passed away at the ripe old age of sixteen. She'd thought about replacing him, even window-shopped a few shelters, but her friends already snickered at her cat-themed socks and her love for all things "kitten." As far as they were concerned, if she got a cat before she got a boyfriend, she might as well apply for her "crazy cat lady" license while she was at it.

So instead, Kara had accompanied them to speed dating, and noisy clubs, and singles mixers, and other forms of torture where no one appreciated her clever feline-related puns. It wasn't that she didn't like people. The right sort of people were awesome; the wrong sort, the sort that wanted to talk sports or politics rather than get into a "Princess Bride" quote-off... Honestly, Kara would just rather hang out with cats.

Friday night was the final straw. Her coworkers had set her up with a blind date who, after about ten minutes of awkward conversation, just gave up and spent the rest of dinner texting. Rude, but she was used to that from humans by now. It was when he set his phone down to pick up his beer and she got a glimpse of his latest text exchange that she'd finally had enough.

DB: How's the date, bro?

M: Meh.

DB: That bad, huh?

M: She's cute but way too fluffy.

Fluffy? And he said it like that was a bad thing? Kara walked out of the date halfway through the meal. Well, she'd got a doggy bag. She wasn't an idiot.

But delicious leftovers aside, she was through with the dating game. She couldn't believe she'd put on contacts and makeup for that jerk.

Who needed men anyway? Who needed people at all? Kara was going to get herself a cat!

So that was why, as soon as her shift was up on Monday, she slipped off to the local animal shelter to meet her new best friend.

Helping Paws Animal Rescue was located in a cold, industrial building that smelled strongly of wood shavings and wet dog. Well, Kara

111

wasn't there for a dog. She knew what she wanted. She pulled open the heavy metal door, pushed her glasses further up her nose, and stared unashamedly into the eyes of the middle-aged volunteer. "I'm here to see your cats."

The husky, gray-haired woman nodded, slowly rose from her office chair, and unhooked a set of keys from the wall.

"Lou," she shouted. "You got the front?"

"Sure, Chris," a muffled voice came from the back office.

Not waiting for Lou, Chris nodded toward another heavy metal door, this one with a fogged glass window. The constant whines and yelps of what had to be a dozen puppies rose from beyond it, tearing at Kara's heartstrings. Well, she didn't have space for a dog, just a cat. Maybe cats weren't as boisterously desperate, but they needed love too.

They walked through a narrow corridor with metal cages on both sides—Kara doing her best to avoid the literal puppy-dog eyes coming at her from all directions—before opening a second door into a quiet room with a Plexiglas divider in the middle. On the other side of the divider rose a forest of carpeted cat trees.

"We had an adoption drive this weekend. Nine lives for nine dollars. Reduced our usual fee for cat adoption from $75 to just $9. Every cat fancier in the county, and some from as far as Portland, swarmed us, so I'm afraid we've only got a few cats left. No kittens." Chris narrowed her eyes, as if testing Kara's resolve with this announcement.

"An adult cat is fine." Kara resisted pressing her nose against the Plexiglas. A bundle of black fur spilled over the sides of one cat bed, and a tabby licked at a water bowl in the center of the room. Not much to choose from. She'd know the "one" when she met him, though, right?

Chris took a binder from a shelf. "These are the stats of our current residents. Do you know what sort of a companion—"

Something buzzed overhead, making Kara jump, then a voice echoed from an intercom speaker. "Chris, we've got a drop-off."

Chris mumbled under her breath. "Sorry, miss, but Lou doesn't have access to the main computer. I need to process the new arrival." She passed Kara the binder. "Why don't you read up on our current guests?"

With that she rushed out of the room, shutting the door behind her and leaving Kara separated from furry goodness by a thick layer of Plexiglas. Kara sighed and opened the folder. The first several pages had appealing pictures of kitties, but all stamped with "adopted." Even if they hadn't been, the paper just listed stats: age, health, whether they'd been turned in or rescued. She wasn't looking for statistics. She was looking for chemistry.

She sank into a nearby folding chair and rubbed her forehead. A prickling sensation rushed through her, like the bite of static electricity, and a haunting scent of cinnamon and ozone filled her nose. Something warm and soft brushed up against her legs. She leaped from her chair with a yelp.

A massive orange tabby cat blinked up at her. She blinked back. The cat rubbed against her ankles then flicked its tail and sat down to wash its paws.

Kara glanced at the Plexiglas. "How'd you get out?" Dropping to her haunches, she stroked the feline's spine. Energy prickled through her fingers. That explained the static. This cat was charged.

A rumbling purr rose from the animal. It gazed up at her with soulful amber eyes. Something about its face said "boy cat."

"Well, aren't you a handsome ginger gentleman," she cooed.

The cat gave an approving "mew" and continued to circle her, his tail tickling her nose. Something within her eased, and before she knew what was happening, she was sitting cross-legged on the cold linoleum floor with a heavy bundle of cat in her lap and purrs vibrating through her entire being. She couldn't remember the last time she'd been so happy.

The scent of cinnamon intensified. Perhaps the shelter had one of those time-release wall plug-ins. They probably needed it to combat all the various animal odors. Closing her eyes, she focused on the hum of the cat and the scent of the cinnamon. A vision came unbidden: one of grassy fields and stone towers. Something from a movie? A book she'd read? Maybe. It was a nice daydream, no matter what had caused it. Every muscle in her body softened, and she slumped against the wall, mechanically stroking the cat's silky fur.

A figure crossed the space before her, tall and willowy. With a deep voice, he called out, "Caius? Caius? Where'd you get to?"

Now that seemed an odd detail to dream up. And come to think of it, she'd never really had daydreams this photo-realistic before. On a whim, she opened her mouth to respond to the dream-man.

"Where did you get a cat? They're all locked up." Chris's question snapped Kara back into the present. The cat meowed in annoyance and hopped from Kara's lap.

Embarrassed at being caught sitting on the floor, Kara stood. "He just showed up. I like him though. Is he up for adoption?"

Chris hoisted the cat off the ground. He yowled and wriggled for freedom.

"Huh. I have no idea where this cat came from. He wasn't here this morning." Chris stuffed the cat beneath one arm like a bag of kitty litter and left the room. Kara scrambled after her, through the gauntlet of desperate dogs, back to the tiny front office. An elderly man in a trucker hat and flannel leaned back in the office chair, scrolling down his smartphone screen.

"Lou, you know you're not supposed to take in new animals without registering them. This one wasn't even in a cage, just wandering around loose." Chris pulled a cat carrier out from under the desk. The cat meowed and splayed his legs, but eventually lost his fight and went into the carrier.

Lou blinked. "I didn't take in any cats this morning." He squinted into the cage. "That's a big orange boy. I'd remember him. Nope. I haven't seen him before. Did he maybe come in last night?"

"No, I locked up last night. We didn't get any new cats yesterday. Just that pit bull and the pair of ferrets."

"Well, he couldn't have gotten in here on his own." The two volunteers continued to discuss the appearance of the strange cat as if Kara wasn't even in the room.

The cat stared through the air holes in the top of the carrier, directly into Kara's heart. Yes, chemistry. She and this cat had chemistry.

She cleared her throat. "Excuse me, but I think that cat is the one I want."

Lou and Chris paused and stared at her.

Kara stepped closer to the cat carrier. Goosebumps popped out over her arms. Yes, she really *was* a crazy cat lady, and she wasn't afraid to admit it. "Can I take him home?"

"I'm afraid it's not that easy," Chris said. "We have procedures. He needs to see a vet, get entered into the system." She opened a file cabinet, her shoulder blocking Kara's view of the cage. Desperation flooded Kara's chest.

"I'll see to his vet bills. I'd just like to...reserve him, to be sure no one else takes him, you know."

"We don't really put holds on our cats. They aren't hotel rooms." Chris sniffed. "What if the vet visit finds a microchip? He'll have to go back to his real family then. Even if he's not chipped, his real family could be looking for him. Wouldn't be responsible for us to promise him to someone before we've held him a while to see if he's claimed."

Stomach tightening, Kara had to admit this made sense. "Oh. Yeah. How long will that take?"

"A week, maybe, depending on what we find in the vet exam." Lou pointed to a wall where a series of printouts advertised the various pets waiting for adoption. "You didn't get a chance to meet the others, though. Maybe one of them will catch your eye."

"No, I think I'll wait." Kara sighed. "I'll keep an eye on the website for him."

With one last longing look at the cat carrier, she turned and left the shelter.

On her way to her second-story apartment, Kara passed the super, Mr. Elliott.

"Hey, Mr. E." She gave him what she hoped was a convincing smile. Mr. E knew the business of all the tenants, including her recent disaster of a first date. The elderly man had been sweetly concerned, but she wasn't in the mood for sympathy right now. No, she just wanted to get in and see if the shelter had updated their "up for adoption" page yet.

"Ah, Kara." Mr. E smiled. "Home a little late tonight. Hot date?" He winked.

"Just with a bottle of wine and a TV marathon." She laughed. "Going to rewatch that episode where the detective has to solve a murder with the victim's cat as the only witness, I think."

"Oh, that's a good one. I might have to rewatch that too. Have a good night."

Unlocking her apartment door, Kara breathed a long sigh. She should've known in the days of modern bureaucracy it wouldn't be as simple as showing up and picking out a cat. For all she knew, cats had to be holistically matched with the ideal owners. No, not owners. That wasn't politically correct. "Human life partners." There, that sounded better. Still, she felt a little foolish for the bag of litter and box of canned food she'd purchased...and the impulse buy of a cat bed and ten-pack of toys that would be arriving via Amazon in the morning...and the "going to meet my new best friend now" tweet she'd sent...

Oh, goodness gracious, she was a mess.

"Maybe there is something wrong with me," Kara whispered, her hand still clenched around the doorknob, her mind unwilling to open it to reveal the cold, empty studio apartment inside with only the cold comforts of a laptop and a half-bottle of zinfandel to welcome her.

No, she couldn't be like that. One bad date and a setback in the cat department wouldn't ruin her day.

She'd get her cat.

Soon.

Maybe the shelter had updated the site already!

She opened the door.

A pair of glowing eyes stared at her from the couch.

Kara shrieked.

Stumbling back into the hallway, she slammed the door shut. Wait. From the size and placement of those eyes, it wasn't a big creature. Not a monster. A rat? A possum? Not great, but not life-threatening. She glanced down the hall. No sign of Mr. E, but it would be good to know what she was dealing with before she called him up. Let him know what size of traps to bring.

Heart pounding, Kara eased the door open while her other hand fumbled for the light switch.

A large orange tabby hopped from her couch and crossed to her. He sat at her feet and gazed up at her with those wise amber eyes.

A cat.

And not just any cat. *The* cat.

She swallowed. But it couldn't be. Even if the cat had managed to escape the shelter, how had it found her apartment and got there before she could? No, this was a really weird coincidence. This had to be a different cat.

"Meow, purr." The cat circled her ankles, throat rumbling like a distant thunderstorm. Tingles shot through her, accompanied by the scent of cinnamon. As ridiculous as it was, she knew, this was the same cat.

This was *her* cat. She gathered him up and squeezed him to her face. "It's all right, Caius," for somehow she was certain that was his name. "You're home. You're home."

A more law-abiding part of Kara's brain wondered if she should call the shelter and let them know she had their cat, but a firm feeling that Caius wasn't *their* cat but *her* cat had implanted itself deep in her soul. As unreasonable as that feeling might be, Kara couldn't risk them taking Caius away from her. Not when he'd come so far to be with her. They had chemistry. All her life, she'd accepted that magic wasn't real, that it was only in her books and movies. Now, however, she knew the truth: magic existed in the form of cats. It was a subtle, everyday sort of magic, of course, but she'd take what she could get.

Kara fell asleep with Caius's claws kneading into her shoulders. It hurt a little, but she didn't mind it. His purrs soothed her soul. In her dreams, she and her new kitty sunbathed in green fields accompanied by the scent of cinnamon and a deep masculine voice calling out, "Caius! Caius!"

Finally her eyes drifted open. Caius rubbed against her face.

"Good morning, dear." She ruffled his stately ears. Rolling over to look for her glasses on the nightstand, she paused. Something glittered beside the paperback of *How to Catch a Unicorn* she'd been reading. She squinted and leaned closer. The object came into focus as a silver flower with frosted leaves and petals. Some sort of Christmas decoration? Where had that come from?

Reaching for her glasses for a better look, her hand brushed the flower, and it crumbled into dust.

What the heck?

Bolting upright, she slammed her glasses onto her face. Nothing. Nothing was there.

Well, she hadn't been wearing her glasses. It was possible she'd just imagined a flower. What was that thing where a person saw faces in appliances? Yeah, that thing. That thing had made her imagine a sparkly flower in the dust.

"I need coffee."

What with seeing things, Kara didn't want to wait for a pot to brew for her caffeine infusion, so she cracked open one of her emergency cans of Liquid Sanity iced coffee. With that chugged, she and Caius settled in for a nice breakfast of eggs and Pawsome brand Chicken and Liver Pate. Caius cleaned his plate then daintily cleaned his paws.

She glanced at her phone. "I'm sorry, boy, but I have to go now. Will you be all right for a few hours on your own? I work right down the street, so I can come back and check on you at lunch, all right?"

Caius paused in his grooming, ears twitching. She patted his head. "I'll leave the TV on, all right? I've got all the best episodes of that fake psychic show recorded. You'll love it."

Caius yawned and settled into a perfect "cat loaf," his tail and paws tucked neatly beneath his body. Kara sighed. He was so, so adorable.

The morning at work crawled along. Between filling customer orders, she closed her eyes and thought about how she finally had someone waiting at home for her. If she allowed her mind to drift, she could smell the cinnamon and hear the voice from her dreams chanting Caius's name. The voice tasted vaguely of cinnamon, which was an odd thing to think, but somehow it felt right.

When lunchtime arrived, she clocked out and zipped to her car. The ten-minute drive to her apartment building might as well have been an hour. What if Caius thought she'd abandoned him? Did cats understand about day jobs? She barreled down the hall, jammed her key into the lock, and yanked the door open.

"I'm home!" she shouted.

Nothing.

Swallowing, she eased the door shut behind her. Well, cats slept a lot. He'd probably found a place to curl up for a nap. She'd make them both something to eat. That would draw him out. She put a Nutritious Options meal in the microwave and pulled back the tab on another can of Pawsome Chicken and Liver Pate.

"Caius?" she called. "I have num nums!"

No answer.

She bit her bottom lip. "Dinner's served, your meow-jesty." She laughed nervously at her own pun. Caius didn't emerge.

Kara panicked. She tore about the apartment, looking under the couch, the bed, in the closet, the bathtub, even checking the various cabinets she doubted he could open on his own. No sign of her cat. Her lunch hour was flitting away, and Caius was nowhere to be seen.

But how? How could he have gotten out? The door was shut. The windows were shut. He couldn't have walked through the walls.

"Caius, where are you?" What if he had gotten out? He'd somehow made it to her home from the shelter, so obviously he could escape buildings. The traffic on her street moved so fast. What if something happened to him?

Grabbing her keys and her phone, she rushed from the apartment and ran smack into Mr. E.

"Whoa there!" He held up his hands, one hand holding a half-empty carton of lightbulbs.

A thought struck her. Mr. E sometimes entered the apartments to fix things. He had a key. While normally he told her if he'd be stopping by for repairs, even while she was out, if something was urgent, he might go ahead and enter. Right? What if he had and Caius had slipped out?

"Have you seen my cat?" she gasped.

He raised his eyebrows. "No. I didn't even know you had a cat. Did you get it recently?"

Forcing herself to draw deep breaths, she fumbled for an explanation as to how Caius had come into her life. He'd just appeared. That wasn't normal, that wasn't natural, but why would anyone expect normal or natural from an extraordinary cat like Caius?

"Yes, I just got him." She opened the door to her apartment. The can of cat food sat untouched on the table. Orange fur coated a section of the fleece throw draped across her couch, so he *had* been there. She wasn't going crazy. She did have a cat.

Mr. E poked around the apartment. "You know, cats can slip through just about anything and wedge themselves in the tightest spots. They have those whiskers for a reason. If their whiskers can fit, the rest of them can too. They're like kitty parking guides." He chuckled.

"I checked the whole apartment though. Twice." She crossed her arms. Caius wasn't just tucked away in some corner. He was missing. She could feel that he wasn't there. Something absent from the air, a thinness she couldn't explain, but which meant no Caius. Still, even as she thought it, she knew how crazy that would sound, and she kept quiet. She couldn't expect Mr. E to understand the magical mystery that was Caius.

"Well, if he did slip out, he wouldn't have gone far. Grab a can of food, and we'll look out by the dumpsters."

Kara and Mr. E circled the building, calling for Caius, but no one came out. Finally they stopped in the parking lot. She set the can of cat food on her car's hood and wiped the gravy from her hand onto her jacket.

"I can help you get the word out, at least." Mr. E smiled sympathetically. "What does this boy of yours look like?"

"Big orange tabby." *Piercing soulful amber eyes, electric energy, deep throaty purr...*

"Huh." Mr. E gazed toward the apartment building. He tilted his head to one side, squinted, then pointed. "You mean like that."

Kara followed his finger to a second-story window. *Her* second-story window if she wasn't mistaken. Sitting, staring out at them, was Caius. She squeaked, "Thank you!" and took off at a run.

Bursting into the apartment, she fell to her knees as Caius hopped down from the windowsill and strolled toward her.

"Where were you? You made me look like an idiot out there. Why didn't you come when I called?"

His tail flicked against her nose. She patted him then glanced at the clock. Even if she left immediately, she'd be late for work. Well, she had a few sick days left, and one could argue there was definitely something wrong with her, getting so overwrought over a cat. "Let me call in, and then we can make some popcorn. Do you like cheese? I think I have some cheese."

Thankfully, Kara's boss accepted that her lunch wasn't agreeing with her without question. Soon Kara and Caius settled down on the couch with the laptop beside them. Caius accepted his backrubs, his gentle purr soothing Kara into a daze. Not feeling like anything challenging, she opened her browser to a "strangely satisfying" video playlist and watched contentedly as hot knives sliced through various substances.

After a bit, Caius stretched out to his full length, yawned, and hopped down from the couch.

"Litter box break?" She smiled. "Yeah, I could use one of those myself."

She headed for the bathroom. Before she could close the door behind her (a habit from growing up with three older brothers), a buzzing noise rose from the room she'd just left. Had her laptop playlist switched to some weird ambient track? She stuck her head out to check.

A bright flash blinded her, and she fell back into the wall, dazzled. Dots flitted about her vision, and the scent of cinnamon burned her nose.

"What was that?" Blinking several times, she cleared her vision. The room looked normal. Nothing out of place. She tiptoed into the middle of the room and paused the video on her laptop. A thought struck her. "Caius?" she called.

He was gone.

Kara sucked in air. *Don't panic. He's just in the kitchen.* She hurried to check, but there was no sign of the cat. *Under the bed?*

She got down on her hands and knees and pulled up the comforter. Nothing. Just dust. A lot of dust. Her eyes watered, and her nose itched. She sat up sneezing.

Flash!

She screamed and toppled to the ground.

"Meow?" Caius poked his head over the side of the bed and peered at her.

"How did you get there?" she snapped.

He hopped down. Two golden points of light whizzed over his head. They zipped around in circles, whistling and screaming...screaming? What sort of light screamed?

Trembling head to toe, Kara stumbled to her feet. The points of light sped toward her, their tone now obviously laughing. One collided with her cheek, burning like a spark from a firecracker. She slapped at it, but it wheeled away, snickering.

Caius hissed and sprang into the air. He thwacked the glowing...*thing* with his paw. It whimpered and hit the ground. The second dot of light zoomed over and pulled the first back into the air, chattering angrily. Caius yawned and flicked his tail. Another burst of light, and the mean light-thingies were gone.

Breath coming in ragged gasps, Kara gaped at Caius. "How did you do that?"

The cat scratched at his ears and disappeared in another flash.

Kara spent the rest of the afternoon huddled on the couch while Caius exploded in and out of her apartment. If she didn't look directly at the blaze of light, she could kind of get the sense of it, like a peephole opening up to reveal the brilliance of the sun. Usually Caius casually slipped through these doorways on his own, but occasionally he brought "guests" with him. A few more of the light-thingies made it through. Kara armed herself with a fly swatter and chased them around the apartment until a second flash allowed them to escape back to wherever they came from.

One time, a part-deer-part-butterfly thing flitted through with iridescent wings and spindly azure legs. The puppy-sized creature frolicked for a bit before tripping over her coffee table and lying with a bewildered look in its big pink eyes, its wings fluttering madly. She'd almost gotten up enough courage to pet the adorably awkward thing when Caius pranced up to it. With a burst of light, both of them were gone.

As the shadows lengthened across her living area, Caius's portals—for what else could she call them?—came further and further between. Finally he curled up beside her, purring contentedly. She hesitantly stroked him.

So that explained how he had managed to make it from the shelter to her home, and maybe how he'd just shown up inside the shelter without any paperwork. Why was a magical, portal-summoning cat following her around, though?

"Why me?" she whispered.

He opened a single amber eye and sniffed.

"Yeah, I guess asking a cat, let alone a magic cat, for explanations is kind of stupid." She adjusted her glasses. "Well, at least I don't have to worry about you getting lost. Not really. You can just appear wherever you want to be, can't you?"

He playfully batted at her hand.

"And so far you haven't brought anything dangerous with you from...from wherever you go." She closed her eyes and remembered the visions of the green fields and the stone towers and the strange man. "I kind of wish you'd take me with you. If it has light...pixies? I think I'll call them pixies, then maybe it has other things I'd like to see. Like unicorns or elves or dragons. Actually, dragons might eat me. Huh." She weighed the positives of seeing elves and fairies against the potential negatives of being a dragon's lunch. Well, it wasn't as if her own world didn't have its dangers. "I guess I don't mind having a magic cat. Though try not to be obvious about it. Don't want the neighbors talking or some weird men in black showing up to recruit you for the Justice League or something." She snorted. "That movie would've been a *lot* more interesting with a teleporting cat."

Caius flicked his tail in obvious agreement.

A pinpoint of light swelled in the middle of the kitchen, but unlike Caius's usual portals, this one didn't burst in and out in a split second of brilliance. Rather it stayed steady, growing from a peephole to a porthole to a wall of radiant light that blocked her view of the refrigerator. She covered her eyes.

"Dangit, Caius. What are you up to now?"

Caius's ears pricked up. Meowing, he hopped off the couch and ran for the portal.

The light blinked out, but this time, Caius hadn't gone anywhere.

And he wasn't alone.

"Eep!" Kara grabbed the only weapon she had on hand—the fly swatter from her fight with the light-pixies—and brandished it in the direction of the tall, lean shadow in her kitchen.

"There you are!" a deep but melodious voice said.

Her eyes adjusted. A willowy man in a silver tunic and leggings leaned down to pat Caius's ears. The cat purred and rubbed against his legs. The strange man had long, flaxen hair, eerily lavender eyes, and pointed ears. He scooped up Caius. "You had me so worried. What were you thinking, staying away for so long?"

There was something decidedly unthreatening in the way he interacted with Caius. She set the flyswatter down and cleared her throat.

"Excuse me, but who are you and how did you get in my house?"

He started. His gaze swept up and down her. Kara shifted from foot to foot, suddenly aware of her pajama bottoms and messy ponytail.

"I'm sorry to intrude, my lady. I am Altair, Lord of the Fields of Light and the Seven Towers of Felancia." He bowed at the waist. "Unfortunately, my companion, Caius, has taken to disappearing of late. Cats are able to slip through the smallest gaps between the mortal and magical realms, so keeping him contained is near impossible. However, he rarely stays away as long as he has this time. Something here must be attracting him."

As if in response, Caius mewed and wriggled out of the stranger's arms. With a rumbling purr, he curled up on top of Kara's fuzzy unicorn slippers.

Altair's eyes widened. "Oh. Oh dear." He cleared his throat. "This is awkward, but apparently my cat has bonded to you."

"He seems to like me. I like him too."

Kara bent down and stroked Caius's chin. The cat shut his eyes, a look of pure contentment on his ginger face.

Yes, Caius belonged to Altair—though could a cat truly be said to belong to anyone? However, he *wanted* to be with Kara, and from the looks of things, Altair couldn't *stop* him from being with Kara. Still, even if the victory was hers, she could be gracious about it. Nothing good could come out of ticking off a gorgeous Elf-Prince, after all. She'd never realized lavender eyes could be so alluring. "I'm fine if he continues to visit. Do you need to take him back now?"

"Well, that's also a little awkward." He scratched his chin. "You see, while Caius can slip through cracks between the worlds as long as they are as wide as his whiskers, I, as an elflord, need a slightly wider opening to make it through. It took all my magic to open a portal large enough to follow him here, and I'm sorry to admit, I'm quite spent. I don't think I'll be able to manage another spell like that for a few more hours." His shoulders slumped.

"Oh!" Kara realized that his cheeks, which she'd just assumed were naturally pale, had a grayish pallor. She motioned to her couch. "Do you want some water?"

He sank onto the couch beside her laptop. "Yes, please. Though if you happen to have some wine, it would be good for my weary spirits."

"Certainly!" Suddenly glad she hadn't consumed her half-bottle of zinfandel, Kara set Caius down on Altair's lap and rushed for the kitchen. Look at her! About to be sipping wine with a handsome elflord. What sort of crazy cat lady would do that? The best sort, of course.

She poured two glasses. As she handed Altair his wine, he brushed a finger across the touchpad of her laptop, stirring to life the paused playlist. This video was a kinetic sand molding compilation. She flushed.

"Interesting." Altair tilted his head. "I had heard of these viewing boxes you mortals are so attached to, but I was under the impression they were for the distribution of information and entertainment. Not...this."

"Um, well, they do information and entertainment too." She sat beside him. The scent of cinnamon wafted from him. "I can switch it to something else, if you'd like. Or turn it off."

"No, this is fine." He stared intently as the silent pair of hands in the video smoothed the kinetic sand into a pleasingly symmetrical shape. "It is...oddly satisfying, in fact. Do you spend many evenings like this?"

Her cheeks warmed. "Not every evening. But some."

"Interesting. Perhaps I shall have to join Caius on his visits more often. Someday I can return the favor and host you in my golden halls. We have musicians and honey cakes. No viewing boxes, but I might be able to find other forms of entertainment to your liking."

"That sounds wonderful," she squeaked.

Altair and Kara sat in silence with Caius's front half on his lap and back half on hers, sipping red wine and watching satisfying videos. As first dates went, it was definitely in Kara's top five.

H. L. Burke is the author of multiple fantasy novels including the Dragon and the Scholar saga, the Nyssa Glass YA Steampunk series, and *Coiled*. She is an admirer of the whimsical, a follower of the Light, and a believer in happily ever after.

Her current project is a Fantasy Romance trilogy called The Green Princess.

The cat in "Whisker Width" is inspired by Bruce, the author's ginger gentleman, a big orange rescue with a heart of gold.

http://www.hlburkeauthor.com/

The Honorable Retrieval of Miss Sunbeam Honeydew

Pamela Sharp

His sword was old, his scabbard was cracked, and his boot heels were worn—all hand-me-downs that bespoke his lowly status as a young and newly accepted guardian of his king's castle. His tabard, however, was brand new.

It would have to be brand new, wouldn't it? Since the tunic had only been recently sewn and the heraldry upon it had only been recently designed. And since he was wearing it for only his third day of duty at the castle.

Only his third day of duty after being accepted into the service of his king and being assigned as a retainer to the Princess Alexia, and already he had been issued a difficult, dangerous task to accomplish. And, already, he had been warned by other, older guards that if he wished to keep his sword and his scabbard and his place at the castle—and possibly even his head—this was a task at which he must not fail!

Gage walked steadily toward the entrance of the private garden—rather, toward the entrance of the other private garden—and cast a wary eye on the guard posted there, another new recruit named Roland. This other boy was no older than himself, his blade and boots were no better, and his tabard was no dirtier.

There was one notable difference between the tunics these equal and opposite retainers wore: the heraldry on Roland's tunic displayed a silhouette of a cat in mid-pounce against a background of green, while the heraldry on Gage's tunic displayed a silhouette of a cat in mid-leap against a background of yellow. That was a significant distinction at the castle these days.

Gage approached. Roland stepped forward to block him. Roland was no older than Gage, but he was a full head taller and far more confident. After all, Gage had been here only three days; Roland had been here a week already.

"State your business!" Roland issued a challenge.

As if he didn't know!

"I've come for the return of Her Highness's cat Sunbeam!" Gage announced.

"You mean you've come to steal Her Highness's cat Honeydew?" his opposite number countered.

"No, I mean I've come for Her Highness the Princess Alexia's cat Sunbeam that was stolen from her private garden the evening before last," Gage said.

"Which is Her Highness the Princess Alexandrina's cat Honeydew that was stolen from this private garden two nights before that," Roland said.

"I wasn't here then," Gage said.

"I was," Roland said smugly.

"Princess Alexia demands that her cat be returned!"

"Princess Alexandrina says her cat will remain in its basket in her garden, and the next thief her sister sends to steal it will be split from ear to ankle!"

Though the threat itself was anatomically dubious, especially given the blades they'd been issued, Roland did sound ready to attempt the feat should Gage try to get past him and into the garden.

The separate gardens of Princess Alexandrina and her twin sister, Princess Alexia, had been created by halving what used to be the entire private garden of the queen and her daughters shortly before these young retainers arrived—which was shortly after the death of the queen. The gardens themselves were separated by a newly built wall on the inside and by the circumference of the castle on the outside.

Gage wanted to make spirited remarks about the silliness of two princesses of the realm arguing over the name and ownership of a motley-coated cat of no particular breed, no particular beauty, or, from what other guards had told Gage, no particular personality. The great attraction of the cat to each of the princesses seemed to be that her twin sister claimed it, too.

Gage said none of the things he was thinking. Young he might be, and new to the job, but he wasn't stupid. He didn't know the strict definition of "treason to the realm"—and couldn't imagine himself committing it! But he wasn't about to test its limits and discover that criticizing the princesses was included.

The obvious next step for Gage was to draw his sword, demand the cat, and duel his opposition when the demand was refused. Poor a blade as it was, it would still slice, stab, maim, and kill as any sword of a soldier should do.

Gage couldn't bring himself to do it. Not over a cat.

"I'll be back," he muttered and turned to leave.

Roland's triumphant (and somewhat relieved) laughter followed his retreat.

Gage walked away from the garden and suffered the mocking calls of "Meow!" and "Cat-boy!" as he passed a pair of older soldiers. He veered sharply into the castle armory. Heskith was there, as Gage hoped he would be. Gage perched on an uncomfortable stool and waited disconsolately for the old, lame soldier to notice him.

Heskith was too old to challenge any castle invaders and too lame to run from station to station issuing orders during a battle. But he had taken an oath to protect this castle as a boy no older than Gage was now, and no one was about to send Heskith away or strip his tabard from him.

And on Heskith that meant a proper tabard worn by a proper soldier that displayed the proper heraldry of their king: the mighty stag and bear in battle against a background of red! Not some ridiculous parody of heraldry displaying the leaping silhouette of a housecat!

Heskith looked over in sympathy. He didn't rise from his place at the table, where he'd laid out a series of daggers to be sharpened on the whetstone in his hand. Heskith didn't move around much unless it was necessary.

"Did you return the dear Miss Sunbeam Honeydew to your princess?" he asked.

"No! And which name is it, anyway? Sunbeam or Honeydew?" Gage asked in irritation.

"Whichever she's called by whoever feeds her," Heskith answered easily.

"This is stupid!" Gage voiced his feelings freely with Heskith, who made life easier for all the new recruits, and whom Gage trusted.

"No, lad, it isn't 'stupid.' It's sad, it's a shame, and it's dangerous," Heskith said very seriously, and wanting Gage to hear it. "The stealing of the cat back and forth matters nothing at all to old soldiers like me who have no part in it, and it matters not nearly enough to the commander who issued you that tunic. He's pleased to regard the trouble of the cat as a training game to weed out any softer lads!

"But there's been one boy already who's had his arm sliced open in all this fun and games, and he's been sent home less healthy because of it," Heskith said. "I'd not like to see another good lad hurt, maybe killed, for a breach between sisters that His Majesty should have stopped the very moment it started! Not waved his permission for them to put up a wall!"

Gage squirmed to hear the outright criticism of the king. Surely that might be treason of a sort? Though he'd force them to cut out his tongue before he'd give Heskith away for saying it.

"I'll have to fight him, you know? If it comes to it? Roland, the guard standing at Princess Alexandrina's garden entrance." Gage watched Heskith's deft sharpening of a knife-edge against the whetstone.

"Roland, aye. A good lad," Heskith approved.

"You think we're all 'good lads.'" Gage smiled.

"Not all of you. But most of you who ask to wear the colors of the king."

"But I'm not wearing the colors of the king! I'm wearing the cat of Princess Alexia!"

"That you are," Heskith agreed.

"I should go back right now to Princess Alexandrina's garden to take the cat. It's my sworn duty to Princess Alexia. I shouldn't have walked away and come in here to talk to you! But I hoped..." Gage sighed.

"You hoped to think of a better way than fighting one of your own?" Heskith guessed. "It's a wise head that stops to think before it throws the body into a fight." He stopped sharpening the dagger he held. "Do you know the story of the cat, lad?"

"I know it's been taken and guarded and taken again!" Gage said.

"No, I don't mean the story of the wall and those silly tunics they've sewn for you to wear! I mean the story of the cat herself and how she came to be valued so high by the two princesses?"

Gage shook his head no.

Heskith told him.

"It was the late queen herself, you see, who found a kitten with a broken paw in the garden while she and her daughters were playing there. By rights, by practice, the maimed kitten should have been drowned or thrown over the wall and left to the wild things of nature.

"But Her Majesty wanted to teach her daughters a lesson about the heart of a queen toward her subjects. So instead of tossing the poor kitten away, they cared for it, the mother and daughters together, so that its broken paw might mend as well as nature would allow.

"You can see, can't you, lad, how the cat is a piece of their mother left behind for the little girls and why both their royal highnesses want her? That is the story of Miss Sunbeam Honeydew," Heskith finished.

Gage frowned. "Then shouldn't they be sharing the cat and keeping the cat together? Isn't that what their mother would have wanted?"

"Aye! No doubt about it!" Heskith said with feeling. "And it would have been share and share alike had their father, the king, told them so! But that isn't what he told them, is it? His Majesty asked his daughters whose cat it was? And when they said 'ours,' he told them that was no proper answer. The cat belonged to the queen, now it belongs to one of them. So *choose!*

"Our king is not a cruel man, but he is a hard one," Heskith said. "He abides no weakness in his eyes. If their mother wanted to teach her daughters care and compassion? Their father wants to teach them what it means to keep a throne!"

Again, Gage shifted position uncomfortably to hear this frank, unflattering story of the king. He was not accustomed to hearing anyone criticize the king. Ever. Perhaps it was treason just to listen to it?

"Well...I guess that makes it even more important that I retrieve the cat." Gage voiced his decision aloud. "If it's the king's own wish that only one of the princesses claim it, my duty is to make sure it is claimed by Princess Alexia!"

With that conflict now settled in his mind, Gage prepared himself to do his duty. He rose from the stool and put a hand on his sword to reassure himself it was there. There was no need to ask Heskith to put an edge on it; the sharpening had been done before it was issued to him. It was as sharp as it would get.

"Gage?" Heskith called to him before he got away. "What oath did you swear to the princess? Do you recall it?"

"To guard her life, her goods, and her honor with all of mine!" he said proudly.

"I don't suppose there was a part about swearing to do what was best for her?" the old soldier asked.

Gage paused a moment to think on the question. "No."

"Too bad," Heskith said with a shake of his head. "Because what would be best for her is to reunite with her sister, wouldn't you think? But you've sworn what you've sworn, and it's your oath to keep."

"And I shall," Gage said.

"Then keep your blade in front of you," Heskith advised him. "Roland will do the same."

A duel over a *cat*!

Gage marched himself back around the circumference of the castle to fight it.

And it wouldn't end here! Oh, no!

Whether he or Roland fell, some other young hopeful would take the oath and inherit the sword and the scabbard and the tabard to go with them, and this same stupid conflict would play itself out again at one garden entrance or the other for as long as the ownership of the cat was in dispute.

And what about the poor cat herself? What life was this for the animal?

Captured and recaptured. Stolen and stolen back.

131

And caged.

Though Princess Alexia called it "Sunbeam's basket," Gage had seen the structure for himself and knew it for what it was. A cage.

A spacious and comfortable cage, yes. A bed secure from wind and weather, yes. A protection to keep a weak-pawed cat safe from any wild predator that might sneak into the garden at night, yes. But still—

A cage.

Though he hadn't yet been in this other private garden to see it for himself, Gage had been told, and could believe, that her sister, Princess Alexandrina, had a similar "basket" for her precious Honeydew.

It was against the nature of a cat to be caged, wasn't it? Against the nature of any cat Gage had ever seen!

What a life!

He felt sorry for the animal to think of it being locked and held by either of the princesses, however lovingly, however treasured.

As though being called by the names of "Sunbeam" and "Honeydew" were not reason enough to have sympathy for the creature!

Gage endured another round of mockery from the guards wearing proper heraldry as he made his return trek. The "cat-boys" were ribbed by the older men just as any new recruit would be, but wearing this ridiculous tunic gave the older soldiers a better joke to tell.

Gage walked steadily forward, his mind clear in the most important respect. Yes, he would demand the cat and draw his sword if he must. It did not matter how silly a fight it seemed to him. The king wished for only one of his daughters to take ownership of the animal; therefore, he would see that the owner was Princess Alexia. That was the oath he had sworn. Hers were the colors he wore. There was nothing silly about that.

"So be it," Gage said grimly as he came into sight of the garden.

Roland stiffened to see him return and again placed himself to block Gage's progress. Gage drew his sword, making his intentions clear.

"In the name of Princess Alexia, I've come for the cat Sunbeam!"

Roland, faced with a drawn blade, blanched a little but did the only thing he could do. He drew his sword as well.

"In the name of Princess Alexandrina, you shall not take the cat Honeydew!"

They stood in opposition to one another, both smart enough boys to feel ridiculous about it, both proud enough soldiers to fight for the oaths they'd made.

"Wait!" Gage said suddenly and lowered his sword.

"What?" Roland looked relieved and lowered his sword also.

"How do I know it's the right cat?"

"What?" Roland asked again, with a different inflection in his voice.

"I need to know it's the right cat," Gage said. "I've not yet seen Sunbeam for myself, but the princess has done a watercolor, and I know Sunbeam's tail has a solid orange tip. Before I fight over her, I want to be sure this is the right cat."

"But— *Of course* it's the right cat!" Roland said with impatience. "We didn't steal the *wrong* one back!"

"Nonetheless, I shall need to see her for myself," Gage insisted primly.

Roland balked, hesitated, and finally surrendered to this totally unexpected condition for battle.

"All right, then! Come and see the cat!"

He started to sheathe his sword but realized that Gage had not sheathed his. Gage followed the look and nodded understanding. The pair of them sheathed their swords simultaneously, each keeping his eye on the other.

As one would expect, the private garden of Princess Alexandrina looked almost exactly like the private garden of Princess Alexia. The only differences were in this particular flower, or that particular bush, or some peculiarity of nature. And, as Gage had expected, Honeydew's "basket"— like Sunbeam's "basket"—was a large, decorative, sumptuous cage. A place with bedding and water and food and a discreet corner of sand and gravel for embarrassing bodily functions—but still a cage by definition.

The motley black, white, and orange cat inside the spacious cage looked out at the two young guardians of the realm with what Gage imagined to be a forlorn expression. For a cat who, as Gage had been told, possessed no great feline beauty to commend her, that forlorn expression did not make her a more attractive prize.

It did make her seem very pampered and very lonely.

And it made Gage sad.

"Cats aren't meant to live like this," he said quietly.

"I know," Roland replied.

The boys looked at one another guiltily, because neither one should have said it.

Roland drew himself up and tried to speak as the adult that he was not. "Are you satisfied this cat is, indeed, Princess Alexandrina's Honeydew?"

Gage drew himself up in kind. "Not until I see the solid orange tip of her tail will I be satisfied the cat is, indeed, Princess Alexia's Sunbeam."

"What does it matter whether you're satisfied or not?!" Roland finally thought to ask in exasperation. "You aren't taking the cat away from here whether you agree she's the right cat or not!"

"Nor need I make the attempt if the tip of her tail is not solid orange!" Gage replied, with the sudden wild hope that somehow, some way, it wouldn't be.

Roland, showing a severe lack of common sense or an overabundance of trust in the opposition, huffed against the request but leaned down to open the cage and cause the cat to display its tail.

Gage, who was fleet of foot and mind both, had a spark of imagination. He imagined himself taking advantage of the moment to trip Roland, grab the cat, and run with it—thereby doing his duty to his princess without bringing a sword into play.

The idea appealed to him greatly.

The prized prisoner cat, Miss Sunbeam Honeydew, had a different plan altogether. When Roland opened the cage door and reached inside, the quick-thinking cat, bad paw and all, raked Roland's hand, sprang over his shoulder, and leapt off his back onto the nearest tree trunk, up which she scrambled until she was sufficiently high to leap over the garden wall and disappear.

To leap over the true garden wall that separated the castle garden from the outside world, not the contrived inner wall which the sisters had lately built between them.

The daring escape took but an instant.

The boys looked at one another in shock.

"I thought that cat had a bad paw!" Gage objected, as though it was unfair of her to use her good ones to such effect.

"The princess will have my head!" Roland squeaked.

He wasn't necessarily wrong.

Gage thought it likely that both princesses would have both their heads if their precious pet cat was lost to them!

The two retainers would not have to wait to find out.

Having direct access through the castle itself, neither princess had to make a long trek to enter her private half of the garden. The opening had been reconfigured to make separate entrances just where their new wall began.

Her Highness the Princess Alexandrina entered her garden and went straight to the spot where she expected to find Honeydew in her basket. She was a little girl of eight years old, with red hair and blue eyes and numerous freckles across her cheekbones. In coordination with her heraldry, she dressed today in light green.

Two older girls of Gage and Roland's age trailed behind the princess as attendants. One carried what looked to Gage like a cloth mouse and a stick with a ball tied on with red yarn. Cat toys.

Roland bowed deeply. "Princess Alexandrina!"

Gage bowed as well.

The princess gasped to see the door of the "basket" wide open.

"Where is she?! Where is Honeydew?!" She looked frantically around the garden as she asked it. "I don't see her!"

Roland tried to answer, but his voice was shaky. "Your Highness, the cat—"

The princess now observed the yellow background and leaping silhouette on Gage's tunic and knew him as the enemy.

"*You!* You came from my sister! *What have you done with my Honeydew*?!" she demanded but didn't wait on his reply. "Go get my sister! *Get my sister right now!*" she commanded her unencumbered attendant.

The attendant curtsied and obeyed.

Princess Alexandrina walked to Gage, marched to Gage, and looked up at him with all the haughty, angry bearing of her eight-year-old rank.

"*Where have you taken my Honeydew*?!" she demanded in a voice near tears.

Roland, with blood dripping from his badly scratched hand, began to answer for his misdeed. "My Princess, I allowed—"

Gage, in a rush of honor and honesty, didn't let him take the brunt of the blame.

"Your Highness, I came to retrieve and return the cat Sunbeam to her home in the garden of your sister, to whom my oath is given. Your loyal retainer would have prevented me from doing this. Your pet wanted no part of either of us, perhaps sensing the fight to come, and leapt away from both of us, and scaled the tree to leap beyond the garden wall into freedom.

"As a cat will leap for freedom when it wishes and is able," he incautiously added and gestured to Roland's hand. "Your loyal retainer was injured while attempting to hold the cat."

That description stretched the truth somewhat, but Roland looked grateful for it. After all, Roland had been touching the cat when it scratched him.

Now, the second of the royal princesses came rushing into the garden, two attendants following her and the messenger who'd been sent. Her Highness the Princess Alexia also had red hair and blue eyes and freckles across her cheekbones. In keeping with her chosen heraldry, she dressed in bright yellow. Had they not been dressed so distinctly, the twin princesses could not at a glance have been told apart.

"Sunbeam is *gone*?!" Princess Alexia cried to her sister.

"*Yes!* And it's *your* fault because *you* sent him!" Princess Alexandrina pointed to Gage.

"My princess," Gage bowed, "the cat escaped me when I tried to retrieve her for you."

"The cat escaped us, Your Highnesses," Roland said, bowing also and taking his share of the blame, because he was, as Heskith had said, "a good lad."

"She has to be *found*! What will she *do*?!" Princess Alexia turned and cried in distress to her sister. "She hasn't been outside in *ages*?!"

"I *know*! She can't live out *there*! Not in the *wild*!" Princess Alexandrina replied with equal distress to her sister. "Not with her crippled paw!"

Gage pictured that leaping, climbing, jumping cat in his mind and said what he was thinking to both the princesses. "You and your good mother, Her late Majesty, must have done an excellent job caring for the animal, Your Highnesses. The cat showed not a trace of an injured paw when she ran up that tree and leapt over the garden wall. Only the desire to return to the life which she had known before your care, and your mother's care, made her well again."

Both the little girls turned to listen upon hearing him speak of their mother.

"Surely, the animal performing such a feat is a tribute to your good mother's power of mercy and healing? And to your own powers of mercy and healing as I've been told she taught you to have?" Gage added hopefully, the idea of mercy being one he wished to plant firmly in both their minds just at present.

"But she's *gone*!" Princess Alexia wailed in yellow.

"Yes, she *is*!" Princess Alexandrina wailed in green.

Whether they meant the cat or their mother, Gage couldn't have said. It worked out as well by either meaning, for the sisters fell into crying and hugged one another in consolation.

And Gage felt that while he had not saved the life of his princess, or her goods, or her honor...he had served her well nonetheless. He felt that he had served her best interests in the way that Heskith had spoken of it.

Unfortunately, his own Princess Alexia was not inclined to agree with him. She wiped great tears from her eyes and condemned her retainer with childish fury.

"*You*! You should be...*roasted*! And...*basted*! And...*burned alive*! Both *of you*!" She added Roland to the burning.

Coming from some other little girl who had just lost a beloved pet, those words would mean only that she was angry. Coming from a princess who could order it done...?

Both Gage and Roland quavered inside and looked steadily down at the grass of the garden in an attempt not to show the quavering. The leaping and pouncing cats on their tunics leaped and pounced a little more violently in a gust of sudden breeze.

"Mother wouldn't say that," a softer voice said. "Mother wouldn't say anything like that. Mother always said that the reason we were making the cat well was so she could go back where she came from, didn't she?" Princess Alexandrina reminded her sister.

"I *know*, but *still*—!" Princess Alexia of the leaping cat in yellow wailed some more. "She was *ours* because Mother *made* her ours, and *then*—!"

"And then Mother didn't get to see her get well. And neither did we," said Princess Alexandrina of the pouncing cat in green, "because we were too busy fighting to notice when she did."

Princess Alexia gulped and wiped great tears away, but she nodded to her sister.

Gage risked raising his gaze and found one of the attendants in green smiling at him, another girl of such red hair and freckles that he thought she must be a royal relation. That attendant nodded to Gage in thanks.

And it occurred to Gage that even as a loyal retainer of Princess Alexia, perhaps he had done Princess Alexandrina a service also?

Then Gage realized that, no, he really hadn't done anything much for either of the princesses when the facts of the matter were examined. It had been Roland who opened the cage and allowed the cat to escape; Gage had only demanded to see the tip of the tail as a stall tactic because he didn't want to fight about a cat.

Perhaps there was some value and service to the kingdom in that, though? In being ready to draw a blade if necessary but not wanting to draw a blade if a way to avoid it could be found?

"Your Highness," said the attendant in green who had caught Gage's eye, "the guard of your garden has been wounded in the fray. Would you wish that he dress the wound?"

"Yes, that's right. See to your hand," Princess Alexandria said to Roland, indicating that he, at least, would not be roasted, basted, or burned alive.

"Thank you, Your Highness."

Roland got out of there in a hurry. He gave Gage a look of sympathy as he left.

Perhaps the threat of roasting was still hanging over Gage's head?

The meow was loud, insistent, and well-timed. All of them turned their attention to the wall, and to the cat sitting upon it, observing the whole group with what Gage read as disfavor and slight chastisement. Then again, was he reading entirely too much into the expression of a cat? Especially one of no great personality? Or so he'd been told.

Gage had his doubts about that now…

"Honeydew!" "Sunbeam!"

The joint cries rang simultaneously, and the princesses faced off as though they would argue the identity of their pet.

Miss Sunbeam Honeydew swished her tail and tensed, as though threatening the princesses that she would jump off that wall and disappear for good should the girls carry their argument any further.

And Gage must not have been reading too much into the expression of the cat after all, because the princesses seemed to get the same message.

"No, it's all right, Honeydew. We aren't going to fight over you anymore," Princess Alexandrina said, making the first grand concession. "You can be Sunbeam when you're on Alexia's side of the garden, and you can be Honeydew when you're on my side of the garden. And I won't make you stay on my side of the garden if you don't want to."

"You won't?" Princess Alexia asked in surprise.

"I won't," her sister said.

"Then I won't make her stay, either. I'll just let Sunbeam decide." Princess Alexia made her grand concession then spoke directly to the cat. "We only wanted to keep you safe because of your paw? And because Mother wanted us to watch over you?"

As if to convince them that they need not worry, the cat licked her paw reassuringly.

"Father won't like it," Princess Alexia reminded her twin.

"We just won't tell him," Princess Alexandrina declared. "And Mother would like it a lot. Mother would probably like it if we did this for a lot of animals!" she added.

The princesses looked at one another and then at Gage.

Princess Alexia lifted her chin and issued her order in a voice of command. "I order you to seek out wounded animals and bring them to my garden to be cared for!"

"Small animals," murmured that red-haired attendant in green whom Gage was certain was a royal cousin and who was fast becoming his favorite person at the castle next to Heskith.

The two attendants in yellow frowned in consternation at the speaker. This was their princess issuing the order, after all.

But Princess Alexia didn't seem to care whose attendant had spoken.

"Seek small animals," she agreed. "And not stinky ones," she added another caveat, suitable for an eight-year-old princess in a garden.

"I'll take the stinky ones," Princess Alexandrina said bravely. "I don't mind."

Gage could have sworn the attendants in yellow gave the attendants in green a pleased, superior look.

"Well! Start looking for them!" Gage's princess demanded of him.

Apparently, he, too, was safe from roasting, basting, and being burned alive for the moment.

Like Roland, Gage didn't waste time for anyone to tell him differently.

"Your Highnesses." He bowed and left them.

As he left the territory of the enemy, he heard cooing and calling to the cat atop the wall as each princess tried to coax their pet to stay. But he also heard, was fairly certain he heard, a remark about "tearing this stupid wall down!"

Gage walked swiftly but proudly from the garden. This time, when the older soldiers mocked him with "Cat-boy!" as he passed, Gage merely said that he had been entrusted with a mission from his princess and this "cat-boy" did not intend to fail her.

Pamela Sharp lives with her husband and son in Texas. Like so many writers, she has more books than she knows what to do with. Like so many writers, that doesn't stop her from collecting more. She is grudgingly accepting the digital alternatives.

The Witch's Cat

RACHEL ANN MICHAEL HARRIS

It was Friday, the thirteenth day of October, and the village was lit with the orange glow of oil lamps against a blackened sky. Deep in the shadows, Onyx purred as his mistress, Vivienne, stroked his long, black fur, her wool cloak enveloping them.

Pressing his cheek against her fingers, Onyx encouraged her to continue petting him. She had gotten distracted again by the barmaid down the dirt road from their alcove. Aurelia was her name. Onyx remembered anyone who snuck him table scraps at the back door. Table scraps of roast lamb soaked in mushroom gravy with hints of pepper and... Onyx licked his nose. Tonight, she stood upon a ladder polishing the sign above the tavern door. As she rubbed the rag in circles, making the wood shine, Aurelia would look down behind her. Every Friday, like the cycle of the moon, she was out here, watching who came just to catch a glimpse.

"Mama, look." A little girl pointed toward Vivienne and pulled on her mother's arm as they passed by. Onyx gave an extra purr. Perhaps he would get a little scratch under the chin.

Vivienne smiled and nodded from beneath the cowl to the girl.

The mother yanked her daughter back. "Stay away from that witch! Do you wish to be cursed?"

Onyx growled, hoping the little girl would step on a crack as the mother hurried them across the road, but Vivienne gently pressed a hand to his side, quieting him, before turning back to the barmaid.

Approaching the tavern was the village lord's son...what was his name...Ethan, dressed with a cape draped over his shoulders and a green tunic with the village lord's insignia stitched in gold. He never had any tidbits for Onyx, just a gentle push of his polished boot to get the cat out of his way. Head held high, he walked toward the tavern without a hitch in his stride...until he got closer to the tavern. His head drooped lower and lower until he passed the ladder. Pausing at the door, he stood for a moment before shaking his head.

Vivienne lifted one finger from Onyx's side and swiped it left to right. Ethan's moneybag fell from his belt, landing just outside with a dull clank as he opened the door and entered the tavern. Lowering her head to Onyx, Vivienne whispered in his ear. With a meow, he jumped down from her lap and sauntered quietly across the road. He could almost feel Vivienne's smile on his back.

Crouching in a corner by the door, Onyx lowered himself to his belly and waited. Twisting and turning his ebony ears, he listened to the loud chatter and bellowing laughs inside, shifting through each voice until he found the one he wanted. That wasn't a very funny joke. That one's had too much to drink. There. That one. Like waiting for a mouse at its hole, he stiffened, listening for Ethan to return to the door. It was only a few moments before his voice grew near. The door swung open and as Ethan took a step outside, Onyx darted between his feet. He yowled as the man's foot caught his side. Tripping forward, Ethan knocked into the ladder.

"Mangy cat!" Ethan howled.

Above, Aurelia screamed as she fell one way and the ladder went the other. Ethan caught her before Aurelia hit the ground.

"Are you all right?"

"I'm so sorry."

They spoke at the same time. Vivienne would take great pleasure in that.

Ethan stared at her, blinked, then gave a lopsided smile. "Hi." Aurelia's arm was wrapped around his neck as he held her for a moment.

Shaking her head like awakening from a dream, Aurelia's brow furrowed before she smiled back. "Hi."

And it was like they stepped back into the past. Onyx remembered them from his kitten days, lounging in Vivienne's young arms while watching from an alley as Aurelia and Ethan, children as well, played in this same road throwing mud balls at each other, laughing and giggling before the lord and the tavern owner grabbed their children and pulled them away to their respective places in society. Now, seeing the two of them together again, the barmaid and the future lord, that time seemed to drift away as they smiled into each other's eyes.

Onyx walked back to Vivienne, a spring in his step, and sat beside her, his tail curling around himself. They watched the two from their dark corner. Flicking his tail, he turned around, his green eyes like glowing orbs out of the darkness, catching yours, and he winked. *Not so unlucky now, am I?"*

Rachel Ann Michael Harris wrote this story in memory of Rockstar "Rocky," the best, sweetest black cat with the greenest eyes you could ever meet.

The Cat-Dragon and the Unicorn

JANEEN IPPOLITO

Humans are peculiar creatures. Also, on occasion, unspeakably cruel creatures.

I should know, for humans made me, cobbled me together in a laboratory in the depths of Erskinel. The Place of Marvels, they called it. The place of devils, more like. More died in Erskinel than ever saw the light of day and the applause of the crowd.

Never for the creature, of course. Always for the creator, the mad scientist who concocted a crazy scheme of magic and technology until the experiments eventually stopped failing. They were patient, these scientists. They had all the time in the world, with their long lives which were also the result of their callous research.

I cannot recall how long they'd kept me in that hideous place with the harsh white lights, the spoiled lemon stench of preservatives with the undertone of rancid flesh. Every morning, I woke in my tiny cage, barely large enough to stretch my wings, and glared at the humans striding by in bleached white aprons and coveralls. Sometimes they would stop by my cage and dare to stick a few of their gloved fingers through the wire squares, as if to pet me.

Amusing. Even after numerous singed fingers from my flames, the humans at this odious establishment still thought of me as their pet, some form of lucky token to their scientific achievements. All because I had managed to survive the hideous experiments that gave me the glimmering golden scales nestled in my orange fur and the magnificent wings emerging from my shoulder blades.

As if the humans could take credit for such marvels. I had no concept of a higher power then—and my attentiveness to such is still tenuous—but I had no intention of holding any gratitude toward the terrible individuals who had inflicted such pain on me. No, I would only use those attributes to escape, at precisely the right time.

Which couldn't conflict with my meals or daily nap time. Such things are important as well. Let those go, and you lose all sense of civility entirely.

As it happened, the unicorns did some of the job for me. Courteous of them. Of course, I would have figured out a way on my own eventually, but capitalizing on opportunities is the mark of excellence. So then, when they raided the laboratory with neighs like screeches of the dying and pounding hooves like thunder, I was ready. Those silver horns, gilded black with some kind of liquid, were more than sufficient to break through the extensive locks on my cage, and the mixture of unicorns in hoof form and skin form attacking all parts of the room was quite impressive.

Until one of the brutes got a bit carried away and stabbed at me, not merely the wire grid that held me. The horn pierced my gut, loosing more entrails and blood than I realized I had. A most undignified but deeply felt mewl escaped me as I puddled at the bottom of my cage, all thoughts of fleeing vanishing in the overwhelming waves of pain. So much for a convenient rescue. After all this time of waiting and scheming, I was reduced to a pile of fur and scales and whimpers. My disappointment was as keen as my shock, although both were quite overtaken by the shadows of unconsciousness blurring the world around me.

The last sight I remembered before darkness claimed me was the vague outline of an olive-toned face, a frown, and violet eyes.

Then all disappeared and good riddance to it.

By life or by death, at least I wouldn't be in that horrid laboratory any more.

When I awoke, I was entrapped in a new cage. A most unusual one, for it held me prisoner without any wires or electricity. Somehow, this terrible device kept me hostage with invisible pressure on all parts of my body. Even my vision was limited to what shaky images I could see from lifting my head a fraction.

Well, at least I could do that much. Perhaps if I could only summon a flame, I would have a small chance of escape.

<You aren't a prisoner.>

If I'd had any mobility, I would have leaped at the sound in my mind. And then pretended like I had done nothing unusual, because of course I could never be surprised.

Now was the time for a spectacular flame of peril. I managed to open my mouth a portion, inhaled through an aching chest—and coughed with the might of a tiny mouse.

Rubbish.

<Foolish animal. You're still healing!> Soft laughter sounded from above me, and a face appeared in front of me. After a few careful blinks, the wavy shapes coalesced into a sharp face with violet eyes, black hair, and pointed ears that stuck out from his head. A child's face.

A young human? No, he smelled different. More like grass and shadows and a tinge of blood. Curiously, none of it set my teeth on edge. Which only increased my nerves.

I hissed weakly. <Go away, you miserable child.>

His dark olive forehead wrinkled. <You want to die then?>

My pulse jolted. The little upstart had heard me! I had a voice. I could talk to humans.

Then I gave the child another look. A bone-colored horn only a few inches long poked out in the middle of his forehead. So he wasn't human?

A memory of screeching neighs and floor-shaking hooves filled my mind. Was the boy a unicorn? But he wore the garb of human bone and skin, not fur and four legs.

The boy was still talking <...my skill is the only thing keeping you alive. The others didn't want to waste resources healing a mere cat, even if they did accidently stab you. Although, are you a cat or a dragon? No, I suppose you're both, aren't you?>

<Yes. I am magnificently both.>

He snorted. <I would say impossibly both.>

<I didn't come here to be insulted by a child.>

<You didn't come here at all. You were rescued during my first raid on the gods and brought to our healing facilities at great risk.>

<A most fortuitous escape on my part.> I twitched my whiskers. <The gods? What's a god? You mean the humans?>

<Yes, the humans who experiment and torture so many so that they can try to make themselves gods. And they already call themselves gods, so we do too. It's shorter and a handy insult. Not all humans are evil. All gods?> The unicorn boy shrugged. <They are all bad. So the herd says, in any case.>

My mouth widened in a jaw-wrenching yawn, and my eyelids were inexplicably heavy. This prison was more powerful than any other.

Unless it wasn't a prison, and instead I was merely coping with the aftereffects of a misplaced unicorn stab. The second was more likely. But that didn't mean I should submit to my injury with any sort of joy. After all, the other beasts had wounded me.

Something touched the area around my ears with a gentle scratch. A purr rumbled within me despite myself. <How long must I stay here?>

<You're still not healed all the way. Maybe another few weeks. Maybe sooner, if Maira will just shift into skin form and assist me.> His face fell.

<But she's still too scared.>

My head was far too heavy. Perhaps the child had misplaced something and put extra weights in my skull. Perhaps I was simply exhausted from the escape. The rescue. In any case, I rested entirely on the surface, realizing for the first time that I had been laid on a soft cushion. For that, I could forgive the unicorn boy his attitude. Slightly.

Still, I needed to escape completely and live entirely of my own volition. Only then I would be free. <Maybe as I improve, I could speak with her.>

<You can try.> The unicorn boy still looked glum. <I don't even get to see her all the time. She's very stubborn.>

<So am I.>

<We'll see.> He started disappearing. No, that must have been my faulty vision again. <I'm Lirome Ukerys. What's your name?>

<...I...don't have...one.>

Belatedly, I realized I should have said that I didn't need one. That would have been far stronger.

I would amend my statement the next time I woke.

For the present, I surrendered to the darkness and comfort.

It would be a full week before I was able to leave the cushioned healing area. During that time I slept a lot, ate when it suited my appetite, drank an absurd amount of water, and in general enjoyed one of the most commodious, civil styles of living I had ever experienced. My space was at least six times larger than the horrid cage at the laboratory and allowed me to extend my wings fully on either side without touching the walls. Truly remarkable.

Of course, I never told Lirome that, especially since the troublesome unicorn boy continued to visit me, speak with me, and—by far the worst part—examine my body for healing. I could have endured the conversation, even if he refused to acknowledge my brilliance. But a cat-dragon has certain boundaries, and that child blithely ignored them in his quest to ensure I was in top-quality shape.

Awful little thing. Yes, I submitted to his ministrations, but only because it would allow me to visit with his sister soon. And once I visited with her and convinced her to shift, then the remainder of my healing would be far quicker and easier. Then I could leave these over-generous, horn-headed creatures and be on my way.

Finally, on the eighth day, Lirome allowed me to leave the facility. Yes, my departure was cradled in his arms, but even a dignified fellow such as myself must endure such things. And it wasn't all that terrible. We walked down a long hallway of plain cream walls and tiled floor, with many doors to rooms that I desperately needed to investigate before I left. Other unicorns walked past, bowing their heads and touching their horns in a gesture of respect, for Lirome was apparently of some notable lineage among his people. I congratulated myself on having the cleverness to be cared for by a child of noble blood. It almost excused the invasive examinations.

Almost.

We walked through a clear entryway that seemed to shimmer then emerged into a forest glade. The air was rich with warmth and growing things, and a gentle breeze stirred my coat. I turned my face into something bright and filled with concentrated heat.

The sun. This was the sun. I knew instantly that we would be very good friends. A part of me wanted to immediately sprawl on the ground and have a restorative nap.

But there would be plenty of time for such things after I escaped.

<This is my sister's special place. Only she and I can come here. No other unicorns.> Lirome paused for a moment, eying me speculatively. <You're not a unicorn, so I'm technically not breaking the rules.>

<Certainly not.>

He bobbed his head in an awkward nod. <All right. I'll call her over, and you can try to talk with her. One bit of unhappiness from Maira, and you're not coming out here again. Ever.>

The fur on my back rose at the fierceness in Lirome's tone. Usually he maintained a steady, thoughtful demeanor with occasional inappropriate humor, often at my expense for reasons I still couldn't fathom. But now, I knew that one wrong move and my plan to convince his sister to shift would be completely undone.

I adjusted myself in his arms until I sat up straight. This required great concentration and skill. A thread of doubt wound through me, and I curled my tail around my feet. My entire life had been devoted to pushing away others and making them fear me. Could I coax this scared unicorn girl into trusting me instead?

Did I even know how?

Hooves rustled in nearby bushes. My whiskers twitched, and my claws emerged from my paws just enough to give me traction.

Then the most exquisite creature I had ever seen walked into the glade. Black fur and mane, a bone-colored horn, and a long face that was both sharp and sensitive. Her head turned, and her violet eyes studied me, the whites showing around the edges. Her small, delicate hooves tripped at the ground, and her ears flicked around. Clearly nervous, from the signs Lirome had explained to me. He still refrained from telling me why. Some nonsense about it being my job to find out, since I was so clever.

Petulant child. At that moment, I would have given anything to know what made this graceful unicorn filly so wary.

<Lirome? What animal is that?>

I lifted my head up. <Not what. Who.>

She snorted and backed up a few steps, her ears flat. <A shifter? I haven't learned about shifters that look like you. I've only learned about seals, wolves, dragons, and unicorns.>

<There are no others like me. And I don't even know if I can shift.>

Maira tossed her head. <It isn't all that special. I'm never doing it again.>

Above me, Lirome sighed. <Maira...>

<I won't!> She stomped the ground. <If this is all you've come to talk about, Lirome, then I'll go back to grazing. The silvagrass is particularly tasty right now.>

Bickering would not do. It was time to take control of this situation. <If you please, I only wanted to get to know you more.>

<Why?> She stepped closer to me again. <You're planning on using me. Don't lie about it. I can feel it from you.>

Unicorns were empaths? I dug my claws into Lirome a little deeper. He had been reading my feelings this entire time and never told me. Another mark against him. There was nothing to do now but tell the unicorn girl the truth. <Forgive me. Yes. I want to leave and journey on my own, and in order to speed my healing, I came here to convince you to shift and assist your brother.>

<Assist him?> Maira walked even closer, until her nose was inches from me. <More like he would assist me.>

She inhaled, sniffing me. Since the girl had initiated, I reciprocated, inhaling a similar scent to her brother: grass, shadows, that tinge of blood. An additional undertone of fresh dew. Even by breathing it in, I felt stronger. Her magic was far stronger than any other I had ever encountered. Even Lirome's.

An odd surge of satisfaction both foreign and familiar came over me, along with a deep purr. I could never imagine living apart from that scent. I never wanted to. Wherever the unicorn girl went, I would be at her side.

Shock rippled through me at the ridiculous turn of my thoughts. In a few weeks, I would be a free cat-dragon, able to follow my own course! Why would I commit to the safety of a fearful unicorn child?

I poked at the resolve that had so recently formed within me. It wouldn't budge. Bother it all. Maybe after Maira healed me, it would disappear.

For her part, the unicorn girl whickered softly and nudged my head with her nose. <You can stay. I won't shift. But you can stay. Both of you, for at least a little while.>

She nudged Lirome as well, backed away, and began nibbling at the grass.

<Thank you.> The unicorn boy set me on the ground, removed his robe, then shifted to hoof form and stood next to his sister. For my part, I curled up in a patch of sunlight and closed my eyes.

Step one was accomplished. Maira had accepted me.

Now all I had to do was get her to talk about what scared her, see that it was all silly nonsense, and get her to shift.

After a nap in this delightful warmth.

It took another few days before Maira gave me the opportunity to ask about her fear. In the meanwhile, I rested, recuperated, and enjoyed sprawling in the sunshine. Sometimes Lirome would leave me there with her, but more often than not, he would stick around as well, shifting into his hoof form and spending time with his sister. It didn't take unicorn empathy to detect how much he missed her. Unicorns as a whole seemed to be a clannish sort.

Which meant Maira's segregation was unhealthy for her and the rest of her people. The thought grieved my heart for some inexplicable reason. Although I was hardly a heartless cat-dragon. Why wouldn't I care about a depressed unicorn? Of course, I cared about the girl, but no more than was reasonable.

She still needed to shift.

At last, one day it rained. I found the vile droplets from the sky most disagreeable. While the unicorns were unmoved at first, when the shower increased to a storm, complete with thunder and lightning, the siblings also grew restless. By that time, we had all moved from the main area in the glade to travel deeper into the forest, so instead of Lirome and me returning to the healing facility, Maira led us to a pavilion tucked between several broad tree trunks.

Well, led is a gentle term. Galloped like a raving mad girl intent on escaping a death knell was more accurate. When we reached her, Maira was shivering in a corner of the pavilion.

She shook out her mane. <Horrible storms. Uncontrollable. Just like in...>

I leapt on her words. <Just like what?>

<...my dream.>

A dream? The soggy state of my fur worsened my irritation. All of this fuss was over a dream? How foolish could this girl be? Lirome stomped his hoof perilously close to my right paw. I glared up at him, and the boy returned it. It was terribly inconvenient to have them reading my emotions all this time.

Maira gave a mental chuckle. <Dreams are the lifeblood of our kind, cat-dragon. They come infrequently, and each one is a true portent for the future.>

<Ah. And yours involved rain? Very disagreeable. Must have put you out quite a bit.> See? I could be quite sympathetic.

A low, sad whinny emerged from her, and then a long period of silence. <I beheld the doom of the great city of Glenalis and the destruction of all. Blood and rainstorm and great clashes of lightning until one could barely see. And I at the middle of the storm, in skin form, standing in a small circle of absolute quiet, watching as the one I cared for deeply was utterly destroyed. All of it my fault.>

Lirome fell completely silent. For my part, there were only more questions. <One you cared for deeply? How?>

<Unlike my caring for you, and unlike my bond with Lirome. Something entirely different and irresistible and vulnerable.>

<Was he a unicorn? A human?>

Maira turned away from both of us. <A god.>

That stole my words as well. That this sweet girl would be entangled somehow with a god, would rue the downfall of one of their kind, would desire him in such a strange way—it was preposterous. I hissed, my fur sticking up on end. It must be some kind of dark magic, to taint her perceptions and twist her mind so. The gods were what those evil humans who tormented me called themselves. They stole magic, they broke Talents, they tortured others for their own gain.

That the unicorn girl would destroy their vast city of Glenalis and crush their kingdom was a great and noble thing. That she would fall in love with a god was disturbing and vile. How could two destinies be wound in the same dream?

<It can't possibly be true,> I snapped.

<I received the dream during my time honoring the great All-Maker at the temple. It is true.> Maira's voice was soft. <But now you understand. If I never shift into skin form, then the dream will be thwarted.>

Lirome walked over to her and hung his head over her back with a gentle whicker. <Yes, but then you won't destroy their terrible kingdom. So many people will die. It's awful what they do to people, Maira.>

<And if I do shift, then I somehow betray all of my kind by taking up in some way with a god. And I will lose their trust forever. How am I to rule and lead them with that kind of destiny?>

Lead? More pieces fell into place in my mind. The reason Maira's magic was so great. The reason why Lirome was held as nobility. His sister was a form of queen. A ruler who was abdicating her throne for the sake of a doomsaying, because she feared either way, she would be alone. Better to choose loneliness now than be cast aside in the future.

A shortsighted vision, especially if the dream proved true. So what if she would be alone? I had been alone so much of my life, and no one cared. Her loneliness might finally bring down the evil we all feared. My irritation and anger must have been violent, for her ears flicked back.

She said, <You still choose isolation, you foolish cat-dragon.>

<So do you. But in your case, the fate of many rests on you accepting this dark future. Is your potential pain truly so much more important?>

<Yours is. At least to you.>

Her words stabbed my heart, far more cruelly than even the unicorn horn. What was this feeling that curled my tail and made me want to hide away? Guilt. Shame. Both of them unfamiliar and decidedly unpleasant emotions that could leave any time they wished.

Yet both of them lingered like heavy stones in my stomach.

Lirome turned his head away from his sister and glared at me. <Leave, cat-dragon. You aren't helping.>

I stared at him a moment longer. The boy dared think he could order me about? I spat and walked over to the edge of the pavilion. Not leaving at all, merely ridding myself of his presence. What did I care that he was displeased or that his sister's dream was gloomy?

None of it was my concern.

And yet, as I curled up to have a good sulk, the stones of guilt and shame sank deeper into my stomach and were joined by a third stone that I liked least of all.

Regret.

After the rainy afternoon, Lirome refused to take me out to meet his sister anymore. He also refused to speak with me more than necessary. Apparently I had quite outlived my welcome, which was just as well for me. Even without Maira's additional assistance, I would be leaving the healing facility soon enough. The exquisite unicorn girl could go and rot away in her hidden glade, ignoring her opportunity to stop the pain of so many.

None of that mattered to me. I would just leave when my time was up and travel alone. Finally free of humans and gods and unicorns. Able to hunt small creatures to my heart's content and answer to no one.

Yes, that suited me just fine.

Unfortunately, the stones in my stomach only grew heavier, and more were added to their number each day. Pity for Maira, who carried such a heavy doom on young shoulders. Admiration for her brother, who remained loyal to her even when she refused to see him. And that same strong, inexplicable devotion that had struck me from the moment I laid eyes on her. An invisible rope tying me to her, no matter what other plans I had made.

She was my unicorn. Lirome might have found me and rescued me, so he claimed, but I wanted to find her and heal her until she was better. I wanted to push her until she did something meaningful with her life and purpose. I was only a cat-dragon, stripped of everything that made me valuable, mutilated in a laboratory, and certainly incapable of doing anything useful.

But I could help the unicorn girl. That would be useful. It would also be a dangerous threat to my freedom, but somehow, I doubted Maira would demand more than I could give. Her weakness seemed to be expecting less of others, not too much of them.

After a while, the heaviness in my gut made it hard to eat, even though I had plenty of space in my stomach. My heart was far too consumed to hold any appetite. Finally, even Lirome noticed and asked after me.

<I want one more chance to see your sister and speak with her.>

The boy's eyes narrowed. <You are nearly healed, cat-dragon. You won't need her help.>

<I want...> The words stuck in my mind.

His violet eyes flashed blood red. <You want a lot of things and give

154

nothing in return.>

<I want to change that. I want to try and get Maira to shift.>

Lirome snorted. <You can't even shift yourself. It was stupid to think you would be able to help her.>

I hissed and clawed at him. <I've never tried!>

The words spun in my mind, disorienting me enough that I had to sit down. Lirome kept talking, but his conversation was meaningless now. Everything was meaningless except for the truth I had somehow missed. I might be able to shift. Then I could have even more freedom. Then I could open all of those doors in the hallway myself and see what lay behind them.

And I'd be able to protect Maira far better than a cat-dragon. My unicorn would be safe, whether I was cuddled in her arms or fighting by her side.

<...you're connected with her, aren't you?> Shock had overtaken Lirome's acerbic tone. <I didn't think it was possible.>

My tail flicked back and forth. The boy always interrupted a good train of thought. <Not in a kissing sense, if that's what you're referring to.>

Yes, I knew about kissing. Laboratory scientists did that on occasion, sneaking around in the dark. Touching mouths looked both absurd and disgusting.

Lirome nodded in empathy, his expression twisting. <I agree, kissing sounds gross. I wasn't talking about that. There are other kinds of bonds. I think you might have one of them. It's not a bad thing. She's my twin sister, so we have an especially close family bond. Yours could be something like that.>

<Family.>

Another peculiar word, but unlike kissing, it was far more pleasant-sounding. It meant home. It meant not being caught unawares. It meant always connected. The ideas sent shivers up my spine that were both pleasurable and terrifying.

But it was too late now. Maira needed my help, and I knew that even if I tried to leave, in the end, I'd turn around and search for her.

I'd even search for Lirome, though I fervently hoped he would never know that. Somehow, the glint in his eyes showed it was already too late. He scooped me up and walked toward the transparent screen. After walking through, he set me on the ground. A few moments later, Maira trotted in. As soon as she saw me, her nostrils flared, and she gave a screechy neigh.

<What are you doing here?>

Even as a filly, she was far larger than me. My heart pounded, and my tail twitched wildly. Nevertheless, I sauntered forward, fixing her with a firm stare.

<I'm here to help you. We're going to shift today.>

She threw her head back. <I told you, no—hold on, *we're* going to shift?>

<Yes. You and I both. Together.>

<*Can* you shift into skin form?>

I gave a rusty meow, projecting all of my natural confidence. <Certainly. I've just never tried.>

Maira turned her head, glancing over at Lirome. <Is this possible?>

<The cat-dragon is very certain.>

<Yes, but why now?> She took a step forward and looked down at me again. <You seem well enough. Why remain here?>

Drat. The unicorn girl was going to make me admit it. I could see the determination in her eyes. She wouldn't accept any of my usual, quite accomplished bluster. Well then, if I was going to do a confession, then I would do it my way.

<You're my unicorn, and I will not have you jeopardizing a promising future where you kill our common enemy simply because you are afraid of your future and of being alone. You won't be alone. I don't care what that rubbish dream says. I will be there, somehow.>

Each word was another nail in the coffin that held my freedom. But at this moment, that didn't matter. I was certain I would have moments of extreme resentment later on, but I was also certain that those moments wouldn't last. Most of all, I was certain that the girl would be equally loyal to me. That even Lirome would continue to care for and about me.

Both of those certainties frightened me almost as much as the whole situation. But I wasn't going to back down now. I would appear even more foolish than I felt.

Maira gave a nicker that was almost a chuckle. <You would thwart destiny itself?>

<Yes. Why not? I'm far cleverer than some mere concept.>

<Very well. You first.>

I padded even closer to her, right next to her hooves. <No. Together.>

<Hmph. All right.>

<...all right?>

Her violet eyes studied me. <Yes. Let's shift. I'm certain you know this, wise cat-dragon, but in order to shift, you must completely let go of one form to receive the other, and the exchange takes place in the Nether, a magical space Between. The first time is said to be a kind of death, until you get used to it.>

My claws emerged, slicing the ground as fear trickled through my brave face. <A kind of death?>

<Oh, a silly thing said by a poet. I'm not even sure a creature like you will notice anything special at all. Just let go and feel through the other side to your skin form.>

Yes. Quite right. Feel through the other side to my skin form. That seemed entirely sensible and tenable. Certainly.

<One.>

I closed my eyes, thinking back to the endless years in the laboratory. The excruciating experiments, the noxious smells, the screams of other victims.

And I let them go. I released the horrors.

<Two.>

I thought back to the unicorn attack. To waking up in the healing facility and verbally sparring with Lirome, a child with the knowledge of someone far older and a deep compassion beneath his quiet wit. I remembered his examinations with careful, thorough fingers. He didn't know how much others before him had hurt me.

And I let the resentment go. I released the scars.

<Three.>

I saw Maira. The first time, a half-grown, exquisite creature filled with fear. A serious young unicorn, carrying the weight of a terrifying destiny that held so much hope for shifters but so much cost to her. I heard the sharp sounds of her laughter in my mind.

And I let everything go.

My body crunched into pieces, broken down into the tiniest bits, bone and marrow and skin reshaping and undoing into something else. A pained yowl ripped out my throat as I lost my wings, my tail, everything that I had known as myself for the last untold years. All of it disappearing into the Nether, replaced instantaneously with something larger and stronger. And strange, oh so strange. Fingers and feet and nails instead of paws and claws. Far finer hair instead of thick fur, except at the top of my head. No whiskers, no wings.

Only bare skin and a vantage point that was far, far taller than I was accustomed to. The world tilted beneath my feet, and I fell to my knees then crouched.

Someone wrapped something soft and warm around me, a large robe.

<It's all right,> Lirome said. I glanced over at him. Instead of being taller, he was a few inches shorter and even more clearly a child next to my full-grown stature. <It can be hard the first time, and I'd think especially so if you were in your scale form all of those years.>

A small hand touched my other knee, comfort and invigorating magic flowing from the contact. I glanced over to see a girl, appearing the same age as Lirome, wrapped in a robe. She had long black hair, pointed ears, a bone horn emerging from her forehead, and a sharp face with twinkling violet eyes.

Her, I knew instantly as my unicorn. My charge.

She grinned. <You weren't what I expected from my dream.>

<...from your...dream?>

Maira's grin widened, and she shrugged. <Yes. You were there too, in my arms in your scale and fur form. Assuring me that somehow, everything would be all right. That no matter what I endured, you would make it all right and help me find those who mattered most. I recognized your voice the moment you spoke.>

My mouth dropped open. Egads, my mouth! What had happened to my teeth? They were blunt and useless. <You never said anything!>

The girl lifted her chin archly, looking every inch the spritely leader. <I wasn't in a good frame of mind, and you weren't either. I decided to wait until events sorted themselves out. And they did.>

At my other side, Lirome chuckled. <Maybe you shouldn't have shifted back. You're just as tricky in this form.>

<It's too late now, brother of mine.> She made a gesture that I assumed was rude, because he mock-glared at her and made the gesture back. <Ademis is here, and now I think I'm quite ready to take up my leader job again.>

<Ademis?> The word sounded unfamiliar, but at the same time, resonated within me as uniquely mine. <Where did you find that name?>

<I called you it in my dream. It means "noble mischief." I think it suits you. Do you agree?>

Hesitation overtook Maira's confidence, and she played with the tie to her robe. Well, let the little unicorn sit in her dread for a moment. I still needed to catch up with everything that she had just revealed. The minx had outwitted me at my own game, all to position me for the greater good.

If I hadn't already been committed to her cause, I would have clawed her face off.

As it stood, I had to admit the name had a certain ring to it. A name for a cat-dragon with a person, a family, a place in the world. Yes, it would suit.

<Ademis it is.>

She grinned again. <Good!>

I agreed. It was very good.

Janeen Ippolito writes steampunk fantasy and urban fantasy with fresh world building, snark, and a side of romance. While she usually writes for an older crowd, she enjoyed writing a YA cat-dragon story set in the past of her steampunk country of Elotrin. For more about Ademis and this steampunk world, older teens and adults are welcome to try The Ironfire Legacy series. You can also find another story of Elotrin in the humorous romance anthology *How to Catch a Unicorn*.

www.janeenippolito.com

Destined for Greatness

Jenelle Leanne Schmidt

Kendall's heart thudded in his chest, pounding out a rhythm of determination. He was destined for greatness, he was sure of it. Though the details of his great destiny were a bit fuzzy in his thoughts, he firmly believed this audition to become the apprentice to the Royal Wizard held the key.

He groaned when he reached the square and saw the long line. Every eligible apprentice or hired hand had turned out for the event. He wished Master Grengle had been more understanding and not insisted he complete all of his chores before allowing him to leave the inn. However, the enormous crowd did not diminish his spirits, nor did the miserable weather. Misty rain clung to his skin, and his breath steamed from his mouth. Dark clouds crept over the little town square, threatening even heavier precipitation soon. Kendall drew his arms around himself and shivered. He detested the rain. But if he won the apprenticeship, it would all be worth it. He stamped his feet for warmth. Clenching his fists, he reminded himself that he would do whatever it took to win the coveted position. Surely if he did his best, it would not matter that he was twelfth in line.

The morning dragged as he awaited his turn. He passed the time contemplating the great things he would achieve once he was a wizard.

Elsie, the butcher's daughter, stood just ahead of him in line. Her curly dark hair had been tamed into rows of braids, and it wasn't until she turned to him, excitement lighting her brown eyes, that Kendall even recognized her.

"He's been staying at your inn," she gushed. "What's he like?"

The question gave Kendall pause. For the past several days, the Royal Wizard Oolumph had indeed been staying at the inn where he worked, and Kendall could honestly say that he did not like the man. He had proven to be an impatient and disagreeable guest. This was unfortunate, as it made the prospect of being his new apprentice less appealing, but Kendall could think of no better situation to put himself in destiny's way. He had always been taught that the Fates wove together a tapestry comprised of the lives of mortals. If this were true, then it was up to him to make sure his life's thread was a vibrant hue impossible to overlook. They could not miss a wizard's apprentice! Not like they could if he remained a lowly hired hand to an innkeeper.

He shrugged. "He keeps to himself, mostly," he replied, not wanting to quell Elsie's excitement by telling her what he really thought of the wizard.

Finally, after an interminable wait, it was Kendall's turn. He stepped up and gave his name with confidence. The tall, somber man and woman in their elegant, velvet robes barely looked at him as they led him inside the mayor's house, which they had requisitioned in order to hold the auditions.

Kendall endeavored to do his best with each task set before him, but some of the things asked of him were beyond ridiculous. Staring at the candle they told him to ponder seemed pointless and boring; he actually dozed off twice! The man set a large tome before him and asked Kendall to turn to a page and tell them what it meant. When he opened the book, all he saw were lines of absolute gibberish. He dutifully read the nonsense words anyway, guessing at the pronunciation to the best of his abilities. The severe-faced woman handed him a tray of various vials filled with liquids and asked him to identify their contents. Kendall smelled them carefully, swirled them about, and even tasted one before he wrote his answers on the parchment provided. Neither administrator indicated whether he had answered correctly. He knew he had done well at categorizing various herbs, and he was confident of the test of his penmanship. The final test was the most confusing one. The administrators left him in the study alone, informing him that he was to do as he liked until they returned. Kendall quickly grew bored and allowed his instincts to take over; he swept and dusted and straightened until the little chamber was so spotless that even Master Grengle would have given a smile of approval. When the administrators told him to return to the waiting area, he pondered his performance with uneasy uncertainty. It was one thing to have determination, but with such vague instructions there was no way for him to know if he had excelled the way he had intended.

It was several more hours before the announcement was made.

Kendall's spirits sank as the name rang out across the square. He didn't even note which name was called. He only knew it wasn't his. Kendall could not bear to stay any longer, even though there were planned festivities afterward. Disheartened, he shuffled back to the stables behind the inn. Nobody could possibly understand the depths of his sorrow, but a tall glass of warm milk might help. And he would be sure to find a sympathetic ear in his friend and fellow stable boy, Bernard. However, upon arriving at the stable, Kendall could not find Bernard anywhere.

"Ah, you're back," Master Grengle said, seeing Kendall's face poke around the doorway.

"Where's Bernard?" Kendall asked glumly.

"Ah, young Bernard." Master Grengle ran a calloused hand through his hair. "That was something else. While you were off at the auditions, Sir Andrew rode through in a great hurry. He needed a page for an important mission he is undertaking for King Sebastian. Was willing to pay good money to buy an apprentice's time. Bernard was the only one around, and though I hated the thought of losing both of you, I couldn't deny the boy his destiny."

Kendall dragged a broom across the floor with a melancholy sigh, his spirits at their absolute lowest. The Wizard Oolumph and his new apprentice had departed that morning. The village had gathered to see them off with excited fanfare, but all Kendall wanted to do was find a miserable hole somewhere, curl up inside it, and remain there forever. He tried to throw himself into his tasks at the inn, but nothing helped take his mind off the missed opportunities of the day before.

Master Grengle entered the room and watched Kendall halfheartedly pushing the broom around and around the same spot on the floor. He frowned. "You've been moping about since yesterday, and neglecting your duties, and I have to admit it's getting old. I know you had your heart set on that apprenticeship, but you didn't get it, and you need to accept that."

Kendall heaved a mournful sigh. How could he explain that the world was just far too unfair?

Master Grengle's mouth twisted into a displeased frown. "I think you need a break, and some fresh air, lad. Here." He reached out and grabbed the broom, then pressed a small pouch and a piece of rolled-up parchment into Kendall's hands. "I want to serve spiced sausages with apples and cinnamon at the evening meal tonight, but I'm out of all the spices I need. Take this list into town and purchase them for me. Can I trust you to do that?"

Kendall nodded glumly and set out toward the market near the center of town. The fresh air and the walk were nice, Kendall had to admit. The clear blue sky above soothed his soul. A butterfly flitted past. A toad hopped across the path, and he watched it make its way into the cool grasses. The flowers were in full bloom. A gentle breeze tickled the back of his neck. Contentment filled his soul as he soaked in the beauty of the day.

A clinking sound drew his attention to the ground, where he had been dragging his toes as he walked. A copper piece lay on the road, abandoned by its owner. Kendall swooped down upon it, pleased with his good fortune. A pastry from the bakery would be just the thing to soothe his disappointment.

When he made it to the heart of the village, Kendall had almost forgotten his woes. He had never liked the Wizard Oolumph, anyway; his face perpetually pursed in a disagreeable scowl, as though he had always just finished biting into a sour lime. Perhaps being a wizard's apprentice wasn't the best place for his destiny to find him, after all. And while he envied Bernard, he wasn't certain that life as a page was what he really wanted, either. Pages were not much better than innkeeper's boys if he was honest with himself. And there was little chance for recognition when you were constantly in the shadow of a knight ... even if the pages were the ones who kept that armor shiny and the weapons sharp. No. That was not at all what he wanted.

While crossing the village square, a woman near the well caught Kendall's eye. Wisps of long gray hair stuck out from beneath her shallow hood above stooped shoulders. She struggled to raise a bucket from the well. He watched her for a moment, curious. It was rare to see anyone in the village he did not know; everyone came to the inn now and then for food or conversation. A memory sparked in his mind.

Hadn't his mother once told him a story about her great-aunt's brother-in-law's cousin's nephew's wife? Yes, he remembered it now. She had grown up in a small village next door to a poor girl who lived with her stepmother and stepsister. It was an awful story. The stepmother mistreated the poor girl and made her do all the work while she and her daughter went to parties every day. And yet, the poor orphan never complained. (Kendall wasn't sure he believed that part.) One day, she encountered an old woman at a well and offered her a drink of water. The old woman turned out to be a fairy in disguise. She blessed the girl so that precious gems came out of her mouth whenever she spoke, and later the girl ended up marrying a prince.

Kendall didn't really want to cough up rocks every time he talked. He imagined that would be uncomfortable. But he wouldn't mind marrying a princess and living in a palace. He changed direction and made his way over to the well.

"Good morning, mother," he said with a polite smile. That story had another part to it, he remembered, and if coughing up rocks sounded distasteful, coughing up lizards and snakes sounded like absolute misery. "Can I help you with that?"

A tiny kitten poked its head out from under the cloak where it was curled up on the woman's shoulder and eyed him haughtily. Kendall smiled at it. Appeased, the kitten retreated back under the cloak.

The woman tottered about, peering up at him with a nearsighted squint. He definitely did not recognize her. "Oh!" Her creaky voice sounded startled. "Well, well, now, well..."

"Yes," Kendall said, nodding and smiling to cover his impatience. "You seem to be having troubles with this well. Would you like me to pull the bucket out for you?"

"Well, now, well, yes. That's very thoughtful of you. Nice lad." She spoke with a pronounced lisp as she let go of the rope and stepped aside.

Kendall hauled the bucket up hand over hand until it sat on the rim of the well. He looked at the woman and felt a sudden pang of concern. If she could not lift the bucket from the well, how could she carry it any distance? Of course, a fairy in disguise would be stronger than this woman looked, but she looked extremely frail. Surely if this were a test of some kind, he could not pass it with a halfhearted effort.

"Mother, can I carry this somewhere for you?"

The woman peered at him for a moment. "I'm not your mother!" she exclaimed, a note of triumph in her voice.

"N-no," Kendall stammered. "I just meant... I was trying to..."

"Granny Mable." The woman stuck out a shaking hand.

"Forgive me, I should have asked your name," Kendall replied. "I'm Kendall. Can I carry this bucket for you?"

She grinned at him. Kendall tried not to wince at the sight of her blackened and missing teeth. "Such a nice lad. Yes, yes." She gave a shaky nod. "This way."

She hobbled off, and Kendall followed, holding the bucket at an awkward angle so as not to spill any of the water.

The old woman lived rather a long way from town, Kendall thought, as he puffed along behind her. They took the road out of the village for several miles until they reached the outskirts of the Verdana Wood. Then the woman turned onto a little trail and dove into the trees, and Kendall was forced to go after her. The bucket weighed heavily in his hand, and he was too tired to be careful any longer; water sloshed out and soaked his right pant leg and shoe. He grimaced as his toes squelched in his wet shoe, his annoyance growing with each step. He hoped this woman was actually a fairy and not a witch who had decided to take him home and eat him.

Though if she was the latter, Kendall was still fairly certain he could overpower her and get away.

"The Fates had better be taking note of this," he mumbled to himself. "They robbed me of my destiny once already, and after I stood in line all day in the rain, too."

A clearing opened before them, and Kendall saw a tidy little cottage at the end of the path. He quickened his pace, eager to set down the heavy bucket and return home. Master Grengle would be worried if he did not return soon, and he still had to purchase the herbs for the evening meal.

The old woman opened the door and beckoned for Kendall to follow her inside. He set the bucket on the floor in the tiny kitchen. A tabby cat lay sleeping before the tiny hearth, but it pricked its ears at their arrival, meandered over to Granny Mable, and wound its way through her legs. The gray kitten leaped down from its perch on the old woman's shoulder and scampered to its dish, where it meowed plaintively.

"Impatient things," Granny Mable muttered.

"If you don't need anything else, I have an errand I need to run," Kendall said. All thoughts of her being a fairy godmother had fled from his mind. There were just as many stories about witches as there were about fairy godmothers. Though he was beginning to think that Granny Mable was just a regular old woman.

"Wait, wait," the woman creaked. "Just a moment now. Just a moment." She puttered about, searching a little shelf that seemed to be the only cluttered thing in the cabin.

Kendall edged toward the door when the woman spun about, her wrinkled face beaming up at him. She grabbed his hand and pressed something into it.

"A nice reward for the nice lad who helped old Granny Mable," she lisped. "Yes, a nice reward indeed."

"Th-thank you," Kendall stammered. He gave a little bob, stuffed the object into his pocket, then turned and fled back the way he had come.

"Beans?" Kendall stared at the little black objects in his hand and tried to figure out when exactly he had done something to so anger the Fates. That was the only explanation he could come up with for why everything kept going wrong.

He returned to the village and purchased the herbs, but the bakery was closed by the time he finished, so he could not get anything for himself. A prickling sensation behind his nose and eyes plagued him all the way back to the inn, but he told himself that he would not burst into tears like a child over something so silly as a pastry. Or rather, the lack of a pastry.

Master Grengle greeted him at the door with a red face and berated him for how long the errand had taken. Then he shouted that Kendall had neglected to get cinnamon, which was the one essential spice he needed for tonight's dinner. Now everything was ruined, and it was all his fault! As he hurled a few more insults about Kendall's lack of common sense and intelligence, Kendall stammered out that cinnamon had not been on the list, but Master Grengle's patience was stretched beyond its limits. He refused to listen to any excuses and sent Kendall up to his little attic room without supper, where he decided to be done with the whole wretched day and go to bed.

Only then, as he shimmied out of his clothes and into his nightshirt, did he remember he had not come away completely emptyhanded from the old woman's house. He dug in his pocket for the small objects she had pressed so urgently into his hand and studied them with ever-increasing dismay.

He peered at them, holding his hand near the candle, hoping his eyes had been playing tricks on him. But they refused to be anything but beans. Five of them. Small, black things that nestled in the palm of his hand. One had a tiny tendril of something greenish poking out of one end.

"What am I supposed to do with these? Plant them?" Kendall muttered to his candle. The candle did not answer. Nothing was turning out like it was supposed to. A tear rolled down his nose, and he swiped it away with the back of his fist and roughly flung the beans away from him. They rolled across the floor and under his bed.

With a tiny, self-pitying whimper, Kendall crawled under the covers. His last thoughts as he fell asleep were of the Fates. He wished with all his heart that he could demand to know why they had chosen such a terrible pattern for his life. If he could only find them, he'd surely give them a piece of his mind!

Troubled, dark dreams plagued Kendall's sleep. He tossed and turned feverishly throughout the night, alternating between being so warm he had to throw his covers off and so cold that his teeth chattered and he had to pull the covers back up under his chin. As dawn broke, he welcomed its light and pushed himself into a sitting position.

His nose prickled with cold in the frosty air, and he wondered if another storm had moved in during the night to cause such a drastic change in temperature. Stretching and yawning, he fumbled about for his clothes and pulled them on while staying as wrapped up in his blankets as possible. He reached his boots without having to put his bare feet on the cold floorboards, which brought a wry grin to his face. This day was already looking up from where the one before had ended. Why did he need a grand destiny, anyway? He had a master who cared for him and even looked out for him. He still had the copper coin in his pocket from yesterday, perhaps today he might slip away to the bakery and get that promised treat. Better late than never. But first, he wanted to let Master Grengle know how much he appreciated him and was grateful for this apprenticeship, and apologize for the way he had been acting. There would be no more self-pity or staring at the horizon longing for something different. Remembering that story the day before had also served to remind Kendall of just how good he had it here. It had been silly to believe that elderly women sat in a room somewhere, spinning out his destiny. No. He would have to determine his own fate and make the best of whatever opportunities came along.

Whistling, Kendall opened the door of his room.

The whistle died on his lips.

Kendall slammed the door and hurled himself back into his bed. Squeezing his eyes shut, he pressed his face into his hands.

"This has to be a nightmare," he mumbled. "I need to wake up, and everything will be fine."

Pinching himself had no effect. Neither did splashing cold water on his face from the pitcher on his nightstand. At last, he sat on his bed and stared at the door. Not a nightmare, then. Curiosity pricked him, urging him to open the door again.

Reluctantly, he cracked it open and looked outside. Instead of a narrow hallway and stairs leading down to the inn, great, green vines and swirling gray mist greeted him.

"What happened?"

The beans! He dove across the floor, ducked his head under the bed-skirt, and gaped. Thick vines snaked down beneath his floorboards. This was obviously where the ones outside originated from. Kendall rubbed the heels of his hands against his eyes and sat on the floor, at a loss. He had no idea what to do next.

"Well?" A lilting voice floated across the room. "Do you plan to waste your wish by sitting on the floor all day?"

Kendall looked up. In the doorway fluttered a tiny person. Pushing himself to his feet, he crossed the room to get a better look at her.

She was no longer than his hand from wrist to fingertips. She had a short mop of curly black hair and flashing brown eyes, and she wore a shimmering blue dress. From her back sprouted two filmy wings that he couldn't get a good look at because they were beating so swiftly.

"Who are you?" It wasn't the most intelligent thing he could have said, but it was the first thing that came to mind.

"Oh..." Her voice changed from its musical lilt to a lisping creak. "Well, well, now ... well..." Then she doubled over laughing, almost turning a somersault in the air.

"Granny Mable?" Kendall gasped. So she had been a fairy!

"You're brighter than you look," the fairy said. "But you can just call me Mable."

"Where am I? What happened? Where did these vines come from? Did they destroy the inn? How do I get back home?"

Mable held up her tiny hands. "Hmm. You ask a lot of questions! And I make it a point never to answer all the questions I'm asked ... but ... let's see. I shall set your mind at ease: the vines did not destroy the inn. As for what happened, I think you can guess that. You are now in the location you most wished to be in when you planted my gift ... really, dear, planting them under your bed was not the wisest idea, though I have to admit to its efficiency. And as for how you should get back home, well, do you really want to?"

"Of course I want to!" Kendall gasped, but a traitorous thought in the back of his mind added a question mark to his protest.

"Do you?" Mable peered deep into his eyes. Then she crossed her arms and tapped a finger against her chin. "Well, if that is the desire of your heart, all you have to do is get yourself to this exact location before the last ray of sunlight slips below the horizon, and all will return to the way it was before."

Kendall breathed a sigh of relief. "So all I have to do is stay right here..."

"Ye-es ... you could do that," the fairy interrupted. She flew about and pushed the door open all the way. "Or you could do a little exploring while you wait."

Now Kendall could see that the mist had cleared. Beyond the vines creeping around his doorway, he glimpsed trees. The morning sun crept above the horizon, casting everything in hues of pink and gold. He could hear birdsong coming from the treetops, and the sound of running water nearby made him aware of a dryness in his throat. Surely it could do no harm to go find the source of that water and get a drink?

Without thinking, Kendall stepped outside. He did not see the satisfied smile on the fairy's face as he left the room.

The woods were as pretty up close as they had been from afar. There were plenty of berries and nuts to eat along the way. He had no trouble finding the little stream, where he enjoyed a drink of the sweetest, coldest water he had ever tasted. He lay back in the grasses and watched the wildlife flit about in the canopy overhead. This was perhaps the most perfect place he'd ever seen. His eyelids grew heavy, and he thought this might be a lovely moment to take a nap. He did not get many days to fritter away like this. The luxury of it overwhelmed him.

"He's going to be late," a voice whispered near his ear.

"Foolish child, wasting a gift like this," an answering voice replied.

Kendall sat up, suddenly very awake. He peered into the grass, searching for the speakers. At first, he thought perhaps he had imagined the voices, until he saw two tiny little men standing beneath a nearby toadstool.

"Excuse me, but I couldn't help but overhear you speaking," Kendall said, keeping his voice low. "Were you talking about me? What gift?"

The two little men exchanged a nervous glance. Then the taller one puffed his chest out.

"Why, the chance to address the Fates! And instead you lie here napping!"

"What?" Kendall leaned closer, not sure he had heard the man correctly.

"The Fates, they live here in this wood. Few from down below get this sort of opportunity. And here you sit, letting it slip by."

Kendall resisted the urge to jump to his feet, worried he might accidentally crush one of the little men. Instead, he leaned closer, until his nose nearly touched the one who had spoken. "Where do they live? Can you show me?"

"That's easy," the little man replied. "Just follow the stream as it flows until you reach the house with a waterwheel attached. That's the home of the Fates."

Galvanized by this new information, Kendall marched through the wood with renewed purpose. Here was his chance to take his destiny into his own hands! He would never get a better opportunity than this.

It did not take him more than an hour to find the house. It was a quaint little cottage, built right next to the stream. The large wheel attached to it turned slowly, the water diving into it and moving it along before leaping back out on the other side. Kendall paused and scooped a handful of water up from the stream, washing his face and slicking his dark hair down. The Fates were said to be powerful, and while he fully planned to tell them exactly what he thought of their work, it would hardly do to rush in there looking like a pauper.

Gathering his courage, Kendall marched up to the front door. His heart pounded in his ears so that he could barely hear his own knocking.

He waited.

One minute. Two minutes. Three minutes.

Kendall's nerves calmed, and his anger rose. He glanced at the sun. It had passed its zenith and was on its way down. There was plenty of time to get back to his room, but not if the old biddies planned to keep him standing on their doorstep all day! He knocked again, much louder this time.

He could hear shuffling around inside. They were home, but they were ignoring him! Taking a deep breath, Kendall reached out and tried the doorknob. It was unlocked.

The door swung in, revealing a large room, unlike anything Kendall had ever seen before.

In the middle of the chamber sat the largest loom Kendall had ever seen. Various colors of yarn and strings and ribbons dangled and fluttered across the heddles in a haphazard mess. Various balls of yarn and long ribbons and pieces of cloth lay about on the floor, covering every square inch of the room. A few chairs, one of them overturned, also graced the chamber, and these, too, were covered in bits and pieces of trimming.

Amid this scene of audacious chaos, four kittens played. They bounced from one ball of yarn to another. They scrambled up the loom, trailing threads from their tiny claws, weaving new bits into the mess of a tapestry, dislodging others.

Kendall stood in the door, gaping. Horror snaked through him at the sight and what it signified.

"You... YOU are the Fates?" he choked out.

At his voice, the kittens paused and looked at him. One of them gave him a quick glance and immediately ignored him, licking her paw with absolute disdain. Two of the kittens batted at a shadow and then scampered over the mess of fabric, their tails disappearing underneath the heap as they dove after some imaginary prey. The fourth kitten prowled over to him, her mien exuding indifference, but she rubbed her face against his ankle and meowed.

Kendall bent down and picked her up in his arms, her striped gray fur feather-soft in his hands. She purred and nuzzled her way up under his chin.

"Grand destiny, ha!" Kendall's soul shriveled within him. "No wonder my life is such a mess. The Fates are a bunch of kittens. There isn't even anyone here to yell at."

Why would you want to yell?

Kendall held the kitten away from his face, staring at it in amazement. It regarded him with quizzical solemnity.

"Did you just...?"

I am one of the Fates, after all.

"Ah..." Kendall did not know how to respond to this revelation.

The kitten rubbed her nose against his wrist. *It is generally polite to bow when addressing a personage of great importance. Or at least ask their name.*

"Oh, I... What is your name?"

Muriel.

Kendall set the kitten down on a nearby chair and scowled, trying to gather his scattered thoughts. It wasn't quite as satisfying, yelling at a bunch of kittens, but that didn't mean he wasn't going to try. He met the kitten's direct gaze. "My life is a mess!" He indicated the loom. "Just look what you're doing! These are people's lives you're playing with and jumping all over! It's not right. You can't do this. If you're the Fates, then surely you are supposed to be taking more care than this."

A wave of amusement from all four kittens washed over him.

172

Two kitten heads popped up from beneath the blanket they had dived under a moment before.

Oh, he's funny. The orange kitten yawned, showing her tiny teeth. She came out from beneath the blanket and crouched, eyeing Kendall's pant leg, her tail lashing back and forth.

Let's keep him, certainly. The little black kitten pounced on the orange kitten's tail. The orange kitten leaped into the air and twisted, and the two of them tumbled together across the floor for a moment. As abruptly as it had started, the wrestling match ended, and each kitten began delicately cleaning themselves, as if the mere idea of roughhousing offended them.

Amerelle? Muriel's voice rang with the question.

All three kittens looked at the one still licking her paw. She continued, ignoring all of them until she had finished. Then she rose. She was the biggest of the felines, though still a kitten. Her fur was pure white, with a black spot on her front paw. She stalked over to Kendall and wound herself through his legs.

I think it would serve him right. Amerelle's thoughts were stronger. They rang in Kendall's head like the gonging of a large bell.

Oh, good! Muriel pounced on Kendall's toes, her claws catching in the hem of his pant leg.

"What are you talking about? You can't keep me," Kendall said. He knelt down and gently removed the gray-striped kitten's claws from his pant leg. "I have to go home. You're just a bunch of silly kittens."

Rude! The chorus of kitten-voices in his head clamored.

We are not silly, Muriel retorted. She clambered up on the loom and stared at him, her bright eyes unblinking. *Cats are the noblest of creatures. This is a well-established fact.*

Kendall snorted derisively. "You're just a bunch of kittens playing with yarn." His shoulders slumped. "I was so certain that the Fates were wise beings, caring for the destiny of mortals. I thought..."

You thought what? Amerelle's imperial voice rang with scorn. *You believed your destiny to be a grand one? Why should it be? Have you slain monsters? Have you healed the sick? Have you fought on the side of justice? What have you done to make your thread shine brighter? What have you done to deserve a better place in the tapestry of life?*

Caught off guard by the directness of her question, Kendall stammered out a few meaningless words.

Destined for greatness, ha! Amerelle sniffed then licked a paw.

The other kittens giggled, their laughter mocking as they tumbled about in the yarn.

An angry flush filled Kendall's head with a throbbing heat. "Well, at least I'm not a cat!" he shouted.

Four sets of gleaming eyes fixated on him with intense glares. The gray-striped kitten leaped down from the loom and stalked over to sit at his feet.

What do you think, sisters? Muriel asked.

Amerelle stretched lazily. *He is certainly insolent.* Was that admiration in her tone?

Muriel wound around his leg, her tail flicking back and forth. She paused in front of him and yawned, her mouth opening ridiculously wide. A strange sensation shuddered through Kendall's body like an itch and then disappeared. He stared at Muriel.

What was that? he thought.

She gave him a sly look, and then her head whipped to the side and she pounced on something to his right. He shook his head. He should have known better than to try to argue with cats. The sun would set soon; it was time to leave. He turned and stumbled, falling over his front paws and landing on his nose. A mew of pain escaped his mouth, and he sat back on his haunches, thoroughly confused.

Something flickered in his peripheral vision. It startled him, and he leaped sideways to get away from it. He landed on his hands and feet and got a better look at the thing that had scared him. It was only his tail.

His tail!

Kendall stared down at his paws and then contorted his neck around, trying to get a better look at himself. Pale, gold-striped fur covered his body. They had turned him into a kitten! A deluge of panic overwhelmed him. He opened his mouth to scream, but the only sound he could manage was a pitiful mewing.

What have you done to me? he all but shouted.

Given you what you wanted, of course, Muriel replied, batting at his nose with a soft paw.

I didn't want this!

You wanted to be greater than you were, no? What is greater than being a cat? Come, play with us!

You... You've... Kendall wanted to scream. He wanted to cry. This was worse than not being chosen as the wizard's apprentice. This was worse than Master Grengle shouting at him for being late. This was worse than...

Something glinted in the floorboards, and he pounced on it. He caught a glimpse of something else that wiggled tantalizingly beneath a pile of yarn, and he scampered after it, scrambling about and tangling himself in scraps of cloth.

His new form was ungainly at first, and he kept forgetting to use his front paws to catch himself as he bounded about the room, landing on his nose. Muriel and the other kittens laughed at him, but he caught on quickly as they led him about, showing him the wonders of the cottage. There was magic here beyond what his human eyes had been able to see.

Muriel sprang at him, but he evaded her and scampered up the loom, his claws finding easy footholds among the weft. When he reached the top, he lost his balance and tumbled to the ground. He twisted easily in the air and landed on his feet on the soft cushion of fabrics covering the floorboards. The other kittens frolicked around him, and they tumbled about together, playing in this glorious land of string and bits of fabric until well after the sun's last ray sank below the horizon.

At long last, the kittens wore themselves out, and Kendall noticed a gnawing hunger in his tiny belly. Before he had a chance to ask about dinner, an enormous bowl of warm milk magically appeared.

After supper, Kendall stretched out near the warm hearth, his tummy pleasantly full. He closed his eyes, basking in the drowsy warmth of the fire. This was a charmed life. He could think of nothing better than being a kitten. It truly was the only thing worth being. A smile curled at the corners of his lips; he had always known he was destined for greatness.

Jenelle Leanne Schmidt first fell in love with stories through her father's voice reading aloud to her before bed each night. A relentless opener-of-doors in hopes of someday finding a passage to Narnia, it was only natural that she soon began making up fantastical realms of her own. "Destined for Greatness" is a bit more tongue-in-cheek than her usual brand of epic fantasy, but Kendall and the Fates are sure to make an appearance in the fairy tale series she has in the works.

www.jenelleschmidt.com

Sammy's Secret

KARIN DE HAVIN

It's been three days of sweat-covered hell since I caught a nasty flu bug. Being sick does have its benefits. First, I don't have to go to work. Unlike the rest of my friends who headed off to grad school, I took a job at a start-up. Big mistake. Chief Marketing Officer sure looks impressive on my business card, but basically all I do is get coffee four times a day for my boss and give endless PowerPoint presentations. My paycheck barely covers my rent, let alone groceries and cat food.

Which brings me to my second silver lining, Sammy. He's my orange tabby cat and current sickbed companion. Normally, my best friend Tara would be playing nurse, but we aren't friends anymore. Not since I lost her sapphire ring three weeks ago. Instead, I'm sure she's working hard on her grad school film. My bit part as Waitress Number Three has surely hit the cutting room floor.

To soothe the pang of loneliness, I reach out to stroke Sammy's puzzle-patterned fur, and the lines undulate like blades of grass under my fingertips. I take a deep breath, thankful the fever-induced hallucinations have improved. Yesterday, Sammy's markings were dancing the highland jig all day. Maybe I'm turning a corner? Jingle Bells plays loudly in my head though Christmas is months away. So much for wishful thinking.

Sammy rolls over, and I scratch his dotted tummy. "This stomach flu is the worst ever. When am I going to feel better?"

A deep male baritone fills the room. "I think your fever has finally peaked. At least that's what I'm hoping, because I sure miss chasing birds around the courtyard."

Goosebumps form on my arms as I push myself up off my pillow. "Who's there?"

Sammy nudges my hand with his paw. "Olivia, it's just me."

My dirty-blond hair falls past my shoulder as I stare into Sammy's large yellow eyes. This can't be happening. "Wow, this fever has really done a number on my brain. Cats can't talk."

Sammy climbs up onto my chest and smiles down at me. "Of course we can."

"But—but—I've never heard you sp-speak before."

"Sure you have. I talk all the time. Your brain just couldn't translate what I said until now."

Sammy sure does meow a lot, but I always thought he was talking to himself, not to me. "So do you think I can understand you now because of my fever?"

"I have no idea. I'm not a doctor."

"Right. But you are a wonderful friend. Thanks for sticking by my side these last couple of days."

"It hasn't been easy." Sammy runs his paw across his nose. "You smell like a can of sardines that sat in the sun for a week."

I knew Sammy had a sassy swagger when he walked. I just didn't know he had a mouth to go with it. "Sorry, I'll clean up when I can see straight."

He nudges his whiskers. "That day couldn't come soon enough."

Guess I owe it to him to at least try to clean up; he's been more than loyal. I lean forward, push off the bed, and stagger to the shower. My apartment is so tiny it doesn't take but ten steps and I'm in the bathroom. "Part of me worries that, if I take a long shower, when I get out I won't hear your voice anymore—the hallucination will be over."

Sammy pads behind me on the squeaky old hardwood floor. "Too bad you're not a cat. Then you could just groom yourself."

I let out a chuckle. "I wish I could."

Trudging back to the bathroom, I hop in the shower. It takes me forever to wash the stench off my body. I step out and wipe myself down. "Thanks for the suggestion, Sammy. I feel so much better."

At first, I don't hear him say anything. I bite my lip, worried that I not only scrubbed myself clean, but also washed away my ability to understand him.

He rubs up against my legs but says nothing. Well, at least we can still communicate as we always have. I lean down to pet him and—

"Much better."

I jump back, and my bath towel puddles to the floor.

"You smell like flowers now," Sammy says.

"Awesome." We meet nose-to-nose as I retrieve my towel. "I can still hear you!"

His eyes grow wide. "Will wonders never cease?"

"I have to call Tara!" I race toward my phone to punch her number, but Sammy puts his paw on my phone and stops me.

"You know she won't answer."

I toss my phone down on the couch. "You're right. If I called Tara and told her that I could talk to my cat, she wouldn't believe me. Unless I find her ring, Tara will never forgive me." So far, my odds weren't looking good. Before I caught the flu, I spent a week searching the local beach where I had lost the ring, but I walked away emptyhanded.

"It's lost forever," I say to Sammy as I trudge back into the bathroom to brush my scuzzy teeth. "I'll never find it after all this time."

"Sure you can." Sammy holds out his foreleg. "With this!"

I stop brushing my teeth and swallow a mint-flavored glob of paste. Rabbits' feet might be lucky, but cat limbs? Surely Sammy isn't suggesting—

"C'mon, Olivia. You didn't spend all that money fixing my broken leg for nothing."

I stuff back a laugh at the notion that the surgical screws and pins holding his bone together possessed some kind of magical power. "You're going to find Tara's ring with your leg?"

"Yes, I am. As soon as I recovered from the surgery, I discovered all the expensive hardware in my leg work like a metal detector. My leg vibrates like crazy when I'm standing on metal. I've been finding all kinds of things with it."

"No way!"

"I can prove it." Sammy saunters over to his cat lounger and flips it over. Under the middle section is a stash of metal objects. I walk over to investigate. His collection is impressive; there's a dime, a bottle cap, a penny, a tiny silver ring, and a clasp from an old purse.

"Wow, did you dig them out yourself? I didn't think cats liked playing in the dirt."

He sticks out his nose. "I certainly don't, but luckily my friend Bruce does. He's a Maine Coon. They're more like dogs than cats." He crinkles up his whiskers. "Can you believe they love to swim? It's outrageous."

I laugh. "I'm glad to hear you have friends. I always feel a bit guilty when I leave you outside alone while I'm at work."

"You know how much I love to hunt. Bruce and I met chasing the same sparrow."

It wasn't strange enough that I was talking to my cat. Now we're chatting about his social life. "Do you have any other friends? I haven't seen too many cats nearby. Most people have small dogs."

"Tell me about it. They're so annoying."

I stare at Sammy's haul and run my finger along the faint tan line still left from wearing Tara's ring at the beach. "Do you think you could help me find her ring? It's the only way she'll talk to me again."

"Of course. That's the least I can do after you sacrificed your dream Paris vacation to pay for the surgery."

The alternative would have been for him to lose his leg or worse—his life. My eyes well up as I reach over and hold him close. "You're more important to me than some stupid vacation in Europe."

He shrugs off my grasp. "I'm ready to help. All I need is a lift to where you lost the ring."

Most cats would dread a ride in a car, but Sammy loves tooling around in my bright red Mini Cooper. "Great, now if only I could remember where it fell off. We hung out at three different places that day. I didn't notice it was gone until we got to Tara's apartment. Then she told me to leave and never speak to her again."

Sammy nods. "I remember. You took it pretty hard."

The thought of our fight still hurt my heart. Tara and I had been friends since grade school. But I understood why she cut me off. The ring was all she had left of her grandmother, and I was the awful reminder that her ring was lost forever.

A grin forms under Sammy's whiskers. "I know someone who can help you remember. I just happen to know Nadya, the top telepath around."

I scrunch up my face. "Is Nadya a cat?"

Sammy makes a strange garbled noise. "Of course she is. There is no way I would trust a human telepath."

I smile at the fluffy Siberian cat eyeing me from across the living room. "So she's going to read my mind and tell me where to look for the ring?"

Sammy nods. "Nadya is well known for her powers. All the celebrity cats go to her."

My jaw drops. "You mean like Taylor's cat Fantasia?"

Sammy puffs out his cheeks. "Of course, and Fubo too. You're extremely lucky Nadya was willing to change her schedule to make a house call."

Nadya's long lashes flutter as a ridge of fur forms a crown behind her ears. In a heavy exotic accent, she says, "It iz my pleazure."

Is she flirting with Sammy? How the heck did my tomcat get hooked up with some fancy celebrity cat telepath, anyway?

Nadya saunters over to me sitting on the couch and gently places her paw on my hand. "Cloze your eyez and think back on ze day you lost ze ring."

I try, but all that pops into my mind is that I've entered some kind of alternate universe where Nadya has her own TV show and all humans can understand cats.

She smacks me with her paw. "Conzentrate. I have another reading in an hour."

I bet. She's acting as high-maintenance and self-absorbed as a human celebrity. I force my eyes shut and think back on the day at the beach with Tara. "We parked and took the long hike to the ocean. It was hot, so we stopped at the refreshment stand to get a cold drink. Then we rented a big umbrella and staked out a nice spot near the water."

I can feel Nadya move her furry paw across my hand. "An image is coming through. Did you go swimming?"

My eyelids flutter open. "No, because Tara wanted me to safeguard her ring. That's why she was so upset with me."

Her fluffy tail brushes against my shoulder. "Yez, but waz it not her fault that zhe took zomething so preciouz to the beach?"

"All this time, I've felt so guilty. I never thought that Tara might carry some blame too."

Nadya nods. "I underztand. Traumatic eventz can cloud the mind. But I need you to be clear now zo I can help you remember the day."

She's right; I really need to buckle down. "Go ahead, ask me another question."

"What did you do while you were waiting for Tara?"

I wrack my mind, but it comes up blank. "I'm sorry, but I just can't remember."

"Cloze your eyez again. I will put you in a deep trance."

Sammy raises his paw like he's in a classroom. "Excuse me, Nadya, but before you do that, I wanted to tell Olivia that I'm going to duck out and get Bruce. We are going to need his help."

She tries to hide her irritation at being interrupted. "If you muzt."

I race over and open the kitchen window. Sammy hops up on the counter and rubs against the window. I scratch his head and give his butt a pat. It's our ritual every time he leaves the house.

"You be careful out there, Mister."

Sammy nods and is gone in a flash.

Nadya's whiskers twitch as she looks at my kitchen clock. "It is almost time to leave for my next appointment."

I stare at the clock, dumbfounded. "Cats can tell time?"

The fur on her back bristles. "Of courze we can. What do take uz for? Zome kind of lowly inzect?"

This Nadya is one tough feline. "Right, sorry, this is all so new to me."

"I have to admit when Zammy told me you could underztand him, I thought he must have gone through a whole bag of catnip."

I chuckle, knowing how much Sammy loves his catnip treats. "I'm still having a hard time understanding how or why it happened."

She jumps up next to me on the kitchen counter, fixing me with her bright green eyes. "It happened because it waz a gift to you from the Egyptian cat god Baztet. You are not the only human who has the ability to understand us. Baztet grantz the gift to humanz who have powerful bondz with uz."

"That makes sense. Sammy and I are best buds. He's like my brother."

She glares at me, and the claws come out. "Only felinez can be ziblingz."

This is going south fast, and I still need her help. I appeal to her better celebrity nature. "I know your time is valuable, so maybe you should go ahead and put me in that trance?"

"Only for Zammy."

My lids slam shut, and I think about where I went while Tara was bodysurfing. Nothing. Only the ocean waves fill my mind.

"Ztop fighting the memory. It iz quite harmlezz."

The wood refreshment stand pops into my mind. "That's it! I went back to the refreshment stand and bought us two more lemonades. A big burly guy bumped into me, and half my lemonade spilled on my hand. The ring must have fallen off then!" My excitement wanes quickly. I hang my head. "It's a priceless sapphire ring. Someone would have surely taken it by now."

A strange smirk forms under Nadya's whiskers. "Something did."

"What?"

"A zeagull. The bird buried the ring by the lamppozt behind the refreshment ztand. He didn't want one of his flock to take it."

In some weird way, it made sense. Birds are attracted to shiny objects. I remember the seagulls were gathered all around the refreshment stand hoping for a stray French fry or potato chip to hit the sand. "But how come you can see the bird in my memory, but I can't?"

"I have ze Gift." With that, she turns up her fluffy tail and waltzes toward the door.

Nadya had certainly proved her worth. No wonder Sammy was gaga over her. I open the door for her. "I don't know what I can do to repay you, but I swear I'll do anything."

She bats her long lashes at me. "A romantic evening alone with Zammy in your apartment would be acceptable. Zome caviar would be nice too."

Great. Next, she'll be asking me for a snazzy rhinestone collar and a queen-sized cat bed. Guess I'll be the one eating the cat food this month, but it will be completely worth it if I can return Tara's ring.

I pull my Mini Cooper out onto the street, and Sammy jumps in and settles down in the passenger seat. While going for a ride is a big treat for Sammy, Bruce is another story. The Maine Coon the size of a cocker spaniel cowers next to my rear fender.

"It's okay, Bruce." I point to Sammy happily gazing out the window. "Riding in the car is going to be fun, right, Sammy?"

"Come on. Get in." He glares at Bruce. "You're embarrassing me."

I open the rear door, and Bruce skulks toward the seat. "All right." He hurls his huge body into the car, and I shut the door. Bruce swats at the back of the passenger seat. "You owe me big time."

Sammy ignores him.

I start the engine, and Bruce wails. "Let me out. You can dig up the ring yourself!"

Sammy jumps over the passenger seat and bats Bruce in the face. "Come on, pull yourself together, cat. If you do this for me, I'll set you up with Candace. Although I don't see what is so great about her. Her markings look like someone spilled a bucket of black paint on a white cat."

Bruce headbutts Sammy. "I don't care what you say, she's my dream girl."

What is it with cats and dating? They are more like people than I could have ever imagined.

Sammy jumps back into the passenger seat, and I speed toward the beach, excited to finally get our mission going. Silence permeates the car as I take a quick turn down a side street. Bruce hasn't uttered one word. Sammy's head cranes back and forth, trying to take in all the birds. My shortcut gets us to the beach in fifteen minutes. I cruise through the parking lot and snag a spot right up front. Luckily, it's an overcast day, so hardly anyone is here. Our mission should go unnoticed. I bound out the door, and Sammy zooms right behind me. I open the back door to find Bruce has managed to wedge himself between the front and back seats.

"Hold on, Bruce." I reach out to help him. "I'll give you a boost."

He snarls at me. "I can do it myself."

Sammy and I watch as he wrestles his twenty-five pounds free.

Bruce catches his breath and then glares at Sammy. "This is the last time I help you, understand."

Sammy makes a snorting noise. "Admit it. You're addicted to the chase as much as I am."

"Guys." I point to a woman over by the curb who is staring at us. "Let's get going."

We waltz by the woman, and she takes a step back up on the curb. I don't blame her. It's not every day that you see two cats off their leashes following a woman who is clearly having a conversation with them.

Seagulls fly overhead, and I wonder if one of them stole the ring. One gull swoops down and squawks at the cats. So much for me being Doctor Doolittle. I can't understand a thing the birds are saying. I guess I'll just have to settle for cat whisperer.

Sammy takes a swipe at the next dive bomber. "Just come an inch closer and you're toast."

The seagull should heed his warning because Sammy is an amazing hunter. I've lost count of how many sparrows and robins I've rescued from his grasp. "Hey, can the birds understand you?"

Sammy shakes his head. "Are you kidding? They have a brain the size of a pea."

"But parrots are really smart," I say. "My neighbor Mrs. Smith's cockatiel could mimic her New York accent."

Sammy stops in his tracks. "Parrots are clever, I'll give you that, but not smart enough to escape me. Remember when Mrs. Smith's cockatiel went missing?"

My stomach sinks. "You didn't."

Bruce headbutts Sammy. "You're my hero."

Talking to cats sure has its downside. As if it isn't enough to surrender my apartment to Sammy and Nadya, how am I ever going to face Mrs. Smith again? I try to shake off the guilt as we continue our journey to the refreshment stand. Several people stop and pull out their phones to take pictures, but nobody approaches us. That is, until we cross in front of the wooden stand. Under the sloping roof, a surfer dude holding a bright orange slushy loiters next to the giant painted starfish.

He smiles at me and crouches down to pet Sammy. "Man, your cats are so well behaved. They follow you like a pair of dogs. Are you an animal trainer?"

I laugh. "How'd you guess?"

"Cool." He reaches over to pet Bruce who is hiding behind my legs. "Hey, big guy, why so shy?"

Bruce does a succession of meows, and I fight back the urge to laugh as he tells the surfer dude to jump into the ocean and ride a wave to Hawaii. The girl at the refreshment stand calls out an order number, and the surfer dude turns back toward the counter. "Hope you and your cats have a nice day."

"Thanks." I wave Sammy and Bruce toward the lamppost. Sammy walks slowly around the base and comes up empty. Bruce lumbers over, and they have a quick conversation. Sammy orbits the post, moving a bit farther out each time. When he's about a foot away, he stops suddenly. Even from a distance, I can see his leg is vibrating like crazy.

Sammy shouts out to me, "I found something."

Bruce moves in and starts digging. I've been concentrating so much on Sammy, I don't notice the seagulls circling above until one poops on my arm. "What the H?"

Sammy races toward me. "Are you okay?"

I point at the growing number of birds hovering like vultures. "We've got company."

Bruce continues to dig, oblivious to the gathering birds. Then I hear, "Jackpot!"

Before I can see if he uncovered Tara's ring, one of the seagulls dives toward the sand and grabs Bruce's find. The seagull flies high above the refreshment stand while his flock cheers him on. The gull with the crooked beak swoops down and lands on the roof of the stand. He struts back and forth with the ring in his beak like he's holding a championship trophy.

With lightning speed, Sammy leaps onto a trashcan and then propels himself onto the roof. In a second, he grabs the seagull by the neck. Sammy shakes the bird until the ring falls from its beak. The ring glides down the metal roof like a kid on a slide. I race to the far edge and catch the ring before it hits the sand and gets lost all over again.

Once it's safely tucked in my jeans pocket, I grab Sammy and twirl him around. "You did it! You're my hero!"

Bruce bats at my leg. "What about me?"

Sammy leaps out of my arms, and I reach down and give Bruce a good petting. "Thanks, Bruce. You're my hero too."

The surfer dude walks over next to me. "Whoa. No wonder your cats are so well-trained. You talk to them like they're people."

185

My feeling of victory dims as I push Tara's doorbell for the fifth time. Maybe she has her headphones on. She's been editing her grad film project for the last month. I had been looking forward to seeing it on the big screen at the university theater, and maybe now I won't have to go in disguise.

I text, *911! I'm at your door*, juggle the ring in my hand, and hold my breath.

The sound of footsteps echoes behind the door then stops.

Sammy looks up at me. "She's not ready to forgive you."

Part of me is just as pessimistic. But the other part hopes that after three weeks Tara has calmed down and our decades' long friendship can be saved.

Sammy lifts his paw and points to the middle of the door. At first, I can't figure out what he wants me to look for. Then I see Tara's ocean blue eyes glaring at me through the peephole. "I'm not letting you in until you tell me what's the big emergency."

I hold her sapphire ring up to the peephole. "I'm sorry for losing something so precious to you."

Tara snaps off the safety chain, opens the door, but blocks my path. She's not going to forgive me that easily. She holds out her hand, and I place the ring back on her finger where it belongs.

"I'll leave. I just wanted to try and make things right."

I turn on my heel, but Tara places her hand on my shoulder. "I can't believe you found Gram's ring—it's been weeks."

"Weeks of missing my best friend."

"Me too." Tara manages a weak smile. "I want to apologize for being so angry with you. The whole thing was my fault. I should have never taken the ring to the beach in the first place." She holds out her hand, and the sapphires glisten under the entryway light. "Thanks again for finding the ring. You're a true friend."

"I can't take all the credit. I had some help." I look down at Sammy who purrs and rubs up against Tara's legs. He seems as happy to see her as I am.

Tara bends down and scratches him between the ears. She knows it's his favorite spot. "Sammy's pretty incredible, almost like a person."

A smile crosses my face. "If you knew how human he really is, you'd put him in your next film."

"Oh, goody," Sammy says to me, getting the last word in, now and forevermore. "I hope I'll have a speaking part."

Karin De Havin writes unique magic-filled short stories like "Sammy's Secret," as well as young adult series. Her books have a unique take on fantasy worlds as they explore everything from the celestial mysteries of a dystopian heaven in The Katran Legacy to the exploits of a time-traveling Victorian genie and his modern-day mistress in the Time is Forever series, as well as the alliance between a girl chameleon shifter and her artist vampire boyfriend as they fight against evil with the help of a team of witches and wizards in The Shifter Vampire Alliance serial.

www.karindehavin.com

Death Always Collects

Jeremy Rodden

I t's my turn to die next. I don't want to die, of course, but when one makes a deal with Death, He always collects. Death doesn't care if the deal was with a group of terrified housecats trying desperately to save their human's life. He has a quota to maintain. The Church will tell you that animals don't have souls. Death disagrees.

I tiptoed around the bottles of pills on the coffee table. Peering inside, I saw they were all empty. This was not normal. It wouldn't even be satisfying to knock them off the table to hear the rattle when they struck the floor. I considered the oddity of the empty bottles for a moment before looking at my sleeping human.

He was barely breathing. Something was wrong. Then it got even more wrong. The temperature of the room grew colder, and I could sense the presence of two new entities in the room.

The first was Skye, my companion of many years. She stood on the stairs, roused from her slumber with our female human and alerted that all was not right. She was a Siamese, like me, but a brighter shade of white.

The other entity that entered the room was something else entirely; not human and not cat, but familiar to all living beings who must one day face Him. Death stood at the head of the couch overlooking our human, whose breath continued to wane. The hooded figure was preparing to retrieve our human's essence for His collection.

Our human took a gasping breath, and I realized what was wrong. He'd been sad for a long time, and the empty pill bottles must have been seen as an escape to him. Over the years, I tried to be a comfort to him, but I suppose I was not enough.

I approached Death and pawed at His dark robe. His seemingly empty hood turned down and, I suppose, glared at me. It was chilling, but not because Death was particularly evil. Skye and I had experienced ghosts before. Cats, like many other animals that choose not to ignore evil spirits, can sense them. Death was no evil spirit. Nor was He a ghost. Other than the cold of the air around Him, He felt unwaveringly neutral.

Death was there to collect a spirit—nothing more, nothing less. He was not the cause of our human's impending demise, just merely a conduit to take his essence to the other plane. Neutral as He may be, Death waits for no man—or beast—so I had to think quickly.

I gazed into the empty hood and mewled, "Take me instead."

Skye shouted, "No!" From her perch on the stairs, she leapt to the floor and padded to my side. "Don't do this, Loki."

"I have to," I pleaded to my companion. "I am his guardian. I must protect him from spirits."

Skye narrowed her blue eyes and glared. She nodded her head toward Death. "He is no spirit." She turned back to our human, who continued to have labored breathing. "And you are not his guardian." She was technically correct about Death not being a spirit, but I also knew she was never as fond of our male human as she was our female human. She was incorrect about my guardianship, however, because she misunderstood who I meant when I said "him."

"Not this one," I said. "The kitten."

Skye's eyes opened in understanding. She looked at our human, then Death, then me, then up to the ceiling above. In the room directly overhead, our human's kitten slept, unaware of the scene playing out at the moment. I had guarded him since the day he arrived home from the hospital, climbing into his crib and binding my spirit with his immediately.

"Feline," came an icy voice from within the vacant hood. "You have little time to decide," Death added.

I rested my head on Skye's and pled, "I must do this. I can only protect him for so long. He needs his father for longer. He will need him in the future. As will the others."

Skye sighed. "She is pregnant with a second son. I am to be his protector."

She was referencing our human's mate. They were, in fact, due for another kitten in the coming months. For all we knew, there may be many more to come, but only if he survived this night. I only thought of my charge overhead. The kitten was special, and I loved him. To offer my life so that he may continue to have a father was an easy decision.

"Take me instead," I repeated.

Death tilted his hooded head momentarily, looking at me and then at my human. "No," he decided, continuing to wait for my human's essence to complete its exodus from his body.

"Why not?!" I cried.

Death ignored me.

I leapt onto his robe and clawed at him. "Answer me!" I screamed.

Death shook me off to the floor with minimal effort. He turned back to me and said, "Not enough. One feline soul is not enough to equal one human soul."

"Then two," Skye said.

"No, Skye, this is not your job," I said.

She held her chin up at me. She always gave off an air of pride and properness. She looked down at me and said, "Just as your charge needs this human, so does mine." She was referring to our human's partner and mother of his kittens.

I couldn't find an argument with her, even though I didn't like it. If she wanted to add her life to mine, what could I say?

Death pondered again, tilting his hood the same way he did when I repeated my offer. Was he doing some sort of mathematical calculation? Who was he to decide on the exchange rate of souls? This system felt pretty arbitrary to me. "Maybe," Death finally answered.

"You bastard," I spat. "Our two lives aren't good enough?"

Death held out his cloaked arms. He moved them up and down, as though he were weighing two different items to gauge which one was heavier. He spoke with his icy voice again, "Balance must be maintained. Exchange must be equal." One of his arms was just slightly lower than the other, suggesting it was nearly even.

"Add mine," a gruff voice came from the kitchen.

Skye, Death, and I turned to the new voice. The old black-and-white tabby, Sparks, who had recently joined the family, stood at the threshold of the kitchen and the living room. We had no idea how old he was, but he couldn't have had much life left to offer. He also was not guardian to anyone in the house.

"Why?" I asked him.

"He was kind to me," Sparks said. "They gave me a home when I had none. If what I have to offer gives Death the balance he needs, then it is a small repayment."

I was shocked. Sparks didn't interact much with Skye and me, and I'd hardly consider him part of the family, but apparently he had a very different perspective. I turned hopefully back to the hooded figure. My human let out a large gasp of air, and I knew time was nearly up.

Death looked at the three of us, simple housecats trying indirectly to keep our charges protected. He looked at the human. Then turned back to us. "Are you sure his life is worth saving?"

"It better be," Skye snarked. "He better learn from this and be who his family needs him to be."

191

"He will," I hoped.

"Agreed," Sparks added with more confidence.

"Then the deal is struck. Soon." Death vanished as quickly as he appeared.

Our human gasped again. With Death not at his post, we knew we had time to act and roused his mate. With intervention, our human was saved. He was alive. Inexplicably, so were we. The three of us sat on edge waiting for Death to return, but a year passed before He came back.

By this time, we had moved to a new home. The second kitten was born to our humans, and the impact of the suicide attempt spurred our male human into a wave of self-improvement. We began to grow complacent until we reached the anniversary of his brush with Death.

As our humans, sobbing, buried Sparks in the backyard, Skye and I realized regretfully that Death would not make the remaining process simple for us. Was this part of His balance? Was He torturing us with anticipation as some sort of vengeance for our interference? I didn't think Death operated with anything but cold logic and neutrality, but I could have been wrong.

Sparks went willingly with Death, and there was no pleading on our part. There was nothing more that we could do other than wait our turn, which we figured was coming.

On the second anniversary of our bargain, Skye went with Death. Again, our humans cried and buried her remains in the yard, near where Sparks was interred the year before. They seemed unaware of the connection to the anniversary of the male's near-Death experience, but I was not.

On the third anniversary, I waited alone for my turn. I was the last remaining from the deal that saved our human's life, and I expected to pay my share that year. Death arrived, but He did not take me with Him. Instead, He sat next to me on the couch where I slept. I didn't know what to say to Him.

"You intrigue me, feline," Death said, his voice causing me to shiver.

"Why?" I asked. "I can't have been the first to offer myself to protect the one I was chosen to guard."

"Hardly," Death replied. "But you offered yourself in a more indirect way. That human that was mine was not your charge. That you saw in him the man he should have been was something most guardians do not see. And he is on his path to becoming that man thanks to you."

"My charge needed him," I explained. "I didn't think further than that."

"I think you did," Death disagreed.

I looked at the hulking, hooded figure sitting next to me. "Is it time for me to go?"

Death shook his hood. "It is too soon. This would not balance the scales. I would be taking more than my share."

"Next year?" I asked.

Death stood and patted me on the head. "Enjoy your remaining time, little Loki. Your humans have one more child to bear, and you must place your mark on him before it is your time. Your spirit is strong and continues to grow stronger. It would be imbalanced of me to deprive the third child your mark." Death vanished again.

Not everyone gets a hint that his or her time is coming. I was practically given an invitation to the end of my life. Death told me that my humans would have one more child before my time was up. Their third son was born just three months ago. We now approach the sixth anniversary of the suicide attempt.

I spent as much time as I could with the third kitten, knowing that it would be short-lived. I have watched the human I helped save grow into the man his mate and children needed him to be. I don't care what Death's mathematical formulas say. I truly believe one cat soul can be equal to many human souls if used properly. In this case, three cat souls have helped many more.

I await my old friend Death with my head held high. I think I did pretty well for a silly little Siamese cat. My life was not wasted. Death, though, is coming now to balance the scales. He always collects.

Jeremy Rodden considers himself a stay-at-home dad first and an author second. He is the author of the middle grade/young adult cartoon fantasy Toonopolis series as well as numerous fantasy and science fiction stories in several anthologies. This particular story is the most personal story he's ever written. Inspired by true events (his own suicide attempt in 2009, followed by subsequent deaths of his cats Sparks and Skye around that anniversary), it serves as both a cautionary tale and a reminder for those struggling that there is hope on the other side, even if you can't see it.

author.to/JeremyRodden

The Wild Hunt

NAOMI P. COHEN

Fog curled around Ciaran as he ran for his life. His legs ached and his lungs burned with the exertion, but he forced himself to move even faster. The baying of the Wild Hunt grew even closer behind him.

Ciaran's fear spiked, and he wheeled around abruptly and dashed across the road, directly in front of an approaching carriage.

The driver cursed and yanked hard on the reins. The horses screamed and tossed their heads while they plunged to the side.

The carriage missed Ciaran by scant inches. The force of its passing buffeted him, and the horses' hooves rang in his ears, but not nearly loud enough to drown out the howling. His tactic hadn't slowed the Hunt at all.

Ciaran sprinted into the nearest alleyway, desperate to find cover. The walls loomed over him on either side like a tomb, pressing in on him and making it more difficult to gasp in air. He squeezed his eyes closed, lowered his head, and charged onward.

A bark sounded directly behind him. Ciaran cursed and ducked. His form shrank instinctively. He darted forward in the guise of a black cat, a Cait Sidhe, the white markings at his throat and the tip of his tail nearly glowing in the darkness. His fur stood on end along his back, and his paws pounded the pavement urgently.

A fence blocked his way. Without hesitation, Ciaran surged up and over it, hissing as the iron burned his paws but sped onward by the jaws that snapped closed just short of his tail. He landed on all fours and continued fleeing.

The howls rose in volume as the Hunt came up to the fence, and then the sounds changed into jeers and barking laughter.

"Yeah, you just keep running, fur ball!" a voice shouted over the clamor. "Come in our territory again, and we'll tear you apart!"

Sophia stood under the eaves of a flower shop and lovingly drew her bow across the strings of the violin, playing harmony with the steady thrum of rain against the wood over her and the bustling New York street.

Over the years, she often wished for wings that she could fly away with. As a girl, her violin provided those wings. Now the music wasn't enough. That couldn't have been more apparent as she poured her soul into her violin for the indifferent pedestrians, simply hurrying by, their faces obscured with hats, and scarves, and pulled-up coats. The old fantasy came to mind and made her bow falter.

She lowered the instrument and for a time simply stood, watched them bustle by, and listened to the unfamiliar words flowing from their mouths. A few cast her odd looks, standing there with a violin held silently.

She didn't blame these people for their unfaltering steps. The storm made the day dreary and gray. Rain fell through the morning, and as the temperature dropped, it turned to sleet. It was relatively dry under the eaves, but it certainly made it unlikely anyone would stop. They continued to stroll by, all shades of brown and gray and black, blending in with the rain and clouds.

Even understanding this, bitterness choked Sophia. She used to play in the grand parlors of Venice. Her music, poetry, and wit entertained nobility. She couldn't believe she now stood on this sidewalk playing for her food day to day.

A man passed her and, like some of the other pedestrians, glanced curiously at her. They paid her more attention now when she wasn't playing. Sophia glared after the man and purposefully tapped her foot three times against the sidewalk as the creaking of carriage wheels grew louder. She flicked her fingers at the passing carriage then leaned slightly out into the rain, eager to see what would happen. The man and several other pedestrians were only a few feet away when the carriage rushed by and sent up a wave of water that doused them.

The sight gave Sophia vindictive pleasure as she raised her violin once more to her chin. This time, an Irish jig flowed from the strings: a fast tempoed and cheerful tune she bartered with an Irishman to teach her since coming to New York. She couldn't play it with the emotion of the classical music, but it might cheer her up.

The black cat with a lick of white fur at his throat that had been skulking by the trash bins for a little while darted across her feet while a knot of men walked by. Several coins clattered into her violin case, striking against something heavier.

Sophia hissed and jerked the violin away from her chin, outraged this piece attracted attention that her more passionate music failed to. Then she caught sight of the watch, and her anger faded. She needed to swallow her pride. It wouldn't keep her fed or pay her rent.

She pocketed the coins and stared at the silver watch, bright against the emerald green velvet lining her violin case. It was a fine piece, engraved with the American eagle on the front. She glanced at the retreating men and traced the silver etching. She popped the watch open and frowned. It was later than she had thought. She remembered the clocks of the Venetian parlors with longing. The coins would be enough for a meal and her overdue rent. The watch she would keep until she needed money badly enough to barter it.

Ciaran watched the violinist disappear into the mass of people on her way to somewhere warm and dry. In his human form, the Cait Sidhe would've grinned. His paws still itched with the desire to dance to the jig. Instead, he crouched down and fluffed his dark fur up against the chill of the wind.

"What are you doing?" The rough voice that spoke suddenly behind him made Ciaran leap several feet in the air. He landed facing the man, his fur standing on end along his spine, his claws out, and his mouth opened in a spitting hiss. His tail lashed once, and then he sat back on his haunches, regarding the man with disdainful green eyes.

The man was fair-skinned, with ginger hair under his hat and freckles spotting his nose and around his eyes. Ciaran recognized him instantly, both by his face and the magic that wrapped the fey like an invisible coat.

The Cait Sidhe turned and stalked stiff-legged down the alleyway.

"You are going to get yourself into trouble, Ciaran," he said conversationally, following a few feet behind. "I heard you picked some pockets in the Wild Hunt's territory last night. Please don't tell me that is what you just dropped in that musician's violin case."

"It is none of your business, Enda," Ciaran hissed and jumped up on a metal bin. "I will not get in over my head. I am going to avoid their streets for a few months. The Wild Hunt will find someone else to bark about and lose interest."

Enda crossed his arms. "And if they come to our court because of this? Your affiliation is not a secret, Ciaran. Our Queen might turn you out for provoking them."

A shiver went down Ciaran's spine at the very suggestion, and he glared balefully at the man.

"Or they might go after the woman. The coins and watch you gave her have your scent on them," Enda added, an amused smile forming. "Is that your game?"

Ciaran leapt from the trash bin, changed his form mid-leap, and landed on two feet. He stood almost a foot taller than Enda, and he glared down at the other man. "I am not playing a game with this mortal. Fly away, Enda," he said, sticking his hands in the pockets of his pants. "You are irritating. Tell the Queen I am going to lay low until the Hunt loses interest."

Enda sighed. "I am not your messenger. The Queen will be less inclined to turn you out if you tell her yourself. She might even let you stay with her until it blows over. Triona has always been fond of the Cait Sidhe in the city."

"I am not going to the court," Ciaran said shortly and strolled away, wiping mud off the sides of his shoes against the trash bins he passed. "Goodbye, Enda."

"Do not be a fool! I do not want to see you get killed!" Enda called after him. Ciaran didn't look back but left the alleyway and sauntered down the street. He paused at a tenement building and looked up.

Ciaran took a deep breath, and a smile touched his lips. He could smell the violinist. A pleasant, foreign scent: something spicy and sweet, like a flower; quite refreshing among the unpleasant odors of the city. His eyes lingered on the window on the third floor, and then he strolled on, a smile on his lips and Enda's warnings forgotten.

Sophia felt wonderful for the first time in several weeks as she ascended the stairs of the tenement building. A loaf of bread, so fresh that it warmed her hand, enticed her with its scent, and coins jangled in her skirt's pocket as she walked. She hopped over the third step from the top of the rickety staircase so that it didn't creak and give her away. She reached the landing at the top of the stairs, knocked on the building owner's door, and smiled with the satisfaction of seeing him surprised by her presence.

The landlord had been tall once, but now he stooped and leaned heavily on his cane. His face was withered and lined with a permanent scowl that made him look like a bulldog. "Sophia," he greeted gruffly with a heavy English accent. "Do you have the rent?"

"Yes." Sophia eagerly dug the coins out of her pocket. She extended her hand, but the landlord didn't remove his hands from his cane. His eyes wandered to the silver watch and chain wrapped around her violin case.

"Ah, good." He nodded his approval and unclamped his gnarled fingers from the cane, turning his hand palm upward so that Sophia could drop the coins into his palm. "This is late, you know," he said, half turning to go back into his room. "Start entertaining more men so that you can pay on time next month. You didn't bring one man up those stairs this month. I don't care if you want to entertain them elsewhere, but get the rent on time."

Sophia's lips compressed. "I'm not a..." Her voice faltered as she struggled to think of the words in English to explain. She didn't know of any American equivalent to Venetian courtesans. Anger burned in her at the suggestion that she was anything like the garishly painted women she saw on street corners in the evenings.

Her face reddened with that fury, and the old man huffed. "No reason to be modest, girl," he said. "I have plenty of your like living here. If you're late again and I don't hear the stairs creak with you bringing guests up to your room, I might have to reconsider our contract."

He closed the door before she could reply. She kicked the wood spitefully, and before she lowered her foot, she heard the old man grunt as he stumbled. This didn't give her the satisfaction causing the pedestrians to be splashed did earlier, though.

Sophia marched indignantly up the stairs toward the third floor, an Italian tirade flowing from her unchecked and uncensored. She made no effort to lower her voice or to not let the stairs creak under her feet. In fact, she stomped down hard on the loudest of the stairs, the one on this flight that she would've hopped over if she didn't want him to hear. For such an old man, the landlord still possessed excellent hearing, and he seemed to have nothing better to do with his time than sit and listen to the comings and goings of his tenants.

"Wretched old man," Sophia muttered, unlocking the door to her room. She slammed the door behind her and made as if to toss her violin case onto the small bed in the corner. At the last moment, she checked and kept her fingers wrapped tightly around the handle to soften the violin's landing. The watch bounced and clattered against the wood, and Sophia glanced at it, then sighed and paced the half dozen steps from the window beside the bed to the door and back, looking around at the tiny room she just spent her earnings on.

The bed was a horrid thing with a straw mattress set on a rusted iron bedframe. She brought a good pillow and blanket with her when she immigrated, and she was grateful for them, but the soft cotton blanket and pillowcase, embroidered with a countryside scene, looked miserable against the thin mattress. A battered chest of drawers scraped the wall in the corner across from the bed. The drawers would not close properly, stuffed full of her clothing. She had struggled with the wretched thing for several hours over the last few months, trying to force it to behave, and finally gave it up. The room bore no other furniture or decoration.

Sophia had been forced to sell most of what she had brought over from Venice to keep this cramped little room. She knew if she lost the contract, the chances of finding another room in the city would be slim, and she would have to go elsewhere in the country.

Sophia turned her eyes miserably out the window, not wanting to look at the room anymore. Dusk rapidly darkened into night, but people still streamed by just as thickly as when she played for those getting off their work shift.

People were constantly walking by below, at all hours of the day and night. Even in the very early morning, men stumbled along, just getting off night shifts in the factories or trying to find the right tenement building in their drunken stupors after trading their hard-earned pay to drown their feelings.

"Wretched old man," Sophia repeated. "Wretched city." She felt her eyes prickle and wiped them surreptitiously as she lay down beside her violin case, stroking the worn wood.

Sophia wouldn't risk leaving the instrument anywhere but on her bed next to her while she slept. Over the last few months, she heard too many of her fellow tenants complain of thievery throughout the building.

Tales of America circulated throughout Europe and even reached as far as Venice. The opportunities seemed too good to be true, but there were too many tales of people returning to Europe rich for the rumors to be utterly discounted.

When a patron told Sophia he intended to make the voyage and wanted her to accompany him, she leapt at the chance.

A fever took the poor man partway through the journey. Upon arriving, Sophia tried to contact the acquaintances he had claimed to have, but his contacts proved to be either fictitious or uninterested in helping her. Possibly both. Either way, she was alone in the foreign city. She sold off her belongings and tried to make her way as best she could, sure that an opportunity to play for the city's elites would arise.

After a month, when she no longer had the funds she needed, she realized she should've immediately booked passage back to Venice. The city was nothing like she had imagined, and it was uninterested in her and her music.

Sophia turned her face against the pillow and again wiped her eyes. She would not cry. In the relative quiet, she heard something padding back and forth outside her door. She recognized the sound as a cat's quiet tread. Many of the patrons she'd stayed with throughout her years in Venice owned mousers. She loved cats for their simple pleasures and useful existences. Feeling safer with the cat outside her door, Sophia slipped into peaceful slumber.

Ciaran paced the dark hallway into the late hours of the night. He could hear the revelry of distant humans and fey. A dog howled somewhere far off, and his ear twitched to listen, but it was a mortal creature, and the sound didn't trouble him further.

He paused at the corner and looked down disdainfully at the dirt that clung to the pads of his paws. His lips curled, and he shook it off, one paw at a time. As soon as he placed each paw back down, he could feel the grits once more.

The Cait Sidhe sighed and padded back over to the violinist's door. He could hear her soft breathing and pressed his head to the wooden barrier.

Ciaran longed to hear the music the Venetian drew from the strings of the violin. The strains of music enchanted him, reminded him of home even when she played classical tunes. The Irish jigs she played made his blood sing. After nearly two weeks of shadowing her, hoping to hear her play, he longed for more.

Being relatively young for a fey, Ciaran didn't remember the old ways that others spoke of. He knew that humans used to leave out tribute though: plates of milk and honey or other food to appease the fey and keep them from causing trouble.

Nobody did that in New York. Irishmen immigrated, and the fey followed, but the old ways stayed in Ireland.

Ciaran curled up, pressed against the door, and had almost dozed off when footsteps creaked up the stairs. A high-pitched laugh echoed up the stairwell and made Ciaran's ears fold back against his head.

The woman reeked of strong perfume. The man smelled of sweat and oil from a factory. He continued to speak to the woman and nearly trod on Ciaran.

The Cait Sidhe lunged forward and sank his claws into the man's calf, just over his work boot. The man gasped and reeled around, aiming a kick at the black cat. The woman exclaimed shrilly, the man shouted, and Ciaran oozed into the shadows until only his green eyes gleamed out of the darkness.

The humans muttered angrily then continued to their own door. Ciaran fluffed his fur out indignantly and returned to his place by the violinist's door.

Sophia often closed her eyes while she played her violin and lost herself in the music. Here in this city, doing so gave her a brief respite from her surroundings. The tactic also prevented her from becoming too irritated with the number of people that hurried past without even a glance as she spent another day playing on the corner.

Sophia didn't want to become bitter. She knew enough bitter old women, both here and in Venice.

When she came to the end of the song and opened her eyes again, her gaze was drawn like an arrow to the man. Sophia couldn't say why he caught her attention, save that he stared right back at her.

He stood on the far side of the street, watching her despite the foot and horse traffic that passed between them. He wore fine attire: a mahogany brown shirt under a bright scarlet vest. A thin gold chain attached to a loop on one side of the vest and stretched over to the pocket of his trousers on the opposite side. His posture was relaxed, his hands tucked into his trousers' pockets, and an air of lazy confidence exuded from him. A smirk played over his lips when he noticed Sophia looking. She couldn't tear her gaze away from the jagged scar that ran from his forehead, over his closed left eye, and down onto his cheek. It gave his face a disorienting, lopsided look that only added to the rakish appearance his unkempt mane of black hair gave him.

Without taking his eyes from her, the man took a step into the street. A horse veered away from him and trotted past, the rider shouting indignantly at him. The man didn't blink. An icy chill slid down Sophia's spine, and an overpowering instinct to run made her tighten her grip on the neck of the violin until the strings dug painfully into her fingers.

Sophia once saw a wolf, bound and in a cage. It glared out through the bars at the gawkers, a harsh and ferocious energy brimming in its tense legs and slightly visible fangs. She could see a similar energy visible in this man's stormy gray gaze. As he came closer, he grinned, baring sharp canine teeth, as if he could smell her fear. Sophia's resolve to stay still snapped. Trembling like a frightened deer, she grabbed up her violin case and fled, heedlessly scattering the few coins resting inside onto the sidewalk.

Faolan watched the girl run, the coins still bouncing down the pavement. He stepped off the road and bent to pick the slivers of metal up. They didn't have her scent, but he didn't need that. He never forgot a scent.

Out on an errand, he was surprised to catch a whiff of a Cait Sidhe's odor. That reek had stayed in his nose for hours after the recent chase, and he still longed to sink his teeth into that sneak thief's dark fur.

He remained unseen, watching the girl for a time, to discover where the scent came from. Finally, he caught sight of the silver pocket watch that a member of the Hunt reported stolen. So, this is why the fool pickpocketed on their turf. Giving wealth to mortals would be laughable if the Hunt wasn't so furious.

An idea began to form in Faolan's head. Bait and traps weren't nearly as fun as a proper chase, but the pursuit could happen after, and there was a certain satisfaction in sitting back and letting the prey come to you. Faolan's mind brimmed with the delightful possibilities, and a spring came into his step when he started off again, following the faint trace of the girl that still wafted through the air.

"Have you heard the news?" Enda's voice made Ciaran twitch. He raised his head off his paws and stared at the man. Enda bounced on the toes of his leather shoes, a smile hovering unpleasantly at the corners of his mouth.

"Obviously not," Ciaran said, unable to hide his irritation. *Why must Enda always play these games?* "Spit it out already and stop dancing around, you wretch."

203

"You would know if you went to the court, like I said you should," Enda taunted in reply. Ciaran hissed, and Enda's smile became more evident. "Okay, okay. I won't torture you anymore," he added in a singsong tone.

"Say it already!" Ciaran leapt to his feet, his tail thrashing furiously and his magic building within him. "If I repeat myself, so help me, Enda..." He let the other fey sense the sharp edge of his magic.

"The Wild Hunt have invited the Queen, and many other fey, to a feast tonight," Enda said in a rush, his grin widening. He paused for dramatic effect while Ciaran pondered this, his tail held to the side mid-swish. "I heard they've captured a Venetian violinist as entertainment."

The fur on Ciaran's shoulders slowly stood on end. Sophia had not come home the night before. He left to do some pickpocketing to get more coins to give her, and when he returned, the corner by the flower shop where she played was vacant. He slipped into the tenement building, but her scent smelled hours old. He had lain down at the end of the hallway and waited, as he often did, but she never came home. The idea she might be taking up with a human male caused him to fret all morning, which made him irritated with himself for being bothered by the notion. He shouldn't be giving a mortal this amount of attention just because he loved her music.

Enda still stood watching him, rolled forward on his toes, with an eager expression on his face.

"Go away, Enda," Ciaran said mechanically and turned his head away so as not to give the fey the satisfaction of seeing the turmoil brewing inside him. "You're blocking my sun!" he roared when Enda did not move, and he leapt up, bringing both his magic and his claws to bear on the fey.

Enda yelped and fled, a hand pressed to the long set of gouges in his arm. Ciaran watched him go with satisfaction. That would not heal quickly and might keep the bird-fey from flying for a time. His gratification proved short-lived, though. *What am I going to do now?* he wondered and sank miserably down onto the frozen ground.

The hours blurred by. Sophia knew she was somewhere bright, with high chandeliers and a long, long table, crowded with a jostling group of men and women. Rough singing, chatter, and barking filled the air alongside the clatter of cutlery against plates.

She was stretched out on something soft, and, despite the noise, the chandeliers reminded her of the grand Venetian palaces. She stared up at the flickering light and wondered if she were waking up from a bad dream. Perhaps her decision to go to the United States had just been a nightmare.

A shadow fell over her face, and she tried to focus her eyes on the man who peered down at her. "Sir?" she asked and sat up slowly, certain if she moved too quickly she would be sick. Her hand fell against plush fabric and the wooden edge of the couch she lay on. "Penso di aver bevuto troppo," she said with a touch of amusement. Her head swam. Yes, surely she drank too much the night before. She wasn't given to inebriation, but it occurred occasionally. She knew the words to claim as much in English, but it felt so delightful to say as much in her own language.

Then her eyes cleared, and she saw that the man standing by her was the same man who had terrified her so badly the day before.

She leapt to her feet, and the room tilted around her, all bright gold light and vibrant colors. The man's hand closed around her upper arm to steady her, and a tremor shook her at the touch. The dizziness slowly abated, leaving her feeling sick.

"Let me go," she said tightly and yanked free of him. Another bout of dizziness struck her, and she struggled to stay on her feet.

The man took a step back and held his hands up soothingly. "Be calm, miss," he said kindly. "I am Faolan, and I brought you to my home to perform tonight. We've been waiting for you to wake up. The feast is already underway, and my guests are anxious for some entertainment."

Sophia's head jerked around. "My violin," she breathed and took a step toward him. "Where is it?"

Faolan smiled and produced it out of thin air with a grand flourish. He bowed as he held it out to her. "I have heard you play often," he said in a silken tone. Sophia frowned as something buzzed in her head. "You should be playing in a concert hall, not on the street. Do well tonight..." His smile widened with the predatory expression she had seen earlier. "And we may just keep you."

"And if I perform badly?" Sophia asked. She set the case down on the chaise lounge and opened it to examine her violin. She breathed a sigh of relief at seeing it wasn't damaged and then plucked it up and brought it up to tune it.

"We shall see," Faolan said lightly, walking off toward the table. "I wouldn't suggest disappointing us on purpose, miss."

Sophia stamped down the sense of danger that thrilled through her at those words. She would not be intimidated. She had played for much grander audiences than this one. She tilted her head and considered the buzzing. It ran like an undercurrent through the room, filling the space, not quite a sound but something akin to it.

The sensation felt terribly familiar. A slow smile to match Faolan's came to her lips when she placed it. *What a delightful challenge,* she thought as she followed Faolan to the head of the table. He called out in Irish, and the revelry quieted into breathless anticipation. Sophia tucked the violin under her chin and began to play.

Sneaking into the Wild Hunt's mansion took first place for the most insane things Ciaran ever tried. That said something, with how curious and mischievous the Cait Sidhe had been in his youth.

His fur stood on end involuntarily as he crept softly along the wall and looked for a way onto the roof. The mansion, brick and covered with ivy, reeked of the fey hounds. The wind changed, blowing the stench straight into his face and making it impossible for him to lift his paws.

Ciaran huddled into the ivy and trembled. This was suicide. The Hunt would be waiting for him as the night's true entertainment.

He very nearly turned to slip away back into the safety of the city beyond the iron fences. Then he heard the violin music drifting through an open window, and an ache filled him. He hissed and resumed inching along the wall toward the window.

The Cait Sidhe hesitated, peering at the square of light that illuminated the ivy and grass below the window. *What now?* The music paused, and he heard Sophia laugh, clear and joyful. He climbed the ivy and peeked in, keeping as much of his head below the sill as possible.

The young woman stood at the front of the Hunt's banquet table, dressed in a sumptuous emerald green gown in the style of an earlier age, the velvet delicate and gleaming in the bright chandelier light. Her dark hair tumbled around her shoulders in curls, and a grin tugged at her mouth as Lord Faolan pressed a drink toward her hand. She stepped back and shook her head.

"No, I will not eat or drink until I am finished playing," she insisted.

Sophia couldn't have noticed the dangerous light in Faolan's eyes above his razor-thin smile. Ciaran sank down below the window again, puzzling out what to do now. He could provide a distraction, but the girl did not know to run. He took a deep breath and caught the scents of many fey mingled with the stink of the Hunt's hounds, including the Queen's. He knew he should expect no aid from that quarter, though.

A small black storm petrel descended out of the darkness and landed in front of Ciaran, its feathers fluffed out and trembling slightly over flying at night.

"Enda," Ciaran breathed and huddled lower, praying that the Hunt would not hear. "What are you doing here?"

"The Queen asked if I would help," the bird whispered. "She offered me a favor and reminded me you would be in my debt if I did." Enda hesitated. "You're fun to tease," he added. "I don't want to see you get ripped apart by the Hunt." He shook his feathers out. "I will not perish for you, Ciaran, but I'll give you a chance to get to the mortal and warn her. After that, it's on you."

"Thank you." Ciaran placed a paw on the bird's head. "I did not expect kindness. From the Queen or you. I will owe you a favor for this."

"May you live to repay it," Enda muttered. "I still think this is folly." He took a deep breath that puffed out his chest, then launched himself through the window, screeching loudly and flapping as hard as he could.

Ciaran surged up and over the window below Enda, a small shadow in the blazing light inside the grand room.

Faolan leapt after Enda, and half the table jumped to their feet, barking at the bird, while the guests looked on in amusement.

The commotion gave Ciaran the chance to slip unnoticed to where Sophia stood, well away from the confusion, with her violin held protectively close. He skidded to a stop at her feet and looked up at her, his eyes wide and large against his dark fur.

"You must escape now!" he yowled and scrabbled around. The Hunt would catch his scent any moment.

Sure enough, Faolan advanced toward them, his grin widening. Ciaran scurried back toward the window, but the man pounced and caught him up, holding him up by the scruff. Ciaran flailed uselessly at him and struggled to draw in breath with the skin pulled tight on his head.

"Enough!" The word rang with magic and caused the room to instantly become still and silent.

Faolan turned slowly and stared indignantly at the human woman. Sophia gently set the violin down in its case and then advanced on him, radiating power.

"You're a witch," Faolan snarled and backed away, his movements slow and jerky with the difficulty of fighting her magic.

"Give him to me," Sophia ordered and slid a hand under Ciaran's belly, alleviating the pressure on his head. When Faolan released him, Ciaran lolled against her and purred instinctively, happy to feel safe so suddenly.

Sophia cradled him against her chest and looked around imperiously, a smile on her lips. "This was delightful," she said and used one hand to curtsy. "I would enjoy playing for all of you again, if you will have me." She nodded to Faolan. "But ask me properly. I do not wish to be carried off again. I know the Irish have more manners than that."

"Enda," Ciaran breathed and peered around over her arm. Where did the storm petrel go?

"The bird flew out," Sophia whispered back as she picked up her violin case and left the banquet hall, keeping her back straight despite the snarling. Animosity chased her out, and her pace sped up despite her determination to not allow them to frighten her.

"Thanks for that," Sophia added. "I wondered when I would use some magic to make my exit." She paused and stroked the cat's ears. "I appreciate what you've been doing for me. Would you like to keep watch inside my room, from now on? I could use a mouser to keep the vermin out. I found a hole behind my bed the other night."

Ciaran snorted. "You're plucky," he said dryly, blinking up at her. "Maybe a few nights." He glanced away haughtily. "If you'll play some songs for me only and leave out a tribute."

"I can do that," Sophia said cheerfully. "The money you gave me will more than pay for some cream and fish." A wistfulness flashed across her face. "I've longed to get in touch with other mages and the fey community in the city, but they're a suspicious lot. I'm delighted you liked my music enough to give me this open door."

Ciaran chuckled and allowed his eyes to drift closed while the scents of the Hunt faded in the clean night air once they were outside. "That is certainly one way to look at what happened here tonight." He paused then added, "I'm the one who should thank you." His purr rumbled deep in his chest as the human woman carried the Cait Sidhe home.

Naomi Cohen was born in the late 10th century, grew up far from any city, and rarely interacted with people outside her clan. She spent her childhood telling herself stories and tending to the many animals her family were fortunate enough to keep, including dogs, chickens, goats, sheep, a donkey, and horses. Her heart is held most by the cats that keep her home mouse free. She eventually discovered a pencil and paper and began actually writing these stories down. She is delighted to share them with you now. One of the above facts is a LIE. Guess which one.

https://www.naomipcohen.com/

Want more? Buy stories and books from these authors. Or get another collection of short stories to sample in previous Fellowship of Fantasy anthologies, *Fantastic Creatures, Hall of Heroes, Mythical Doorways,* and *Tales of Ever After.*

Find more stories from these authors and others at www.FellowshipOfFantasy.com.

Made in the USA
Middletown, DE
25 June 2019